MYSTIC VISIONS

Rosanne Bittner

TOR®

A TOM DOHERTY ASSOCIATES BOOK
NEW YORK

This is a work of fiction. All the characters and events portrayed in this book are either products of the author's imagination or are used fictitiously.

MYSTIC VISIONS

Map by Mark Stein Studios

A Tor Book
Published by Tom Doherty Associates, LLC
175 Fifth Avenue
New York, NY 10010

www.tor.com

Tor® is a registered trademark of Tom Doherty Associates, LLC.

ISBN: 0-812-56542-8

First edition: May 2000
First mass market edition: April 2001

Printed in the United States of America

0   9   8   7   6   5   4   3   2   1

To my very patient husband, Larry, who understands
my need to write, my passion for telling the real story of
the West and its Native Americans, and for twice taking
me to Wyoming to visit the sacred Medicine Wheel on
Medicine Mountain, which became the inspiration
for my Mystic Indian series.

PART ONE

Innocence

I see the land, and all is gifted to me by Wakan-Tanka.
*Only the Great Spirit owns Mother Earth and all her creatures,
the four-leggeds . . . and the two-leggeds . . .*

JUNE 1836

The Month of Making Fat

CHAPTER ONE

EMERGING FROM SWIRLING clouds, the warriors rode out of the sky toward Buffalo Dreamer. Their bodies glimmered a ghostly white. Coup feathers and quilled ornaments decorated their hair. Colorful quills adorned lance covers, quivers, leggings, moccasins, and armbands. Each man wore a bone hairpipe breastplate tied to his otherwise naked chest. Some wore a bearclaw necklace. Their faces were painted black, making the whites of their eyes seem to glow.

Buffalo Dreamer watched them, astounded and afraid. War shields of buffalo hide hung at the sides of their painted horses, the shields decorated with hand-drawn pictures of personal spirit guides: eagles, horses, wolves, bears, birds, beavers, suns, stars, lightning bolts.

As the warriors charged forward in thundering glory, their long black hair trailed in the wind. Eagles circled above them like sentinels. The hooves of galloping warhorses rumbled like thunder, but even though the riders' mouths were open as though shouting war cries, there was no sound.

Buffalo Dreamer tried to run, but she couldn't move. Sod sprayed in all directions as panting steeds charged past her, determination on the faces of the warriors, who stared straight ahead as though unaware of her. Now she could see they were Lakota, but men of another nation rode with them—Shihenna, those the white man called Cheyenne.

Suddenly the terrain changed, and Buffalo Dreamer found herself standing on a ridge, looking down at many white men wearing blue coats. More Lakota and Cheyenne rode out of the sky, until they numbered in the thousands. The fierce warriors surrounded the men in blue coats, circling, killing, until the white men were pounded into the earth and disappeared in a pool of blood. The warriors rode back into the clouds, carrying scalps and sabers, their eyes gleaming with victory.

The clouds swirled around and engulfed them, then fell to the ground and took the form of a white buffalo. The sacred beast stared at Buffalo Dreamer, its eyes bright red. Crimson tears of blood trickled down the white hairs of its face.

"It is the beginning of the end," it spoke. *"When next I appear to you, I will die. Eat of my heart, and keep my robe with you always, for protection. And beware of the men in blue coats."*

Buffalo Dreamer awoke with a gasp and sat up. Taking a moment to gather her thoughts, she was almost startled to find herself in her own tepee. Big Little Boy, two summers old, still slept quietly nearby.

After hearing the thundering hooves of the warriors' horses, everything seemed too quiet, and Buffalo Dreamer found it difficult to remove herself from the very real dream she had just experienced. She shivered, for her dreams carried great significance. Though only nineteen summers in age, she was considered a holy woman by the Lakota. In her medicine bag she carried the hairs of her spirit guide, the white buffalo. Among all living Lakota, she alone had seen and touched the sacred beast.

She pulled a wolfskin shawl around her naked body and looked at her husband, who slept soundly beside her. Because Rising Eagle was a man of vision and possessed great spiritual power, she knew she must tell him about her dream. She watched him quietly for a moment longer, reluctant to disturb him. In sleep, he appeared just a common man: peaceful, calm. Awake, no man could match him in strength and bravery, in hunting or in raiding. He had even fought the great humpback bear to win her hand in marriage, for her father had demanded the hide of a grizzly as part of her marriage price. Rising Eagle still bore scars on his throat, chest, and back from his struggle with the fearsome beast.

Other markings spoke further of Rising Eagle's prowess: a deep scar on his left calf from a battle with Crow warriors; a narrow white scar ran from above his left eye over his nose and across his right cheek, making him appear fierce and intimidating. He had sacrificed his flesh more than once at the annual Sun Dance. And twice *Wakan-Tanka*'s messenger, the Feathered One, had spoken to Rising Eagle in a vision, making Rising Eagle a highly honored man among the Lakota, one whose prayers were heard beyond the farthest clouds. No other Lakota man had ever seen or spoken with the Feathered One; and so, at twenty-eight summers, Rising Eagle already claimed the status of *Naca,* a very important leader among the Oglala and the entire Lakota Nation. Red hands painted on the rumps of Rising Eagle's most prized horses depicted his many wounds suffered at the hands of the enemy. Black hands represented the number of enemy warriors killed.

Buffalo Dreamer touched his shoulder. "Rising Eagle," she whispered.

He started awake, frowning at being disturbed. "What is wrong?"

"I had a dream," Buffalo Dreamer said softly. She still expected to hear the thundering of horses' hooves go charging through the Oglala camp. "I saw the blue coats again."

Rising Eagle rubbed his eyes as he sat up to face her. With concern in his voice, he said. "Tell me."

Buffalo Dreamer explained what she had seen in her dream. "It is surely an omen. When you saw the Feathered One in your vision at Medicine Mountain, he warned us of the *wasicus.* I think it is those who wear the blue coats we must fear the most, more than any enemy we have now."

Rising Eagle lay back down. "You said that in the dream

the warriors destroyed those who wore the blue coats. Surely that is a sign that there is nothing to fear from them."

Buffalo Dreamer pulled her knees up and wrapped her arms around them. "But this time the Sacred White also appeared, and it told me to beware of men in blue coats. When the warriors disappeared into the clouds, it said, 'It is the beginning of the end.' You know that this is not the first time I have dreamed about the men in blue coats."

Rising Eagle reached up and teasingly yanked at her hair. "Lie down, woman. I enjoy lying beside you in the early hours, when the camp is still quiet."

Buffalo Dreamer obeyed. "There is more." She told her husband about the words of the white buffalo, that when she saw it again, she must eat of its heart.

Rising Eagle breathed a long sigh, then turned on his side and ran a hand over her nakedness. "I will speak with Runs With The Deer about your dream. My uncle is wise in his old age. We must decide what to do about the men in blue coats when finally we see them in life."

Buffalo Dreamer traced her fingers along his firm jawline. "When I have a dream that frightens me, it is good to wake up to the safety of your strong arms. I know that with you by my side, nothing can harm me, not even the blue coats." She watched the love sparkle in his handsome dark eyes. A vision had led him to her, and she had feared and hated him when he first came to claim her, a man she had never before set eyes on. Now she loved him beyond her own life.

"I would die for you, and for my sons," he said softly.

Buffalo Dreamer smiled. He'd said *sons,* not son. He considered Never Sleeps, their adopted son, as much their son as Big Little Boy, even though Never Sleeps bore no blood relationship to them.

"Never Sleeps might as well belong to my mother," she told him. "Since she agreed to care for him while I still nursed Big Little Boy, she has come to love him like her own son, the son she was never able to bear."

Rising Eagle nodded. "Never Sleeps has been good for Tall Woman, and also for your father. Every man wants a son. Since Never Sleeps has no uncle to teach him the warrior way, I have asked Looking Horse to train him."

Buffalo Dreamer drew in her breath with joy. "I know my father will be happy and honored to lead our son to manhood. And my mother will also be pleased."

Rising Eagle moved on top of her, laughing lightly. "Looking Horse often jokes that Never Sleeps is in his tepee so often that he cannot enjoy your mother's company at night. Often she takes Never Sleeps to bed with her so the child can sleep close to her." He leaned down and licked her neck. "There is, however, nothing between you and me right now, Buffalo Dreamer. I wish to enjoy *you* at this moment."

He moved his mouth to lick and taste her lips, and Buffalo Dreamer tasted his in return. They did not know what to call this touching of lips and tongues, but they had discovered once, during lovemaking, that it was very pleasant. It usually led to the exploring of other, more secret places. She had only recently stopped nursing Big Little Boy, and so they had renewed their lovemaking only a few days ago. Passions still ran high.

Rising Eagle caressed her breasts, her belly, and her private places that had always belonged only to him. She breathed deeply with the want of him, enjoyed the scent of him. Soon she felt the rising exotic pulse that made her ache to be filled with this man who had taught her the glory and delight of mating.

"I need you, my husband."

Rising Eagle mounted her, grasping her hips and thrusting his most virile self into her with movements that made her groan with pleasure. For the moment, Buffalo Dreamer forgot about her strange dream. All that mattered was the ecstasy of mating with this most honored warrior. For many moons after first marrying him, she had refused his advances. Now she rued the pleasure she had missed by being so stubborn.

They twined in sweet rhythm; then Rising Eagle rose to his knees, moving even deeper and faster, the gleam of a conquering warrior in his eyes. Finally, Buffalo Dreamer felt the rush of his life pour into her, and Rising Eagle groaned in his own pleasure. He held himself deep within her for a moment before pulling away and lying down next to her again.

The morning sun began to brighten the inside of the te-pee then, and they lay there a moment longer, each lost in their own thoughts, until a small voice broke the early morning quiet.

"Ate."

Buffalo Dreamer turned at her son's call to his father. Big Little Boy was awake and watching them. She thought that the boy truly fit his name. The husky child had walked sooner than others his age, and he was a bundle of energy, always ready for mischief. Once he had run into the nearby river and was caught by Buffalo Dreamer just in time; otherwise he surely would have drowned. All the Oglala took great joy in his antics, everyone agreeing that Big Little Boy was definitely his father's son when it came to fearing nothing.

Rising Eagle sat up and gave Big Little Boy a frown in mock scolding. "You are awake too soon, my son."

Big Little Boy giggled and jumped up. He ran outside naked, and Rising Eagle shook his head. "It is a good thing the weather has warmed." He reached for his breechcloth and rose, tying it on. "I will catch him for you this time. You can stay here and dress. I will wash myself in the river."

He ducked out of the tepee, and Buffalo Dreamer lay still, feeling pleasantly happy, until suddenly a flash of ap-prehension moved through her. She sat up, whispering Big Little Boy's name, deciding to hurriedly wash and dress. Perhaps it was just a reaction to her still-vivid dream, but something felt very wrong.

CHAPTER TWO

RISING EAGLE CHASED Big Little Boy into the tall grass beyond the camp, where he caught the child urinating.

"You must do this farther away from camp," Rising Eagle scolded. He leaned down to grab his son, teasingly letting Big Little Boy scamper off again. The boy laughed with glee, and Rising Eagle smiled at the child's excitement in thinking he could outrun his father. He shook his head and took his time following, allowing his son to play his game of tag. After all, it was not too soon for the boy to begin to learn how to hide from the enemy.

Rising Eagle stopped to also urinate, then casually traced the pathway of trampled, broken spring grass left by Big Little Boy.

"So!" he shouted. "You think you can hide from me!" He heard another giggle. He noticed that the pathway led toward the thicker brush and trees that bordered the river, and he felt a sudden alarm. Later in the summer, the river near where they were camped would be shallow and sandy, but heavy spring rains, mixed with snowmelt from the mountains far to the west, had caused it to swell way beyond its banks.

"My son!" he shouted. "You know you are not to go near the river! You will cut your feet running into the tangle of brush there, and you must not go into the water!"

Somewhere deep in the heavier brush he heard more laughter, then a light shriek. It sounded like a child's normal shout of excitement, yet something about it made him wary.

"Big Little Boy!" he yelled, but there came no reply. He did, however, hear a loud splashing sound. He began running, ignoring the sticks and stones that gouged his bare feet. He reached the north riverbank, but Big Little Boy was nowhere in sight. Again he called for him. He heard voices behind him then, and realized that his shouts of alarm had disturbed the rest of the camp. He ran alongside the riverbank, desperately searching the rushing water. He saw nothing, but as he ran farther, he spotted a lance stuck in the ground on the opposite bank.

A new dread charged through him when he looked down to see fresh hoofprints in the soft sand along the riverbank. No Oglala horses had grazed in this area since making camp, and none were in sight now. He looked across the river at the lance, then hurriedly waded into the chilly water. Worry obliterated all sensation of cold.

My son! Not my only true son! He swam toward the opposite bank, still hearing voices somewhere behind him. He heard Buffalo Dreamer scream her son's name.

Fighting the strong current, he headed toward the lance that had been left stuck in the ground. The rushing water slammed him against a boulder, knocking the breath out of him. He clung to the cold, slippery rock until his breath returned, then struggled to the opposite bank. He crawled out onto the sandy ground, where he saw moccasin prints. He studied them closely, and he knew from their shape that the prints did not belong to the Oglala, nor to any other Sioux band.

After scanning the immediate area, he rose and walked over to the lance. He yanked it from the ground and studied the beaded edge of the buffalo hide wrapped around the upper half. The Oglala had only recently begun trading for the white man's colorful beads. No Lakota man yet decorated his lance with beads, but only with quills. One other tribe, however, now traded frequently with the *wasicu,* and he knew the design of his most hated enemy.

"*Pawnee,*" he growled. The surrounding trampled grass was an obvious sign that several men had been hiding here. A deep rage began to swell in his soul.

"Rising Eagle!" Buffalo Dreamer shouted from the opposite bank. "Where is our son?"

Rising Eagle's gaze fell upon a wide pathway left by many horses. He turned to see the look of terror on Buffalo Dreamer's face, and it made his heart ache. He held up the enemy's lance.

"Pawnee!" he shouted. "They have taken our son!"

CHAPTER THREE

"GREAT SPIRIT, TO whom I will one day return; Wakan-Tanka, *Ruler of the Earth, of all we see and taste and touch, save my son!"*

Buffalo Dreamer repeated the same prayer she had sung for the last five hours. A rush of cool wind blew her hair away from her face as she spoke, and she believed it to be a sign of the presence of another power. Below the bluff where she knelt praying, Rising Eagle shared a sweat lodge with other esteemed men of the Oglala *Akicitas* and equally honored Shihenna men, all participating in *Inipi,* the rite of purification.

The Oglala and Shihenna had begun trading with one another over the past few years, resulting in several inter-tribal marriages. They often shared the Sun Dance celebration, and they supported each other in warfare, especially against the Pawnee, an ancient, hated enemy of both nations. Unsure of how many men rode with the Pawnee who had stolen Big Little Boy, and because most of the Oglala clan was scattered farther north on its own hunting expeditions, Rising Eagle appealed to the Shihenna for help in finding his son. Many Shihenna men gladly agreed to join the search, hoping to retrieve sacred arrows stolen in an earlier attack by the Pawnee that had resulted in the death of many Shihenna women and children.

Prayers and fasting were always important before going to war. In a sweat lodge, the Oglala men prayed to the all-powerful one, *Wakan-Tanka,* the same god the Shihenna called *Maheo.* Buffalo Dreamer took hope in the power of their prayers. The men would smoke sacred tobacco in an offering of the prayer pipe to the Great Spirit, and would be cleansed by perspiring from the heat of rocks taken from *peta owihankeshni,* the sacred fire, making them pure in the eyes of the Great Spirit.

Surely Rising Eagle's petitions for the safety and rescue of his son would be heard by the Feathered One himself, that Being who was half man, half eagle, the Being who had once come to Rising Eagle in a flash of lightning on top of Medicine Mountain, enveloping Rising Eagle and Never Sleeps, healing their adopted son's deformed fingers and toes. The miraculous healing had proved the power of Rising Eagle's faith and prayers. Surely a man whose prayers could heal the lame could bring about the rescue of his own flesh and blood.

"Hi ho! Hi ho! Pila miya," Buffalo Dreamer prayed, bowing low so that her face touched Mother Earth. "I thank you, *Wakan-Tanka,* for all your good gifts. I am nothing in your presence. I come to you to plead for mercy for my son. He is helpless among the enemy without you to protect him. Holy One, you came in answer to my husband's prayers and healed Never Sleeps. You gave the child all his fingers and all his toes. Now I ask for still another answered prayer, that my husband can find and save our son."

She took her skinning knife from its sheath at her waist and held it toward the sky. Adding her own prayers to those of the *Nacas* could help ensure they would find Big Little Boy.

"Do you see me, *Wakan-Tanka?* I will show you how I am willing to sacrifice my own flesh for your generosity." She slashed her left arm twice, grimacing with the pain, determined to do anything, even to die if she must, to save her son from the Pawnee. She did the same to her right arm, then held out her arms and let the blood drip onto Mother Earth. "Grandmother, you gave me life, and I give part of it back to you. Speak to *Wakan-Tanka* for me. Plead with the Great Spirit for the life of my son. Ask him to place my child back into my arms, these arms that now bleed in sacrifice for my son. Bring me a sign, a powerful sign, that I might know my son will live and be returned to me."

She made fists so that her arms would bleed more. Over the past three days, they had ridden from dawn to dark to come this far. She had not eaten in all that time, having decided to begin fasting immediately upon the abduction of her son. As the Oglala warriors tracked the Pawnee southward, they'd come upon this camp of Shihenna, who hunted buffalo close to Pawnee country. When the Shihenna warriors heard Rising Eagle's story, they had come alive with a fierce desire to help the Oglala avenge Big Little Boy's kidnapping.

Scouts from both tribes had immediately ridden out to search for the Pawnee camp, while Rising Eagle and the others remained behind to pray and a war party of Shihenna danced. Drumming and singing filled the air with excitement, while weapons and war ponies were made ready. As soon as scouts returned with news of the enemy's location, they would all ride, thirsty for Pawnee blood. Rarely did a woman join a war party, but Buffalo Dreamer intended to ride with them, even though hunger raked her belly and exhaustion consumed her.

Sounds from the war dance grew more distant, as though she were only dreaming now. Buffalo Dreamer felt herself floating, and when she looked down at her arms, she saw red wings. She smiled, for the red bird *was* her favorite of all feathered creatures, its brilliant color such a contrast to its surrounding terrain.

She spread her arms, feeling like a bird herself. Then, in the distance, something white rose from the earth, taking the form of a buffalo. Perched on its side was the same red bird of which she had been dreaming. The buffalo suddenly went to its knees, letting out a kind of groan, as though in pain.

Concerned, Buffalo Dreamer stumbled toward the animal, soon realizing that it was truly alive and not a vision. The red bird became blood, oozing from a wound in the buffalo's side. Twice in her life, Buffalo Dreamer had been gifted with the presence of the white buffalo. Now she saw that indeed, the sacred beast had appeared to her yet a third time.

Her vision cleared, and she looked down to see that her arms were flesh again, rather than feathered, and that the bleeding was slowing. Her legs wavered with weakness, and she again dropped to her knees. She dared to reach out and touch the thick, soft mane of the white buffalo. Its eyes rolled back and she could see their whites. The huge animal snorted and groaned again, kicking out so that Buffalo Dreamer jerked back. It was the biggest female she had ever seen, even among the more common and darker buffalo.

Her heart ached at the sight of the wounded animal. Who would do such a thing? Again she reached out and touched the animal's thick mane, stroking it gently. "How can I help you, Sacred One?"

She felt a voice speaking to her, not loud and distinct, but rather from her own heart.

The wasicu *has done this to me,* she felt the spirit of the beast tell her. *Far off. I ran with my brothers and sisters so that they could not catch me, but now I am weak and dying. Someday it will be the same for you and the Oglala. It is wise not to trust the white man, but as long as you possess the hide of the Sacred White, the Oglala will be protected. I leave you now. Eat of my heart, and your son will be saved. You will not see me again, Buffalo Dreamer, until the day of your own death, when I will come to take you away with me.*

The buffalo snorted, stirring dust with the breath from its nostrils. Its eyes rolled farther back, then closed. The animal shuddered with a last groaning sigh and died. Buffalo Dreamer felt horror at the thought that any man would dare to kill such a magnificent and sacred beast. Here was another reason to be wary of the white man. Anyone who had such little respect for this magnificent animal must be careless and ignorant, most certainly a man of little or no wisdom or heart.

Her hand weak and shaking, she took her skinning knife

from the belt at her waist and cut as deep and hard as she could, obeying the command to skin the buffalo and eat of its heart. However, her hungry, worn condition left her too feeble to cut through its tough hide. Knowing she must partake of the animal's heart while it was still fresh, she struggled to her feet, then staggered down the hill toward camp. She fell, got up again, called to a Shihenna woman to come and help. The woman did not understand, but she ran to an Oglala warrior, Rising Eagle's uncle Bold Fox, and she pointed to Buffalo Dreamer. Breaking away from the war dance, Bold Fox approached her with a scowl.

"It is bad luck to leave the war dance," he chided. "Why do you call to me, Buffalo Dreamer?"

"This will bring you *good* things," she answered. She grasped his arm to keep from falling, then turned and pointed toward the rise. "There. Do you see it?"

Bold Fox followed her command. Even from below, one could see the white buffalo's body lying near the edge of the bluff. Bold Fox's eyes widened. "Is it—"

"The Sacred White," Buffalo Dreamer answered for him. "I asked . . . for a sign, and then she was there. She has died from a wound inflicted by a white man."

Bold Fox gasped. "A *white* man killed her? How could any man be such a fool?"

"She *told* me it was a white man who did this. I am to eat of her heart, but I am too weak to cut into her hide. I need help, Bold Fox. Send some women to help me skin the beast for I am bidden to keep its hide. As long as I do that, the Oglala will be safe from the white man."

Bold Fox stepped back, looking at her as though afraid to touch her. "You are truly gifted, Buffalo Dreamer, a holy woman of great power! I will get help for you, and I will send word into the sweat lodge, so that the elders and leaders there shall know what has happened. We can all take great hope in this."

He turned and ran toward the sweat lodge, shouting to others that the sacred white buffalo had again appeared to their holy woman, that they would now be victorious in battle with the Pawnee.

Buffalo Dreamer sank to the ground, feeling burdened with responsibility. Having been visited and protected by the sacred white buffalo, she was highly obligated for the safety, success, and vitality of the Oglala. She must protect the sacred hide with her life.

Women came running. Apparently finished with their prayers and sacrifices, honored warriors exited the sweat lodge. They, too, offered their help. She saw Rising Eagle, and she managed to stand again as he approached. When he reached her, she stepped back. He had just finished the rite of purification, and now he would not want her to touch him until after his battle with the Pawnee. She looked from him to where the white buffalo's body lay on the edge of the bluff. Meeting her husband's gaze again, she held her chin proudly as she spoke. "It is a good sign, my husband. Our son will be saved. The Sacred White has said so."

Hope shone in Rising Eagle's dark eyes. "This is indeed a great sign!"

"You must cut out her heart," Buffalo Dreamer told her husband. "I am to eat of it, but I am too weak to pierce the tough skin and muscle."

Rising Eagle nodded. "Let us go quickly!" He walked past her and up the hill. Helped by Shihenna women, Buffalo Dreamer followed, along with Bold Fox, Many Horses, and old Runs With The Deer. Upon reaching the white buffalo, the Shihenna women began adeptly gutting the sacred animal. They whispered reverently as they worked, rather than talking in the usual loud, joking manner used when happily gutting and skinning many buffalo after a hunt. This was different. This was an event that would be spoken of for generations.

Both Shihenna and Oglala warriors watched in wonder. Once they cleaned out the animal, the women would go about the task of skinning it.

"The meat must be divided so that every man, woman, and child eats of it," Runs With The Deer announced, his fading voice and white hair giving away his advanced years. "And more must be smoked and saved to take back to the Oglala, so that they, too, can eat of it. It will make each of us wiser and stronger."

The Shihenna women moved away when Rising Eagle knelt before the buffalo. He took his hunting knife from its sheath at his waist, then held it up to the heavens.

> *Guardian of the Universe,* he sang.
> *I offer you this knife.*
> *With it I remove the heart of the Sacred White.*
> *And thus I remove its spirit,*
> *That Buffalo Dreamer may eat of it*
> *And thus receive the spirit of the White Buffalo.*
> *Keep us strong. Make us wise.*

Rising Eagle leaned down and deftly cut into the already-open rib cage, slicing around the animal's still-warm heart. He reached inside the beast then and grasped hold of the bloody muscle, holding it up to the heavens as he rose, singing again:

> *Keeper of the Universe,*
> *I hold up to you the spirit of the Sacred White.*

Blood from the fresh-cut heart ran down his arms.

> *Bless us, Great Spirit!*
> *Make us strong! Make us wise!*

He turned to Buffalo Dreamer and held out the heart. Her own heart pounding with the weight of her responsibility, Buffalo Dreamer stepped forward. Rising Eagle handed her the slippery-soft muscle and she grasped it gingerly. She brought it to her lips and bit off a piece, savoring the sweet meat, then swallowed it and held up the heart.

"Death to the Pawnee!" she shouted.

The warriors broke into shrieking war cries, repeating her chant. "Death to the Pawnee!"

The women trilled in their own songs of war and assured victory. Now their husbands and sons could join the Oglala in war against the Pawnee, and they would not have to worry about defeat. The Sacred White had appeared to all of them through Buffalo Dreamer, most holy woman of the Lakota Nation. They had been allowed to touch the sacred animal, and all would eat of its meat. Gladly they would skin the animal and begin drying and curing the hide for Buffalo Dreamer, whom they were honored to know.

Bold Fox, Many Horses, and Runs With The Deer joined in the shouting and celebrating, all three men still strong and fierce enough to ride into battle against the Pawnee. Buffalo Dreamer watched and listened, holding the warm heart in her hands, still reveling in this most glorious moment. She held out the heart to Rising Eagle, indicating that he, too, should eat of it. He placed his hands over her own so that the heart remained in her grasp. Buffalo Dreamer felt greatly honored at his touch. Now she, too, was purified.

Rising Eagle bent down to eat of the raw heart, then met her gaze, again with a look she had never seen before in his dark eyes.

"Death to the Pawnee," he said quietly to Buffalo Dreamer, "and to the *wasicu* who would dare to kill the Sacred White!"

CHAPTER FOUR

BUFFALO DREAMER PROUDLY rode her sturdy black mare, a gift from Rising Eagle. Captured from the Crow, the horse, named "Sotaju" for its smoky black color, was among many other fine gifts, including the grizzly bear's hide, that Rising Eagle had presented to her father for her hand in marriage.

The band of Oglala and the Shihenna warriors with whom they rode, at least thirty strong, followed the two scouts who had returned earlier, after four days of tracking. Arrow Runner, the lead scout and Rising Eagle's brother-in-law, was sure he had spotted his nephew in the Pawnee camp they intended to raid. Arrow Runner was a member of the Badger Society, and no one doubted his keen eyesight and his clever abilities to spy on enemy camps.

Rising Eagle slowed his horse as he followed his brother-in-law into a grassy ravine. Experience at waging war and surprising the enemy had taught these men how to be nearly silent in such moments of danger. Rising Eagle's well-trained war pony stepped lightly.

Sotaju also moved with graceful stealth through the high grass. Buffalo Dreamer's heart raced with excitement at the prospect of holding Big Little Boy in her arms again. Surely he must be alive. After all, the child's conception and birth were the result of another of Rising Eagle's sacrificial prayer vigils atop Medicine Mountain. They considered their son to be a gift from the Feathered One.

"Our enemy is near," she heard Arrow Runner tell Rising Eagle as Sotaju moved closer. "We can go no farther without their lookouts seeing us. Their camp is over another rise beyond this ravine. One or two men can easily sneak through the tall grass to spy on them, but a war party on horseback cannot approach without being seen."

Rising Eagle's horse shook its head and turned in a circle. Named "Olute" for its exceptionally large-muscled and powerful legs, the spotted gray-and-white gelding had been chosen by Rising Eagle for its speed and agility. Olute was the most dependable of all his horses in times of war and hunting.

"We must strike swiftly," Rising Eagle told Arrow Runner, his eyes glittering with eagerness. "My son will not spend one more day among the arrogant Pawnee."

Buffalo Dreamer shared his eagerness. Two days of rest following her fast had brought back most of her strength, aided by her burning desire to find her son. She was prepared to ride against the Pawnee with her husband, excited about participating in a daring adventure usually reserved only for the men. Now it would be each man for himself, to count coup or to kill, to capture whatever horses they could, and to dare the enemy in battle.

"It is a large camp," Arrow Runner explained. "They have more men than we, but about half of them are younger warriors. There are not many women. I think it is a hunting party and that those who took your son had broken away from the others to search for buffalo when they came upon our camp."

"That means there could be a much bigger camp not far away," Rising Eagle surmised. "We must hit them hard, find my son, then quickly ride north again. We do not have enough men to face a bigger camp."

"There is one more thing," Arrow Runner warned, keeping his voice low. "When I first spied on the Pawnee camp, I saw them trading hides and furs, as well as women, to white men, who gave them long guns in return. It was not like when we once traded skins for a few of the white man's guns. I saw them laugh together, and the Pawnee gave their young women to the white men to take inside their tepees. They drank something together, as though they were great friends, and it made all of them laugh more and begin behaving wildly, dancing around a fire. I think perhaps it is the white man's firewater they drank."

Rising Eagle glanced at Buffalo Dreamer. She knew how much he hated the white man's evil drink. He had seen what it did to some of the Lakota who'd chosen to live near the white man's forts and settlements farther east. They became lazy and worthless, shaming themselves just to get more of the firewater that made them act like fools. Never Sleeps's real mother, Fall Leaf Woman, had given them her baby boy because she herself was addicted to the firewater. Her white husband had been abusive and cruel, yet Fall Leaf Woman had chosen to stay with him because he could provide her with the drink, which she craved above all else in her life. Rising Eagle had killed her husband, but Fall Leaf Woman had still given them her son, choosing to stay on the settlement and sell herself to white men in exchange for more whiskey.

"So, the Pawnee are now friendly with the *wasicus*." Rising Eagle stiffened. "Drinking the white man's firewater will only make them weak and useless!"

Arrow Runner nodded. "I also saw them trade for many guns. I think most every man in the camp owns a white man's weapon, able to kill from a distance. We have only a few of the long guns among ourselves."

Again Olute shifted nervously, as though anxious to be off.

"I do not fear any Pawnee man, no matter *what* his weapon." Rising Eagle replied. "The Sacred White told Buffalo Dreamer that we will find and rescue my son, and I will do so *without* using the white man's weapons." He raised his war shield. "Death to the Pawnee!" he shouted again to the others, not caring now that he might be heard. The time for battle was at hand.

Yips and shouts answered him as the others raised their

fists and war shields. Among them was Standing Rock, Rising Eagle's young cousin of twenty summers, eager for his first real battle; Buffalo Dreamer's own father, Looking Horse; Owl Crier, a Kit Fox leader; and Wind In Grass, an esteemed Shirt Wearer, married to Standing Rock's sister.

Runs With The Deer and Bold Fox raised their lances and tomahawks. Several other Oglala warriors, combined with the many Shihenna men, made them a strong war party.

Rising Eagle turned his horse to face Buffalo Dreamer. He tied the braided-rawhide reins around the animal's neck so they could not hang loose. Then he removed his tomahawk, affixing his war shield to his left arm. Watching him—virile, handsome, and heated for battle—strengthened Buffalo Dreamer's courage. Her husband would ride Olute into battle using no reins.

"Watch out for yourself," Rising Eagle told her. "If you see Big Little Boy, grab him and ride away from danger. I cannot keep my eyes on you every moment."

Buffalo Dreamer tossed her hair behind her shoulders. "You do not need to watch over me," she answered proudly. "The white buffalo has promised our safety. Take many of their horses, Rising Eagle, and count many coup!"

Rising Eagle's dark eyes shone with revenge. He shouted a war cry and charged away, sitting his horse as though a part of the animal. The magnificent gelding galloped off, maneuvered only by signals from Rising Eagle's thighs, knees, and feet.

Buffalo Dreamer kicked Sotaju into a hard run, and the rest of the warriors followed. Buffalo Dreamer felt no fear, only excitement at the prospect of finding her son, and at the great honor of riding into battle with some of the most highly esteemed men of the Oglala clan. She had no doubt that part of Rising Eagle's fury in this attack stemmed from the humiliation of having had his son captured from under his nose. Besides finding Big Little Boy, Rising Eagle would regain lost pride by counting many coup and taking many horses.

Buffalo Dreamer's heart pounded as the Pawnee village came into sight. They were almost upon their enemy!

CHAPTER FIVE

OGLALA AND SHIHENNA warriors alike charged ahead. Buffalo Dreamer sensed that Sotaju was as eager as she was, and she drove the sleek black mare at full gallop, holding neck and neck with Olute. As they moved closer, Buffalo Dreamer noticed little puffs of smoke in the distance, followed shortly by loud cracking sounds. The Pawnee were shooting at her and the others with their long guns, yet she felt no fear, only confidence.

Olute ran full-out, his neck stretched, mane flying in the wind. Out of the corner of her eye, Buffalo Dreamer saw Rising Eagle lean forward, defying the gunfire. Although the Oglala also possessed several of the white man's long guns, they were still training themselves to be adept with the weapons, and only a few men, including Rising Eagle, owned one. But for a hard, fast attack on horseback, Rising Eagle and most of the others still preferred using bow and arrow and tomahawk, weapons with which they were best experienced.

They were nearly in the midst of the Pawnee now, yet still no bullets touched them. Again *Wakan-Tanka* seemed to be blessing them with magical powers. Never had Buffalo Dreamer felt so close to her husband. The excitement was unlike anything she had ever known. Behind them, the rest of the Oglala and Shihenna screamed war whoops and calls of attack; ahead of them, the few women and children in camp scattered, a few of the Pawnee men hurrying behind to protect them. Other Pawnee warriors scrambled to mount their horses, some trying to grab the ropes of several mounts at once to keep them from being stolen. Buffalo Dreamer pulled out the knife she normally used for gutting game, not caring if she had to kill even women and children to get to her son. Such was the risk the enemy took when stealing a child.

A powerful-looking Pawnee buck headed toward Rising Eagle on horseback, lance raised. The man gave out a gutteral roar as he charged Rising Eagle, the whites of his wild eyes gleaming with determination. Buffalo Dreamer winced when they clashed. Rising Eagle whacked the Pawnee man's lance with his tomahawk and cut it in half, then hit the warrior on a back swing, landing the tomahawk into the nape of the Pawnee's neck. The enemy warrior let out a chilling cry of pain and fell from his horse.

Now they were in the thick of battle—gunfire, grunts, and screams of pain all around, blood splattering everywhere. There was no time for Buffalo Dreamer to look to anything but her own safety, and to search for her son. She heard gunfire close by, and out of the corner of her eye, she saw a Shihenna warrior fall, together with his horse.

A Pawnee warrior grabbed her leg then and tried to pull her off Sotaju. She slashed at him with her knife, cutting him across the eyes. He screamed and fell to the ground, his hands over his face. He had barely landed before another warrior came at Buffalo Dreamer, grasping her right wrist before she could stab at him. Quickly, Buffalo Dreamer used her left hand to jerk out a stone war club Rising Eagle had given her. She brought it down hard over the man's skull, knowing she could not hesitate or fail to use her full strength. She heard a cracking sound, but the warrior still clung to her wrist. Fearing he might yet pull her off her horse she smashed at his skull several more times, fiercely clinging tightly to the knife. Finally the warrior let go of her wrist and fell to the ground, his skull caved in.

Buffalo Dreamer realized then that the rest of the Pawnee men still in camp were engrossed in hand-to-hand combat with the Oglala and Shihenna. She took the opportunity to charge Sotaju through the camp, knocking down a woman who slashed at her with a knife, then ducking down when she galloped toward a Pawnee man pointing a long gun at her. For some reason, the gun would not fire, and she continued to feel confident that the buffalo spirit protected her. She ran the man over with Sotaju. He gave out a short scream and then a grunt, followed by silence.

Buffalo Dreamer headed for the area where she had seen women and children running. Over and over, she screamed out Big Little Boy's name. Behind her, she heard more gunshots and shouts, war whoops, grunts and thuds, horses whinnying, and the screams of the few women still in camp. Dogs were barking and children crying, most of those sounds coming from the high grass surrounding the camp.

Again she called out Big Little Boy's name, charging Sotaju back and forth, searching the tall grass, fearing nothing now. A warrior protecting the women suddenly rose up from the grass and ran full-speed toward her, raising a tomahawk. Before he reached her, Buffalo Dreamer flinched at a sudden movement to her right, realizing only after his lance landed in the approaching warrior's neck that the movement was Rising Eagle, charging to her rescue. He yanked the lance from the warrior's neck and rode Olute farther into the high grass, causing the Pawnee women to run screaming from their hiding places. One of them carried a husky young boy.

"Big Little Boy!" Buffalo Dreamer screamed. At the same time, Rising Eagle raced past her and rode down on the fleeing woman. He stuck out his foot and knocked her to the ground. Woman and boy went tumbling, and Rising Eagle leaned over his horse and yelled for Big Little Boy to grab hold of his arm. The child obeyed, scrambling up and reaching for his father. He was laughing with excitement, and Buffalo Dreamer realized that her son likely had no idea of the danger he was in. He probably thought this was all just a game.

Rising Eagle rode back to Buffalo Dreamer and plunked

Big Little Boy into her arms. "Ride to the left!" he ordered. Blood ran in a stream down his face from a wound on his forehead. "Circle around the fighting and head back toward where we came from. When you reach safety, wait for me."

He rode off, and Buffalo Dreamer obeyed his command. She clung tightly to Big Little Boy with one arm and galloped away from the scene, riding as hard as she could in case other women or another warrior tried to stop her. Suddenly she felt a hard thud on her right calf, and Sotaju stumbled slightly.

"Go! Go!" she screamed at the horse. She dared not stop now. A dog ran in front of the horse, but Sotaju did not spook easily. He simply ran over the dog, and Buffalo Dreamer heard a yelp. She did not look back, nor did she bother to look at her leg. Her son's safety was all that mattered at the moment.

After several minutes of riding, the sounds of fighting dimmed. Buffalo Dreamer saw nothing but vast, open grassland for miles ahead. She knew by the sun that she was headed north, and she kept going until she was sure she was safe, then turned a panting, sweaty Sotaju to look back.

She breathed hard with a mixture of relief and apprehension, as well as pain that was beginning to throb fiercely through her right calf. Far in the distance she could still hear gunshots and shouts, screams and whinnying. Rising Eagle was continuing the fight. The Pawnee would not give up easily, but neither did they realize whose son they had kidnapped. He was not just any Lakota boy. He was the son of Rising Eagle and Buffalo Dreamer, and the Pawnee would suffer for what they had done.

Tears welled in her eyes as she hugged Big Little Boy close. "My son!" she wept. "I shall have to tie a rope around you so that you can never get away from me or your father again," she chided. At the same time, she kissed his chubby cheek several times over, squeezing the boy tightly in utter relief that he was still alive.

Big Little Boy giggled, entirely unaffected by his abduction and ensuing rescue.

Buffalo Dreamer smiled through tears and shook her head. "I have a feeling you are going to cause me great worry as you grow older and more adventurous," she said, clinging to him. "You are truly your father's son, knowing no fear."

She quickly inspected him to be sure he bore no bruises or wounds, then finally looked down and saw that her leg was bleeding heavily. She'd been so intent on her mission that she had not even been aware of how badly she was injured. Blood ran into her moccasin. She took off her rawhide belt and tied it around her leg above the wound to slow the bleeding. It was a strange-looking wound, a hole rather than a cut, and she realized that she must have been hit by one of the round balls that were shot from the white man's long guns. There were actually two holes in the fleshy part of her calf, and she could tell that the ball must have gone right through her leg. She ran a hand carefully over her shin bone. It did not seem to be broken, and she realized she was fortunate the injury was not worse.

She inspected Sotaju, relieved to learn that her leg had apparently kept the lead ball from hurting the horse.

"Indeed," she murmured, "the white buffalo is with me."

She looked toward the warring camp again; in truth, she was proud of her wound—she was now a full-fledged Lakota warrior! She breathed deeply at the good feeling that gave her. She, a woman, would have a story of battle to share with others over campfires!

"Rising Eagle," she whispered, anxiously waiting and watching.

"*Ate*," Big Little Boy said, pointing.

Several Oglala and Shihenna warriors rode toward them then. Buffalo Dreamer prayed that her husband would be among them. A few of the victorious warriors led stolen horses, and as they came closer, she could see Rising Eagle. She hugged her son with relief. Olute's hooves sprayed sod as a bloody Rising Eagle, still heated with battle, halted his horse from a full gallop and studied his wife and son. He glanced at her leg.

"You are wounded!"

"It will be all right. I think it is from the ball of a long gun, but the bone is not broken. Your wounds are worse."

"I suffer them proudly! We have our son back, and I took two Pawnee scalps and counted many coup. I have with me four Pawnee horses. Now the Pawnee know that we will hunt as far south into Pawnee country as we please, and that they will suffer if they dare make trouble for us again!"

Buffalo Dreamer did not mention that she also had counted coup and had probably killed at least two warriors. This was not the time to tell her husband such a thing. Rising Eagle was a *Naca*. He was strong not just in body, but also in spirit, too, and now his tortured pride could heal. She would not harm it by declaring her own accomplishments.

Rising Eagle came closer, leaning over to study her wounded leg. "Can you keep riding?"

"I have no choice. We must leave quickly, Rising Eagle. The Pawnee might get help and follow us."

Rising Eagle nodded. "We will stop as soon as we can and dress our wounds." He breathed deeply. "I will not soon forget that my woman was wounded by a white man's long gun. We hardly ever see the *wasicus,* yet already they begin to intrude on our lives, and we have not even yet seen those who wear the blue coats. It is as though they are an unseen enemy, able to strike without even being present. I consider them just as much an enemy as the Pawnee or Shoshoni or Crow!"

More Oglala and Shihenna warriors rode past them, some of them herding stolen horses. Rising Eagle reached out and touched Buffalo Dreamer's arm, then stroked Big Little Boy's soft cheek. "My son," he murmured. "Never again will I fail you." He glanced at Buffalo Dreamer. "Or you." He turned his horse. "Come!"

Buffalo Dreamer whipped Sotaju into another run, following her husband north, away from Pawnee country, while Big Little Boy laughed and screamed with delight as the wind whistled past his face.

SEPTEMBER 1836

Moon of the Drying Meat

CHAPTER SIX

FLORENCE LANGUISHED ON the steps that led to Newt Porter's tavern, sipping on a pint of whiskey. She no longer felt shame at being a nightly fixture at Fort Pierre, having become numb to any feelings at all. The precious whiskey dulled all emotions, especially the pain in her heart.

She missed her son. Little Wolf was just a baby when she had given him to Rising Eagle to raise. He was small and deformed, and for all she knew, he might not have survived. If he had, he probably carried a new name now, for it was custom among the Lakota to rename the children as they grew. It was useless to wonder. She would never know.

She stared at the brown bottle in her hand. Once she was called Fall Leaf Woman, a proud Oglala woman. Now she felt no pride, and the Oglala no longer wanted her. Here, she had taken a white name, and here she was doomed to stay. She had given up her son for this. She never could have properly cared for him. She needed her whiskey, and Little Wolf needed a better life than he would have had here at Fort Pierre, scorned by the whites as a half-breed and a bastard. She had done her son a favor when she gave him to Rising Eagle.

She took another swallow. Rising Eagle was one more part of her life she needed to forget. She had loved him, but she and her brother, Gray Owl, had betrayed him out of anger that he'd wed someone else. That betrayal had led the Lakota Nation to ostracize them and so they had come here to Fort Pierre. Later when Rising Eagle found them, he beat and disfigured her brother, cutting off Gray Owl's nose and ears, then killed her abusive white husband before leaving with Little Wolf. Months later, Gray Owl, lost in humiliation and whiskey, had killed himself.

She took another swallow of whiskey, consoling herself with the thought that her son would be taught the Lakota way, and would be much happier than he ever would have been living here, watching his shameless mother sell herself for whiskey money. It was an easy trade in which a woman could earn her way in this place. White men seemed to have a never-ending need for a woman, and she filled that need for many of the single men who lived in or about the fort, and not a few married ones also, both white and Indian. Some of the Indian men called her *witkowin,* a crazy, immoral woman, and she supposed she was exactly that. Occasionally she took in laundry, but it was back-breaking work that left her knuckles sore and red. If the white men would wear skins instead of cloth, they would not have to wash their clothing so often—although from the smell of them, it still was not often enough.

She tossed her black, tangled hair away from her face, then pulled the neck of her plain blue cotton blouse down over her shoulders, thinking of how Rising Eagle had once desired her when they were both young. If not for his vision all those years ago, foretelling that he must wed another, she would probably still be sharing his bed, the wife of an honored Lakota warrior.

She pulled one side of her skirt up over a knee to expose a slender, dark leg, eyeing the driver of a trade wagon that clattered past. She offered him a sly, fetching smile, but after a look of curiosity, then of derision, the man looked away, whistling to the mules pulling the wagon. Dust rolled into the air and when it cleared, Florence noticed a man in a dark suit and hat approaching. The stiff white collar of his shirt looked uncomfortable.

"Reverend Kingsley," she muttered. She had seen the missionary man several times since he had come to Fort

Pierre to build a ministry, but she had never spoken to him, nor had he addressed her; but whenever they did pass one another, he always gave her a second glance. It occurred to her that in those glances, she never saw any scorn in his eyes, and this struck her as odd. Most of the other "respectable" whites around here certainly did scorn her. White women stayed out of her way, sometimes crossing to the other side of the fort grounds whenever they saw her coming. If their husbands stopped to look or speak, the women gave them a tug and an angry look.

She drank more, keeping her eyes on the reverend, beginning to feel uneasy when it appeared that he meant to come closer and talk to her this time. She felt suddenly self-conscious under his scrutiny as he approached, confused and uneasy about the look of true concern in his eyes. When he reached her, she stood up, backing away slightly.

"Florence Dundee?" he asked.

What on earth did the man want of her? She nodded. "That is the white-woman name my husband gave me."

The reverend actually smiled. "So, you *do* speak English."

Florence frowned. "I have lived here among the whites for many years."

"I know." He tipped his hat slightly. "I am Reverend Abel Kingsley. You probably already know that. You've seen me around here for the last month or so." The man stepped onto the first wooden step, and Florence moved farther back on the boardwalk, watching his friendly smile warily. No one around here ever smiled at her like that.

She had never given the reverend a second look, until now. She guessed him to be perhaps in his mid-thirties. For a white man, he was decent looking, with gray eyes and thick, brown, wavy hair. He was not as big and strong looking as her husband, John Dundee, had been, but he had a presentable build. Of course no man could ever compare to Rising Eagle in either physique or looks, but Kingsley had a square jawline and fine bone structure, a deep yet gentle voice.

When she made no reply to his comment, he removed his hat and came up the other two steps, moving even closer to her. Florence was tempted to turn and run.

"Florence, I would like to talk with you. Would you consider coming over to the little church the settlers have built for me? We could certainly talk better there than here in front of the tavern."

Florence moved her whiskey bottle behind her skirt. "What would we talk about?"

The man shrugged. "Oh, I just . . . I've been watching you. I've asked around about you, and I know your story, how you came here and how your husband gave your son to the Lakota, who proceeded to kill the man before they made off with your baby."

That was not quite the truth, the part about John giving away Little Wolf. She had done it herself, but was too ashamed to admit it. Let people believe what they wanted. Everyone knew her husband had hated his half-breed son anyway, had even threatened to kill him. But why explain it all to this man? And why did he even care?

"I still do not understand why you wish to talk with me," she answered. She caught the look of appreciation in Abel Kingsley's eyes as he quickly scanned her appearance, yet she did not feel offended, nor did she feel that he looked at her as a man hungry for a woman would do.

"I see hope in you, Florence. I see someone who can help me reach your people with my faith. I can help them give up their heathen practices and follow my religion and learn the white man's way. That is, after all, how they will eventually have to live. I can see it coming, Florence, the day when all the Lakota and other Indian tribes will have to learn to live alongside the white man in peace."

Florence thought about Rising Eagle living this way, and it made her smile with the humor of it. "That will never happen," she answered.

Kingsley smiled in return. "Well, maybe you can help me understand why not. Help me understand the Lakota. But most important, I would like to understand you. I want to know what happened that caused you to be living here and wasting yourself as you do. You are a very beautiful woman, and you are still young. You have much to offer in this life, and I need help in reaching the Lakota. You can help me learn their language, learn how they think. Will you consider it?"

Florence frowned, baffled by the surprising request. "Maybe," she shrugged.

Kingsley folded his arms. "You would first have to give up your sinful ways, Florence. I can help you stop drinking whiskey. I can teach you about my faith, and teach you how to write, read, things like that. Would you like to learn those things?"

Florence fingered the whiskey bottle she still held behind her skirt. She both loved and hated the firewater. It soothed her sore heart, but it had also caused her son to be born deformed, she was sure. And her need of it made her do bad things just to have more. Still, the thought of never taking another drink was close to horrifying.

"I can't stop drinking the whiskey," she answered. "I need it."

Kingsley shook his head. "You only *think* you need it. I can show you a way to quit, Florence. All you need to do is learn to trust in my *God* and pray to him. He will help you, and so will I, if you will let me." He reached out his hand. "Please, come over to the church with me for a while and we will talk. You can even bring your whiskey. I promise not to force you to do anything. I just want to talk. I came out here to save the Lakota, and I have to start somewhere. I've not had much luck with those who camp around the fort. I've been watching you, and I feel sure that you are the key to my making progress here. Will you just give it a try?"

Florence stared at his hand, solid and strong. Something deep inside told her to take it, that her only hope of rising above her dreary, abusive situation was to go with this man. How strange, for he was a white man, and so different from any of the others around here.

She cautiously reached out. He took her hand and squeezed it gently as he led her down the steps. Filled with curiosity and wonder, she walked with him toward the crudely-built church, her bottle of whiskey still gripped tightly behind her.

JULY 1838

Moon When the Chokecherries Ripen

CHAPTER SEVEN

BUFFALO DREAMER, ALONG with several other women, stood on a hill watching the hunters in the distance. The Oglala were camped in the land of the shallow river, high on the grassy plains where buffalo abounded. After two weeks of scouring the land, a large herd of bison had appeared this morning, just over the rise from the Oglala camp.

Eagerly the men had ridden out, and the women had hurried up the hill to watch the hunt. If the kill was successful, the women would be busy for many long days to come, skinning the carcasses and dividing up the meat, as well as carving hundreds of weapons and utensils from the bones and making clothing, shelter, and medicine from all the other parts of the animals.

"*Wakan-Tanka* has answered our prayers, bringing brother buffalo almost right into our camp!" Yellow Turtle Woman said in a near whisper.

"It is because of the white buffalo robe," Buffalo Dreamer answered Rising Eagle's aunt. "Look at how many there are! Soon our camp will be filled with the smoke from curing meat, and hides will be staked for drying as far as the eye can see. For the next several days, our men will truly feast." She rubbed her pregnant belly. "Yes, *Wakan-Tanka* has given us many fine blessings."

The past winter had been one of deep snows and long hours spent inside the tepees, a time for storytelling and games . . . a time when a man and a woman made love often. Now Rising Eagle's seed again grew within Buffalo

Dreamer, and it was with great joy that she looked forward to giving him another child.

The hunters approached the herd on horseback, quietly and slowly surrounding it, some actually walking their horses right into the midst of the great beasts. A buffalo hunt was both exciting and frightening, for it was not uncommon that a hunter was knocked from his horse and trampled. Riding among a thundering herd of buffalo was a very dangerous thing to do, but Buffalo Dreamer had faith in Rising Eagle's abilities. Even though he owned a white man's long gun, he hunted with bow and arrow. He did not want to shoot into a herd from a distance, risking scaring them off in the wrong direction, or perhaps hitting one of the hunters who rode among the herd. Besides, hunting in the midst of the great shaggy bison with bow and arrow was a true test of a man's abilities and bravery. The white man's way of hunting, Rising Eagle said, seemed almost cowardly. To shoot an animal from a distance gave the sacred creature no chance to run or to challenge its predator.

"There is Standing Rock," Yellow Turtle Woman said, pointing to her oldest son, now twenty-three summers in age. "He has become such an honored man, one of our best scouts," she bragged. Then she sighed. "Time goes too swiftly, I think. My daughter, Sweet Root Woman, is now twenty-one summers and married to a Shirt Wearer."

"Wind In Grass has truly gained much honor," Buffalo Dreamer said, "and he and Sweet Root Woman have given you two fine grandsons. I am anxious for the day I will be a grandmother, too."

Yellow Turtle Woman smiled. "Even Little Black Horse is already seventeen summers. But I am lucky to have been able to conceive late in life. I have my little son, Two Feet Dancing, still only six summers in age."

Buffalo Dreamer sighed, realizing that she herself was already twenty-one summers. "It seems only yesterday I was still thinking like a child, frightened by the prospect of marrying a complete stranger," she told her friend. "I was so afraid of Rising Eagle when he took me for a wife."

"And now *you* give *him* the orders inside the tepee, hmmm?"

Both women giggled, excited by the view of the hunt, happy over the peace and prosperity the Oglala enjoyed these days. Buffalo Dreamer spotted Arrow Runner among the hunters. He and Many Robes Woman had given Rising Eagle two nephews since they married. Little Beaver was just a few days older than her own son, and Fox Running had been born only last year.

All the children played in the village below the hill, watched over by several of the elders, including Buffalo Dreamer's mother, who never seemed to tire of tending to the young ones. Because of the danger of spooking the buffalo herd on the other side of the rise, the children had not been allowed to come and watch. The little ones simply had too much energy to remain still and quiet while their fathers approached the great beasts. The elders were prepared to grab up the children, mount their horses and run if it became necessary because of a stampede in the wrong direction. However, the hunters were doing a good job of coaxing the buffalo away from the hill and toward wide, flat, open land. Normally, the hunt was conducted far from camp to avoid such danger, but this herd had practically walked right up to them. The temptation had been too great for the hunters to worry about the danger.

"It is as though the Great Spirit sent them right to us," Many Robes Woman said, walking up beside her aunt and her sister-in-law. Fox Running slept soundly in the cradleboard that Many Robes Woman wore tied to her back. "I wonder who will get the most buffalo this time," she pondered, then added teasingly, "My brother, or my husband?"

Buffalo Dreamer smiled. "Rising Eagle enjoys arguing with his brother-in-law," she said. "They both like to stretch the truth about their kill, but we can watch the hunt this time. We will help them remember it the right way."

All three women struggled to stifle their laughter so they wouldn't startle the herd. Even though the great shaggy beasts were a good half mile away, the women knew that in this land, sound became magnified when carried on the wind.

The hunters drew ever closer, and the buffalo continued to graze as though oblivious to the intruders. One of the men raised his bow. From her vantage point, Buffalo Dreamer could not tell which man it was. He released an arrow, and it landed in the animal's side. The buffalo shuffled sideways, ducked its head and shook it hard. Even from this distance, Buffalo Dreamer could see dust fly from its shaggy mane. A second hunter drew his bow and fired an arrow into the neck of yet another buffalo.

Finally, the first buffalo fell, but its killer had to shoot again into its side before it lay still in death. The second buffalo also fell, and Buffalo Dreamer could sense the alarm that spread among the remaining herd. Those closest to the two fallen animals began to shuffle about and paw the earth, and finally one started running.

Within moments, the entire herd was in motion, and it was as though the ground suddenly shook under a great burst of thunder. Huge clouds of dust rolled into the air, and it was not long before it became impossible to distinguish man from beast. The hunters vanished from view in the dizzying swirl of brown shaggy backs and thick dust. Amid the noise of pounding hooves, snorting buffalo, and whinnying horses, the women could hear the excited shouts of the hunters, and all prayed that none of their loved ones would be among those who would end up hurt or killed.

The great herd, spread out as far as the eye could see, veered first to the right, below the hill and directly past where the women stood watching. Then it swirled, going back to the left, heading away from the camp. Several of the hunters followed, making sure the beasts kept going in that direction. As the herd thundered into the distance, its stampede making the earth tremble, a wall of dust followed it. As the dust settled, Buffalo Dreamer quickly counted at least ten downed buffalo. She and the others hurried back to camp to mount their horses, left tied near the tepees for just this moment.

In spite of being seven months with child, Buffalo Dreamer gladly joined the other women in the work that lay ahead. The travois tied to Sotaju was packed with knives for skinning and carving, and with old hides that would be spread on the ground for wrapping the meat. The older women in camp were already pounding stakes into the ground for stretching the hides, and preparing fires for smoking the meat.

Five-summers-old Big Little Boy hurried up to his mother, begging to go along.

"One day you will be out hunting the buffalo with your father and grandfather," Buffalo Dreamer promised him. "But for now, you must stay here with your *uncheedah*."

Never Sleeps ran up beside Big Little Boy, quietly watching and listening. Buffalo Dreamer's adopted son followed Big Little Boy around worshipfully, playing whatever his stepbrother wanted to play, at his side constantly. "We will practice with our bows and arrows," Never Sleeps told his mother with a smile, holding up the small bow Rising Eagle had made for him. "We will hunt good, too, someday."

"Yes you will, my son," Buffalo Dreamer answered, noticing how startlingly blue the child's eyes were against his dark skin. "Later, you and Big Little Boy can help sort the meat that we will share with others. I will show you how to cure and smoke the meat."

Never Sleeps smiled eagerly, but Big Little Boy frowned. "That is woman's work. I would rather hunt."

Buffalo Dreamer shook her head. "You are too eager for your age, my son. But that is the sign of a proud warrior in the making. I will tell Rising Eagle how anxious you are to hunt with him."

Big Little Boy finally broke into a beaming smile. He and Never Sleeps ran off, toy bows and small, blunt arrows in hand. Some of the other women, including Yellow Turtle

Woman and Many Robes Woman, led their horses over beside Buffalo Dreamer, pulling their own supplies on travois, ready for many days of hard work.

Buffalo Dreamer smiled with happiness. Life squirmed in her belly, her sons were healthy and eager, and tonight the camp would be alive with dancing and the celebration of the hunt, the air filled with the wonderful smell of roasting meat. The magnificent herd that *Wakan-Tanka* had sent them would provide enough meat and hides for the rest of the summer, and probably for most of the winter, as well as extra hides for trading.

In spite of all the warnings against the white man in her own and Rising Eagle's dreams and visions, Buffalo Dreamer had seen no real sign of danger from the *wasicu*, nor had she seen any wearing the blue coats she so dreaded. Few whites from Fort Pierre, far to the east, had ventured into Oglala land. Perhaps they were wiser than she thought, and had decided to stay away.

Sotaju crested the hill, and now the herd could barely be seen to the north, a handful of the hunters still chasing it. She and the other women stared in awe at what lay below: perhaps fifty or sixty slain buffalo. A few warriors rode among the bodies and upon seeing the women above, one raised his arm and gave forth a loud cry of joy and victory, rejoicing over a good hunt. Buffalo Dreamer could see that it was Rising Eagle. As she and the other women began descending the hill, he dismounted and knelt beside one of the dead beasts. Buffalo Dreamer knew it would be one that he had killed, identified by the specific markings on Rising Eagle's arrows. He would begin counting his kill, and at the same time, he would touch each dead buffalo and thank its spirit. Every animal that offered itself so that the Oglala might live and prosper must be honored for its sacrifice.

Buffalo Dreamer thought how beautiful was the scene before her: a great big land in which the Lakota could live and hunt, a deep blue sky, green grass offered by Mother Earth to feed the many horses of the Oglala, a good buffalo kill. What a wonderful gift the buffalo was, an animal that sustained their every need. Even from this distance, she detected the bright smile on Rising Eagle's face. This moment and this place were surely very much like the heavenly abode where they would all someday go after death to be with the Feathered One and their beloved ancestors.

AUGUST 1838

Time of the Hot Moon

CHAPTER EIGHT

FLORENCE FINISHED READING a chapter from the Old Testament of the King James Bible. She sat with Abel Kingsley at the kitchen table of the small house he shared with his sister, Belinda, who had come to Fort Pierre from Illinois to join her brother in his missionary efforts.

"That was very good, Florence," Abel told her. "I can't believe how fast and how well you have learned to read and write. Tomorrow I would like you to read from the New Testament. The more you learn and remember, the easier it will be for you to help me teach." He leaned across the table, resting his elbows on it as he continued. "You have already been a wonderful help, and an inspiration to people like me who want so much to teach the Lakota a new way."

Florence smiled with satisfaction and pride. Life here at Fort Pierre was now more bearable, and she attributed her newfound happiness to Reverend Kingsley, a devoted Christian who genuinely cared about people, no matter their race and no matter their station in life. During those few months after their first meeting, she had resented his intrusion into her life. How *dare* the white man with his strange religion try to impose his way of life on her? Once he had even locked her in a windowless back room of the church to keep her from drinking. Never had she suffered such agony. No one else at the fort had cared how she was being treated, so no one had interfered. Her screams from pain and those awful hallucinations meant nothing to others. She often heard some, both men and women, laughing outside the barricaded door.

"Thank you," she told Abel. She felt her cheeks grow warm at her next words. "And I have never really thanked you for helping me stop drinking. I know that you also suffered during that time . . . from cruel remarks." She swallowed. "Your sister has told me that some of the men around here spoke insultingly about . . . about what you were really doing with me. It hurts my heart to think of how that must have wounded you, being the honorable, caring man that you are."

Abel cast her a gentle smile. "I never worry about what others say," he told her. "I know in my heart I am doing what is right. That's all that matters. And that is all that should matter to you."

Florence thought of how different Abel was from her former husband. She never imagined that a white man could be so kind and understanding. Abel Kingsley was sometimes quite stern and unbending, but he always made his point without yelling or inflicting physical abuse. He was a rather plain but pleasant-looking man, always clean in appearance, his soft brown eyes rarely showing anger or dissatisfaction.

She met his gaze then, but he quickly looked away. What was it she had seen in his look just then? Could it really have been a new admiration, the kind of admiration a man held for the woman he loved, rather than just for a friend?

Of course not! In spite of her reformation, a man like Abel Kingsley could never love her that way.

"You have instilled in me a new pride," she told him aloud. "A pride I never thought I could feel. And I . . . there are some things you should know about me, things we have never talked about. I have committed more sin than just drinking and . . . selling myself to men, Reverend Kingsley."

"Florence, you don't need—"

"Yes I do, Reverend," she interrupted, determined this time to tell him the things she had never admitted to him.

Abel leaned back in his chair, folding his hands behind his head. "How many times do I have to ask you to call me Abel, Florence?"

She shrugged shyly, staring at the table. "It just does not seem right. I am not worthy—"

"No. Don't ever say that, Florence. I am just a man, no more important than the next, and I am certainly not without sin. But if it's going to make you feel better, tell me whatever it is you think I should know."

Somewhere deep inside she knew she was falling in love. She could not let this happen, not with a man like Abel, especially not with a man who could never love her back . . . once he knew the truth.

"I want to tell you about my life with the Lakota, and what really happened with my son. John Dundee did not give him to the Lakota. *I* did. I gave up my own son because I knew I could not properly care for him since I was drunk most of the time. I would do anything for whiskey then, even stay married to an abusive man who threatened to kill our little boy." She traced her finger over a daisy in the fabric of the tablecloth. "Little Wolf was deformed. Did you know that?"

"You told me once."

"That, too, was probably my fault. I drank heavily the whole time I was with child, and he was born early and small, with some fingers and some toes missing. My husband and others believed it was because I drank, and so it was my fault that my baby boy suffered deformities."

She blinked back tears before continuing. "I gave him away because I loved him. You should know that. I was afraid John would kill him, and I knew that growing up here would mean the lad would suffer being called names. He would never have had a good life, even though John was . . . killed after all. I gave Little Wolf to the Lakota because I knew he would be loved, and he would be raised to be proud of who he was."

She met his eyes again. "I gave my son to a Lakota man called Rising Eagle. I loved Rising Eagle once, and I slept with him several times. You should know that is something young Lakota women do not ordinarily do—chastity and honor are very important to the people. After the age of twelve or so, young Lakota women are not allowed to be alone with a young man. They are always chaperoned. But I had a very strong desire for Rising Eagle, who was then called Night Hunter. I tempted him flagrantly, and he was then a very young man, eager and curious."

She rose and folded her arms, her cheeks burning. She walked away to look out the window at the little church next door, where Abel preached every Sunday and some weekdays about the sins of the flesh.

"I lost the respect of all the Lakota, men and women alike, including Rising Eagle's. Later, he became a man of vision and power. One vision caused him to change his name to Stalking Wolf, and in that vision, he was told he must marry a certain woman, a Brule woman." She faced Abel again. "You have to realize how important dreams and visions are to the Lakota. You say you want to understand us, so understand this, Abel. A man like Rising Eagle will act on anything he is told in his dreams, even if it means giving up his life. To do anything else is dishonorable. Lakota men cannot live with dishonor. And so Rising Eagle went searching for this special woman. He found her, and he risked his life killing a dangerous grizzly bear for her, because her father required the skin of the humpback bear for her hand. Besides that, Rising Eagle was on his way to becoming a *Naca,* a very high-ranking man among the Lakota. That meant I could no longer be a part of his life."

She looked at the floor and paced. "I was not worthy," she added quietly. She put her head back and breathed deeply before continuing. "I was jealous when Rising Eagle returned to the Oglala with his new wife. I told lies about her, tried to shame her. She proved herself most honorable, and because lying and spreading false rumors are not allowed among the Lakota, no one would speak to me after that." She finally walked back and sat down again.

"Then my brother, Gray Owl, betrayed the Lakota by helping our enemy, the Crow, steal Rising Eagle's wife. He thought that if she was no longer there, Rising Eagle would take me for a wife instead. She was to be killed, but she was saved . . . by a miracle."

Abel frowned. "A miracle?"

Florence smiled sadly. "The more you learn about my people, Reverend Kingsley, the more you will see that their religion is not so different from yours . . . I mean, ours. Buffalo Dreamer's prayers have much power, just as Rising Eagle's do. I am sure she did much praying when she was stolen away, and she was saved by a herd of stampeding buffalo. It trampled the village and killed many Crow people. The rest of the Crow ran away, and the herd of buffalo parted when it came to Rising Eagle's wife. Even though she was caught in the midst of the animals, she was not harmed. Oglala men found her and brought her back, and again her prayers worked a miracle. Rising Eagle had been horribly wounded while fighting the men who had abducted her, but her prayers saved him."

Abel sighed and shook his head. "I am sure it was all a coincidence, Florence. Heathens do not work miracles."

Florence raised her eyebrows, feeling defensive. "There is your first mistake, Abel. If you want me to help you teach my people, you must not think of them as heathens. And I tell you again that you must understand and respect their ability to stay in touch with a great power, the one you call Jehovah, and his son, Jesus Christ. The Lakota call their god *Wakan-Tanka,* and there is one he sends to us as a messenger, just as Jehovah sent Jesus. Rising Eagle has seen this messenger, and it is from him that Rising Eagle got his name. We call this messenger the Feathered One. He is part man, part eagle, and he spoke to Rising Eagle in his vision. A man whose prayers are strong enough to invoke the presence of the Feathered One can indeed sometimes work miracles. I suppose it is a bit like Moses speaking to God. And I have seen miracles happen among the Lakota, several times."

She took up the Bible and leafed through it absently. "The way to reach my people is simply to explain to them that the one whom they call *Wakan-Tanka*, we call Jehovah, that they are one and the same. Then they will listen."

Abel put a hand to his chin, fingering his mustache as he thought quietly for several long seconds. "All right. We will try that, but I am not so sure it is right." He sighed thoughtfully. "You haven't told me why the Lakota killed your husband—at least that's what people around here say. He was found dead, his throat slit."

The memory both thrilled and shamed Florence. It thrilled her because of the way Rising Eagle had defended her that night; but it shamed her to remember how drunk she had been, how she had crawled around searching for the bottle of whiskey Rising Eagle had grabbed from her and thrown away.

"John came out to the Lakota, where I had brought Little Wolf to give to Rising Eagle. He was drunk and wild, and he thought I had gone to Rising Eagle to . . . sleep with him. John knew about Rising Eagle and what he had once meant to me, and he was jealous. When he found me, he threatened to harm our little boy. He hit me, knocking me down. Rising Eagle defended me. He killed John Dundee, and then he and Buffalo Dreamer took Little Wolf and fled."

"And your brother? Is Rising Eagle the one who cut off his nose and ears?"

She nodded. "Gray Owl had sneaked away from the Lakota because of his betrayal—he knew that Rising Eagle wanted to kill him for it. Because I had no one else, and the Lakota would have nothing to do with me, I had come here to live with Gray Owl. That is how I met John Dundee. He and Gray Owl hunted and trapped together. When Rising Eagle came here looking for us and found Gray Owl, he attacked him, intending to kill him. It was a brutal fight, a horrible thing to see. My brother was no match for Rising Eagle, and Rising Eagle decided to shame and humiliate him instead of killing him. In

Rising Eagle's eyes, that was a more proper and satisfying punishment. Gray Owl had stolen his wife, and that is cause for death among the Lakota, second only to stealing another man's horses."

She paused, and Abel's eyebrows shot up in astonishment. *"Horses?"*

Florence could not help sharing his laughter then, and the moment of humor helped ease her guilt over her part in the events she had revealed to the reverend. But then her smile faded as she finished.

"I am not sure why I felt you should know these things," she told him, realizing that deep inside she *did* know why. Reverend Kingsley was too good for her, and he had to understand that, before both of them began allowing feelings that should be forbidden. "I was never wed to John Dundee in the Christian way, and in the eyes of your people, we lived in sin. I gave away my only son so that I could stay here and keep on drinking. I sold myself to men for whiskey. And it all came about because I had betrayed my own people, betrayed the only man I ever truly loved."

She lifted her head to meet his gaze, and still she saw something there that surprised and worried her. All she had told this man apparently had had no effect. She still saw no condemnation in his eyes.

"I already know that you have asked God to forgive all your past sins, Florence. You didn't need to tell me these things. You have told them to God, who knows every single sin any of us has ever committed. He has forgiven you, and so it is as though none of these things ever happened."

She frowned. "It is not God I worry about. It is you, and your friendship."

He smiled and shook his head. "Do you think that telling me all of this means I would turn away from you as the Lakota did?"

She shrugged. "Maybe."

"No, Florence. That will never happen. You have come so far, and I am proud of your accomplishments. You have become good friends with my sister, and now you are ready to help us teach the Lakota and the other tribes who live around Fort Pierre a new way, the white man's way, the white man's religion. And you of all people can be a great help in aiding those who wish to stop drinking. Belinda and I need you, Florence."

And I need you, she thought, *in more ways than you know. But I will never tell you . . . unless . . .*

"It is possible," he continued, "that Belinda will go home to Illinois in a year or so, at which time I might move even farther west. There is talk of a trading post out on the Platte River—I think they call it Fort John now, though it used to be called Fort William—that some think will eventually become an army post. More and more whites are migrating west for one reason or another, and this trading post has become quite a popular rest stop. Not only is there a need for spiritual guidance for weary emigrants who stop there, but out there I would also be in the midst of many different Indian tribes. Other priests and preachers now work diligently at reforming the Indians. I feel it is my calling to do the same. I am hoping you will agree to go there with me. You have plenty of time to think about it. I am going home myself for a while, to visit relatives and such. You can give me your decision when I return."

Florence felt alarm. She did not want him to go, but she did not want to admit to herself, and certainly not to Abel Kingsley, the reason why. She simply nodded in agreement. "I will think about it."

Abel rose. "And to show you how much confidence I have in you, I would like you to continue on here. Move out of that little cabin where you still have so many bad memories and move into this place after I leave. Take care of it for me. I would like you to begin teaching the Indian children around here. Lord knows, none of their parents trust any white teachers. Maybe they will let you teach them a little of the white man's writing and reading, some simple arithmetic. Will you try that for me?"

Florence's heart leaped with pride and shock. "You truly want me to do this?"

"I just asked, didn't I?" His smile was heartwarming.

"Yes. I would like very much to take care of your home and the church. And I am honored that you would ask me to teach the children."

He came around and stood behind her, putting a hand on her shoulder. He squeezed her shoulder lightly, and his touch warmed her. "I have full faith in you, Florence." He withdrew his hand and walked to the door.

In all their hours of working and studying together, usually with Belinda, but sometimes alone, Abel Kingsley had never made one wrong move toward her, showing only respect and kindness. Florence supposed that was what she loved about him. She rose to face him. "Thank you, Reverend—I mean, Abel. I will try to oblige you by calling you Abel, since you said you would prefer that. It just sounds too . . . too familiar, I guess." She felt herself blushing.

"We're good friends now, Florence. I've told you about my life, certainly not as colorful and exciting a story as your own, but enough that I think we know each other pretty well. I look forward to returning after my visit home, and I especially look forward to going even farther west. We'll travel with traders, and you'll have your own wagon, so it will all be quite proper, I assure you. You should enjoy it, since you will be closer to the surroundings in which you grew up."

"Yes." Florence's heart quickened at the realization that it was quite possible she might see Rising Eagle again. Did he ever go to Fort John to trade? It was even possible she might see Little Wolf again! "I am excited at the thought of going back into the land where I grew up. But I go back as a changed woman." *Except that I will always love Rising Eagle.*

Abel nodded. "Indeed you will." He looked her over in a way he had never looked at her before, then left.

Florence put a hand to her heart. "My goodness," she muttered. What a strange and wonderful turn her life had taken.

SEPTEMBER 1838

Moon of the Drying Meat

CHAPTER NINE

BUFFALO DREAMER WAS surprised and relieved at how quickly her first daughter came into the world. Contrary to the difficult birth she had experienced with Big Little Boy, her labor did not last as long for this second child, who nearly fell out of her in a bloody little heap, her first cry reminding Buffalo Dreamer of the squeal of a puppy. Tall Woman quickly cut the cord of life and took her new granddaughter away to bathe her.

Yellow Turtle Woman and Many Robes Woman helped with the afterbirth, which would be wrapped with deer hide and hung high in a tree, an offering to *Wakan-Tanka* in thanksgiving for another life.

Many Robes Woman packed Buffalo Dreamer with cattail down tied in place by rawhide, then wrapped her stomach with deerskin to support it until her muscles would strengthen and her skin become firm again. Buffalo Dreamer lay down on her bed of robes. The sacred white buffalo robe hung nearby over a wooden rack, and she touched it, thanking the buffalo spirit for bringing her another child, the daughter she had so dearly wanted.

Tall Woman brought the baby to her, and Buffalo Dreamer eagerly opened the deer-hide blanket around her daughter. A swath of deerskin was wrapped tightly around the baby's belly to protect her navel, and her tiny body glowed with buffalo fat, which Tall Woman had smeared on her to protect her tender skin and keep it soft.

"She is beautiful," Buffalo Dreamer said softly.

"Like her mother," Tall Woman added, smoothing a

strand of hair back from her daughter's face. "I remember when you were born. It seems such a short time ago, and now here you are giving birth to your own daughter. I know how much you miss your *uncheedah.* You were so close to my mother. Now it will be that way for me and your daughter. I will be her *uncheedah,* and I will train her in the ways of a woman. This makes me very happy."

Buffalo Dreamer smiled. "I am glad you and Father chose to leave the Brule and come to live among the Oglala for my sake. It is good that my children will have their grandmother and grandfather close to them."

Tall Woman nodded. "I will leave now so that Rising Eagle may come in and see his new daughter." She and Many Robes Woman, holding hands in delight at the birth, left together. After a moment, Buffalo Dreamer heard a war whoop, followed by a barrage of yips and piercing cries, as well as women trilling. She knew it was Rising Eagle celebrating the birth of another of his seed with the others who had waited to hear the outcome of her labor, another healthy child for Rising Eagle. Moments later, he came inside, carrying a cradleboard. He hesitated for a moment, looking at mother and child as though wanting to remember the moment. Then he came closer, setting the cradleboard beside Buffalo Dreamer. "Many Robes Woman made it for you, but I directed her in how I wanted it done."

Buffalo Dreamer smiled with pleasure. The cradleboard was covered with bleached buckskin and decorated with colorful quills. She was well aware of the many hours of labor it must have taken to produce such lovely quillwork, and she had no doubt that, as was custom, she would find many more cradleboards outside her tepee over the next few days, gifts from other Oglala women friends and relatives.

"I felt in my heart that this one would be a girl," Rising Eagle continued, "and I decided that she should be carried in the most beautiful cradle in camp, since her mother is so special. That is why I had Many Robes Woman use bleached skins."

"It is lovely, Rising Eagle. And my heart feels warm at knowing you are happy to have a daughter."

Rising Eagle leaned closer, studying the tiny girl. "She is beautiful, and she looks healthy."

Buffalo Dreamer touched his muscled arm. "I never thought I could be this happy among the Oglala. And the birth was so fast! I nearly fainted because she was born so quickly, so different from Big Little Boy."

Rising Eagle laughed lightly. "Our son has been trouble ever since he came into this world, always challenging us in some way." He touched his new daughter's tiny, soft cheek. "We will hold a feast, and Runs With The Deer will again name a child for us. We have much to celebrate, Buffalo Dreamer. Three times we hunted and found buffalo this season, and our tepees are full of smoked and cured meat for the winter, and we have many hides to trade. I think we have enough to trade with the *wasicus* for many more of their long guns. Because of the warnings about the white man we have received in our dreams, we must have more of his weapons and learn to use them, in case the time comes when we must make war with him. If he can kill from afar with these guns, then we must be able to do the same. The balls from the guns travel farther than our arrows do."

Buffalo Dreamer closed her eyes. "I do not want to think about it. I want to believe that such a thing will not happen, not in our lifetime, or our children's lifetime. This is a big land, plenty big enough for us to live here forever, even if a few white men do arrive, and in my dream, the men in blue coats were trampled into blood by the Oglala. Surely that means they can never be a true threat to us."

Rising Eagle sighed. "Perhaps." He leaned down and took the baby into his arms. "But for now, our bellies are full, our tepees are full, our *hearts* are full!"

He rose and carried the baby outside, and Buffalo

Dreamer laughed when she heard him shout to the others that he had a daughter. There followed more shouting, and drummers began beating rhythmically, singing songs of celebration. The circle of life continued, whole and strong.

PART TWO

Truth

I admit that there are good white men, but they bear no proportion to the bad; the bad must be the strongest, for they rule. They do what they please. . . . They will say to an Indian, "My friend! My brother!" They will take him by the hand, and at the same moment destroy him. . . . Remember that this day I have warned you to beware of such friends as these. I know the long knives; they are not to be trusted.

—PACHGANTSCHILHILAS,
   HEAD WARRIOR OF THE DELAWARES, EARLY 1700s

OCTOBER 1838

Moon of the Changing Seasons

CHAPTER TEN

BUFFALO DREAMER LOOKED up from her cook fire, where a thick buffalo hide filled with stewed buffalo meat and turnips hung from a tripod over hot coals. The day was sunny and relatively warm for October. Because of the dry air and bright sun, she had made a rack out of tree branches and draped several buffalo robes over it to air out before the coming winter.

Nearby, Many Robes Woman pounded more pemmican, a mixture of buffalo and deer meat, berries, and meat fat. Pemmican lasted for months, even years, and was kept in supply for emergencies and for warriors to carry on the hunt or in making war, times when there were seldom women along to cook for them.

Buffalo Dreamer's gaze moved from her sister-in-law's work when she noticed a commotion east of camp. Women were shouting and leaving their cook fires, dogs began barking wildly, and men gathered, taking up their weapons. Soon she saw the reason. Two teams of horses approached the Oglala camp, which was nestled in the Black Hills. The horses pulled two huge covered wagons.

"What is it?" Many Robes Woman asked, walking over to pick up her youngest son, Fox Running. In the distance, her first son, Little Beaver, played with Big Little Boy and Never Sleeps.

"*Wasicu*," Buffalo Dreamer answered, feeling a pang of alarm. It was more than two winters since she and Rising Eagle and several hundred Oglala had visited Fort Pierre. She remembered being repelled by the noise of all the clat-

tering wagons and the shrill whistle of the monstrous fire-
boats on the nearby river. It was at Fort Pierre that Rising
Eagle had killed Never Sleeps's white father, John Dundee.
They had never gone back to that place or traded there
again with the *wasicus*. Now here came white men, right
into their camp!

She picked up her daughter, whom Runs With The
Deer had named Pretty Feather. "There are plenty of men
in camp," she said. "We will go and find out what these
white men want."

Tall Woman hurried to her side then and took Pretty
Feather from her. "I will watch the children, my daughter.
The *wasicus* are probably here to trade. Go and see what
they have. Bring me something pretty."

Buffalo Dreamer smiled and waited for Many Robes
Woman to set Fox Running on his deerskin blanket. Tired,
the baby rolled onto his side and began sucking his fist. His
mother left then with Buffalo Dreamer. "This is exciting! It
is the first time white men have come right into our camp."

"I do not like it," Buffalo Dreamer said. "I have been
happy not seeing *any* white men. I thought perhaps they
had decided never to come into the Black Hills."

"You worry too much," Many Robes Woman told her.
"What does it matter? There are many more of us than
there are of them. And I would like more of the pretty colored beads we traded skins for when we visited Fort Pierre.
You liked them, too."

"Yes." Buffalo Dreamer felt a rush of indecision, repulsed
by the white men themselves, yet anxious to see what they
might have brought to trade.

The traders, dressed in buckskins, unloaded a treasure
of wonderful, unusual items, spreading them out on blankets on the ground. They stacked more of the soft, colorful
blankets on the gates of the wagons and set out pans filled
with beads of every size, shape, and color. They also displayed black cook pots. One of them brought out fancy
cloth, bright ribbons, wonderful items for decorating tu-

nics and cradleboards, things that could be tied into a woman's or a warrior's hair.

Buffalo Dreamer noticed Rising Eagle watching the white men guardedly as they also brought out long guns. There were four traders, none of whom appeared to have bathed or groomed himself anytime recently. The hair on their faces repulsed her. Their buckskins were worn and shiny and soiled from obvious constant wear. Three of them wore beaver hats. The fourth, who had graying hair and a grizzled beard, sported a wide-brimmed leather hat. It was he who appeared to understand the Oglala tongue and who conversed with Runs With The Deer in a mixture of that and sign language.

"Look at the fine beads!" Many Robes Woman exclaimed. "And the hard black pots we saw them using at Fort Pierre to cook in. You can put them directly into the flames and they do not burn up or melt."

The man in the leather hat announced that if the Oglala had plenty of buffalo robes and beaver skins to trade, they could gather around and pick out items they would like to have. Runs With The Deer looked at Rising Eagle. "What do you say, my nephew? It is you who has received warnings in your visions and dreams about the *wasicus*."

"We *need* the long guns," Bold Fox added.

Rising Eagle strutted around the blankets covered with interesting items. He moved close to the traders, looking down his nose at all four of them. "We have plenty of robes to trade," he said, addressing the one who understood the Oglala language. "The women can choose whatever makes their work easier. I and my uncles and some of the other men will trade for your long guns, but we must also have the round balls that they shoot, and the black powder that makes them fire."

"Of course," the man answered, nodding. He waved his hand toward where the guns lay.

Rising Eagle moved his gaze back to Bold Fox. "I agree that we should have the long guns." He stepped aside, and men and women alike, including Buffalo Dreamer and Many Robes Woman, began eagerly sorting through the bounty, the women talking excitedly then, many laughing joyfully at the many things they could use to brighten clothes and hair.

Rising Eagle joined the men in picking up the long guns, getting the feel of them, raising them to check their aim. Some of the women took trinkets and wares to the man in the leather hat, who determined how many robes or furs he would need in exchange for the items they had selected.

The camp came alive with visiting, laughing women, who began hurrying to their tepees to grab furs and buffalo robes to bring to the traders. Camp dogs continued their chorus of barking over all the excitement, and men, young and old alike, compared guns, discussing the merits of such weapons as opposed to bow and arrow.

After determining the value of the black kettle Buffalo Dreamer chose, which she had filled with beads of every color, as well as the worth of the bolt of bright red cloth she carried on her other arm, the bearded trader let her go back to her tepee so she could load Sotaju with robes and furs for the trade. One of the other white men followed. Buffalo Dreamer supposed he intended to look over her furs, but when she set down her pot of beads and her bolt of cloth, she was not comfortable with the way he looked at her when she turned to face him.

Many Robes Woman joined her, and the man studied both of them with obvious lust in his eyes. To the surprise and disgust of both women, the man pointed to his privates, cupping his hand and moving it back and forth to indicate intercourse. He stuck out his tongue and wiggled it, using his other hand to point to Buffalo Dreamer and back to himself.

There was no mistaking what he wanted. Buffalo Dreamer scowled at him, and Many Robes Woman giggled. "He stinks," she said. "And he is so hairy. Our men are much more handsome and smell much better." She giggled again, and apparently the man mistook her laughter for meaning she was interested. He grinned, grabbing her and yanking her close, burying his face in her neck while he tried to force her inside the nearest tepee.

The smile on Many Robes Woman's face turned to a snarl as she began pounding on her attacker in rage. Buffalo Dreamer joined her, beating the amorous trader with a fist while she pulled at his hair with her other hand. The man yelled and struck at her with an elbow, landing a hard blow to her ribs.

Then Yellow Turtle Woman joined in the melee, as did several other women, who dragged the man, now screaming and thrashing wildly, away from the tepee. A fist crashed into Buffalo Dreamer's left cheek, and she ducked away from the scuffle, giving the other women a turn at teaching the trader a lesson.

The rest of the women continued kicking and beating the man, and the commotion brought several of the Oglala men running, accompanied by the other traders. Buffalo Dreamer ran up to Rising Eagle to explain.

"He tried to force himself on your sister," she announced, still panting. A bruise was forming on her cheek where the trader had hit her with his fist. "First he made the offer to me, gesturing at his manpart with his hand!"

Dark anger flared in Rising Eagle's eyes. He shouted to the other men the story of what had happened, and they all broke into war whoops and cheers as they circled the women, who continued to beat the man with fists, feet, rocks, and sticks. How dare a white man try to steal an Oglala man's wife! He deserved to die!

The man in the leather hat ran up to Rising Eagle. "Stop them!" he pleaded. The other two traders stood nearby, nervously fingering their long guns.

Rising Eagle managed to explain to the man what had happened. "We said we would trade furs and hides, not our *women*," he finished. "A man asks for death when he tries to take another man's wife!"

"No! Wait!" The man ran to the mob of women, trying fruitlessly to work his way among them and rescue his friend. Instead, two of the women turned on him fiercely and chased him away running. The other two men laughed at him, beginning to see humor in the situation. But when the man in the leather hat barked something at them, they lost their smiles. The three men argued among each other; then one of them ran back to the wagons. He returned with a crate filled with brown bottles.

The women finally began backing away, and the three traders pulled the brown bottles from the crate and ran amid the Indian men, holding up the bottles and grinning.

"Firewater! We are sorry about what our friend did," the one in the leather hat told them. "We give you this firewater as a peace offering, free! All we ask is that you do not kill our friend. We came here in peace!"

The Oglala men just looked at each other in wonder, many not even sure of what it was the white men were offering them. However, Buffalo Dreamer knew the meaning of firewater, and so did Rising Eagle. The desire for the white man's drink had destroyed one of their own, Fall Leaf Woman, and it caused men to act like fools.

Buffalo Dreamer watched as Rising Eagle approached the man in the leather hat. He yanked the brown bottle out of the man's hand and threw it against a stump, where it shattered. "No firewater!" he yelled. "It is bad! You *go!*" He gestured violently. *"Niksapa hantans ecanu kte!"*

The man backed away, apparently understanding Rising Eagle's hotly spoken advice: *If you are wise, you will do what I say.* He looked over at the other two men, telling them something in their own tongue. One of them pointed to their bloody, beaten partner, who lay prone on the ground, some of the women occasionally poking at him with sticks. He said something in obvious anger, then turned and pointed to the rack of buffalo robes Buffalo Dreamer had hung to air out. The man in the leather hat looked at Rising Eagle and Runs With The Deer, who had come to stand beside his nephew.

"We will take our friend and leave," the man said. "You

can have all the items your women have chosen, but we deserve some of your robes and furs in trade."

"His friend stays with us!" It was Arrow Runner who spoke up. "He attacked my wife. He deserves to die!"

Rising Eagle folded his muscular arms and looked arrogantly at the man. "The woman your friend tried to steal is my sister and Arrow Runner's wife. He wishes your friend to die, and so do I. We will kill him slowly for what he has done."

Buffalo Dreamer remained silent. This was a matter for the men to settle. The white trader in the leather hat gasped, as if horrified at the words.

"Why?" he asked. "Your women have already beaten him nearly to death! He did not try to *steal* the woman. He only meant to have a little fun with her. He probably just misunderstood something she did, or a look she gave him. We did not come here to make trouble. We came only to trade."

"You spoke of trading for buffalo robes and furs, not for women," Runs With The Deer told him. "Take some of our robes in trade, as offered. Then go!" He gestured with his hand. "Your friend stays with us."

The white man looked helplessly at his friends, who now stood near him. The three men talked, argued. Finally their apparent leader turned to Rising Eagle again. "I beg of you to let us take our friend with us. He has received his punishment. Now he understands your ways. This will never happen again. Let us take him and we will give you another crate of guns, and more blankets. We are sorry for what he did. We . . . we just have to get used to your ways."

Rising Eagle looked at Arrow Runner. "It is your decision."

Arrow Runner walked over and kicked at the nearly lifeless body of the beaten man. He knelt down, pulling a hunting knife from its sheath at his side and deftly whacking off the end of a finger. The man let out a pitiful groan, moving only slightly.

"Hey! What the hell—" one of the traders protested.

Arrow Runner faced him, still holding the knife in his hand, indicating that the man had better not protest or he, too, could lose an appendage. The man gripped his long gun as though prepared to use it, but the trader in the leather hat shouted some kind of warning.

Rising Eagle cast a haughty look at the man, then looked back at the one who spoke his language. "She was my sister," was all he said. With that, he walked over to the beaten man and also knelt down and cut off the entire little finger of the man's other hand.

"Jesus!" one of the other traders yelped, sounding ready to cry.

Buffalo Dreamer had no idea what any of their words meant, but it was obvious that the white men were shocked. Why should they be so surprised at the treatment of a man who had tried to seduce and steal another man's wife? Rising Eagle walked back to the trader in the leather hat.

"He also tried to attack *my* wife!" he told the man. "For this, I take a *whole* finger. Take your robes now and leave, before more harm is done."

The man sighed, a deep scowl on his face. He barked something at the other two men, and they quickly ran over to pick up their beaten comrade. Blood dripped profusely from where his fingers had been severed, leaving a trail of red droplets as they hurriedly carried him to the trade wagons and hoisted him inside one of them. The man in the leather hat, obviously older and more experienced than the others, yelled something more to them, and the three men began helping some of the Oglala women carry buffalo robes and furs to the wagons. The man then walked over to the rack where Buffalo Dreamer aired out her own robes, noticing the albino robes. He walked closer, studying it for a moment. Alarmed, Buffalo Dreamer ran over and stood between him and the robe.

"Do not touch it!" she ordered. "It is holy! Sacred! No white man should touch this robe. It is *mine!*"

The man stepped back, turning to Rising Eagle. "I will give you five boxes of guns for this robe. Blankets. Anything you need."

Rising Eagle walked to where he stood, followed by most of the Oglala men present. "There is nothing you can give me that would equal the value of the hide of the white buffalo."

Frustration showed in the man's eyes. "That robe is worth a lot of money to the white man. Where did you get it?"

Rising Eagle stepped closer to his wife. "The white buffalo died from a white man's bullet. If I knew who that man was, I would *kill* him for what he did. The white buffalo is sacred. This robe belongs to my wife, who is a holy woman. Do not touch it!"

The man turned defiant. "I want that robe! I'll pay *anything* for it!"

Rising Eagle lowered his arms, stepping very close to him. "I told you, no value can be put on it. Leave now, before my anger becomes directed at you instead of your friend. I have told you how it is. You have your robes and furs, and we let you take your friend with you. Give us the extra guns and blankets and go! There is nothing more to say!"

The obviously unsatisfied man clenched his fists, then stepped back, glaring at the rest of the Oglala men. He swallowed, and Buffalo Dreamer could tell he was suddenly afraid. He stalked over to the wagons and climbed into one of them, throwing out more blankets, then shoving out a crate of guns and ammunition. He scrambled into the wagon seat then and picked up the reins. He kicked at the brake and whipped the horses into motion. A second man drove the other wagon, while the third man sat in the back with their wounded friend, who was beginning to yell with pain and agony.

All the Oglala men followed on foot behind the wagons until the traders were well on their way. Buffalo Dreamer felt a slight chill at how eager the white trader had been to get his hands on the white buffalo robe. She thought of what the white buffalo had told her about the Oglala prospering as long as she possessed the robe, and about the warnings in her husband's visions that the white man must never be trusted. Seeing how insistent the trader had been about having the white robe brought grave concern to her heart. She took down the robe, which was quite large and heavy, and half carried and half dragged it inside her tepee where it would be out of sight, deciding that from now on, she would never let any white man see it.

MAY 1840

Moon of the Greening Grass

CHAPTER ELEVEN

FLORENCE TOOK ONE last look in the mirror. Her feelings for Abel Kingsley had definitely grown beyond friendship, and by his eyes and actions over the last few months, she could tell that he had come to feel the same way about her; but Abel was a proud, quiet, reserved man who had a hard time expressing deep feelings.

She liked what she saw in the mirror now. She looked healthy, and she wore dresses that were plain but nicely fitted, the kind of dresses respectable white women wore. Her hair was clean and wound into curls at the crown of her head. Belinda had taught her the proper way to dress and wear her hair, proper manners in speaking, makeup, eating, and general conduct. She had learned to wear jewelry in a subtle way that enhanced her beauty and made her appear more refined, rather than in the gaudy, colorful way she had once worn such ornaments.

She turned in the mirror, admiring the way her green gingham dress fit her. She had discovered that she actually had a talent for sewing, and now she supported herself by doing seamstress work for others at Fort Pierre.

Once Abel had returned from his visit home, she'd moved back to her old cabin, which she'd painted and cleaned up and furnished with a davenport and a table and chairs ordered from the fort's supply store. The items were shipped from a mysterious "city" in the East called Philadelphia. Abel had told her about other cities, like New York and Pittsburgh, but hard as she tried, she could not truly visualize what they must be like, nor the great numbers of white people who lived there. She thought of how surprised the Lakota would be to realize just how many *wasicus* there were in the land of the Great White Father, which Abel called the United States.

She supposed she would never see such places, but she was perfectly happy here now, and secretly delighted that Abel was finally back. When he had first left, she'd been afraid he would never return. He and Belinda had stayed away for nearly two years, and although Abel had written to her several times, assuring her he would come back, part of her had not been able to help wondering if that was true.

It was not until Abel finally returned, having stayed in Illinois because of a long illness his father suffered, that Florence fully realized why she had been so worried about his absence. As soon as she set eyes on him again, she knew that she loved him. She had missed him more than she thought possible, and it was all she could do to keep from running up and throwing her arms around him. But until she saw the same desire in his eyes, and heard words of love from his lips, she simply could not bring herself to speak first.

She took hope, however, at the special look she had sometimes seen in his eyes over these past two weeks. She sensed that he, too, was holding back a greater joy at seeing her than he let on.

All of which made her nervous now. Abel had told her earlier in the day that he wanted to call on her this evening . . . that he had something "special" to talk about.

Did she dare think it could be about them? Perhaps something deeper than just how to plan for their trip west? If the man didn't know by now what he wanted . . . or that she loved him . . . he would never know. Four years had passed since the day he took her away from the tavern steps and changed her life. She had already decided that if Abel Kingsley did not own up to his feelings soon, she would not go to Fort John with him after all. It was just too hard, loving him as she did and not being able to act on that love. Still, Belinda had stayed in Illinois with her widowed mother, which meant that Abel would have to go on to Fort John alone. She was not sure she could let him do that, knowing she might never see him again.

A knock at the door interrupted her thoughts. She knew it would be Abel, and her heart pounded so hard she feared he would hear it. She answered the door with a smile to see him standing there in his usual black frock coat, buttoned to the neck and setting off his white-collared shirt. He removed his stiff black hat and nodded to her.

"You look very nice, Florence."

Florence felt suddenly awkward and flustered—silly feelings to have around someone she had known for so long. She noticed that he appeared just as uncomfortable and nervous. He smiled, and to Florence, he seemed to have grown more handsome during his absence. She was used to his mustache now, realizing that most white men were simply hairy creatures and that most of them were as adamant about their beards and mustaches as Indian men were about plucking all hairs from their faces.

"Thank you, Abel," she said in reply to his compliment.

"If you would step outside, Florence, I would like to discuss something with you. It wouldn't look proper if I came in."

Curious, Florence obeyed, stepping out onto her porch.

"Would you sit down?" Abel motioned to one of the two wooden rockers on the small front stoop.

Florence complied, and Abel sat down in the other rocker, leaning forward and resting his elbows on his knees. "Florence, I've been thinking very seriously about something. I, uh, I missed you while I was gone—very much, in fact."

Florence felt hope building in her heart. "And I missed you." She twisted her fingers nervously in her lap. How strange, she thought, that after all the men she had shamed herself with, she should be so nervous around this man.

"I have to admit that part of the reason I stayed away so long—" Abel's face reddened slightly, and he looked at the wooden boards of the porch floor as he continued. "Well, it wasn't just because of my father. I was almost afraid to come back, afraid of my own feelings, not sure of yours. I had a lot of thinking to do, and to be honest, I wanted to see if I could bear not having you in my life."

Florence's surprise was difficult to hide, but she was not sure if she should be happy or sad. Was he about to tell her he discovered he *could* live without her?

"I am thirty-six years old, Florence," he continued, "perhaps an old man in your eyes, as you are only twenty-four, or so you believe. I had a wife, back in Illinois. She died several years ago from a heart ailment . . . the doctors could do nothing for her. I guess I told you that a long time ago."

"You did, Abel, and I'm very sorry for that."

He fidgeted with his hat, then glanced at her almost bashfully before looking away again. "Well, what I am saying is . . . I would like to marry again. And I have come to know you so well. I have observed how easily you learn. You are a bright woman, Florence, and still young and healthy. I have grown . . . well . . . quite fond of you over these four years. I have felt that way much longer than you know, but I hid it, not sure of how on earth a beautiful young Lakota woman would feel about a hairy old white man like me." He straightened, finally turning to meet her gaze again. "I would consider it an honor if you agreed to be my wife."

Florence just stared at him for a moment, astonished at the unexpected offer.

"I understand that you may not have the right feelings for me," he added. "Please don't feel obligated to—"

"On the contrary, Abel," Florence interrupted. "I have had deep feelings for you for quite some time now." She blurted out the words with no hesitation. It felt good to be able to actually say them. Now that she was free to do so, she quickly decided she was not going to be shy about it. "I admit that I have sometimes . . . wished . . . that I was your wife."

Abel grinned almost bashfully, staring at his hat as he

began twirling it in his hands. "Well." He sighed, appearing greatly relieved. "That is very good news." He looked squarely at her. "I am in love with you, Florence. You are exotically beautiful. There are those who would say it isn't right to marry one from another race, but out here . . . well, since coming here . . . it's just a different way of life, isn't it? So different. And besides, if I am going to be working with your people, why shouldn't my own wife be Lakota? You can be such a big help to me, act as my interpreter, that sort of thing. I discussed it with Belinda before I left, and she is delighted with the idea."

How different he was from Rising Eagle, who was so wild and bold . . . so very, very different. She would never love that way again, but she also could not expect that kind of love twice in her life. She truly did love Abel, though, as much as she could love or desire anyone after having lost Rising Eagle.

"I love you, too, Abel, and I would be proud to be your wife."

Abel grinned and shook his head. "This was a lot easier than I thought it would be."

They both shared light laughter, and Abel rose, coming over and taking her hand, urging her to rise also. He put a hand on her waist.

"A minister will be visiting us soon from Illinois. Would you be willing to marry me as soon as he gets here?"

His grip was gentle, and Florence felt a surge of sweet desire. "Yes. As soon as he arrives." She did not mind his slightly crooked teeth, or that he was not built nearly as magnificently as Rising Eagle. Abel Kingsley was a solid man, good-looking, dependable, kind, and respectful. He was not a warrior. He did not sport an array of weapons. His hair was not black and shiny and long. It was not decorated with coup feathers. His face was not scarred from battle, and his body was not scarred from making blood sacrifices at the Sun Dance. She would never love this man quite the same as she had loved Rising Eagle, but love him she would. It would just be a different kind of love.

For the first time since they had known each other, Abel pulled her close and put his arms around her. Florence rested her head on his shoulder and took comfort in his embrace.

APRIL 1842

Grass Moon

CHAPTER TWELVE

BUFFALO DREAMER DEARLY loved spring in *Paha-Sapa*. The scent of pine, still wet from melting snows, filled the air, and open land became an array of wildflowers. The sun's warmth made her feel more alive, and when she first discarded her heavy winter robes and knee-high moccasins, she felt light and free. Children ran and played outside, free spirits who were glad to cut loose from the confines of the tepees.

She casually walked some distance from the main camp, looking for particular wildflowers that could be used for food and for medicinal purposes, then reached a bluff overlooking a vast expanse of land to the south, void of trees. Spring rains had created there a sea of wildflowers, yet behind her, a thick forest stretched over many miles of hills and valleys.

She sat down at the edge of the bluff to enjoy the scene and serenity, thinking about her children. At eight summers of age, Big Little Boy was now so agile on horseback that during a special ceremony, Rising Eagle had renamed him Brave Horse. And because over the past winter Never Sleeps had begun occasionally walking in his sleep, the old medicine man, Moon Painter, had declared he should be called Spirit Walker. Buffalo Dreamer thought of how proud Fall Leaf Woman would be of her son if she could see him now.

Both boys kept their grandfather, Looking Horse, busy with teachings of wisdom and warfare, and four-summers-old Pretty Feather occupied a good deal of her grandmother's time watching Tall Woman quill and listening to her tell stories about proud Lakota women.

"So, here you are, my wife."

Buffalo Dreamer turned at the words, spoken from a distance. Rising Eagle stood in the trees behind her.

"You are too good at sneaking up on someone," she answered.

"Something every warrior must know how to do," he replied. "Besides, I am aware of your favorite place to sit and think good thoughts."

Rising Eagle walked toward her. He wore only leggings, with no shirt and no moccasins. A bone hairpipe necklace graced his throat, and his hair was gathered to one side of his neck, its only adornments a round, beaded hairpiece to hold it in place and a quilled leather tie wound through the tail. A blanket was draped over his arm. He opened it and spread it out on the grass when he reached Buffalo Dreamer, then sat down on it.

"Soon it will be time to hunt again," he said. "Spring and summer bring much work for all. I decided to spend this day with you, before you become too busy with skinning and tanning and making pemmican." He patted the blanket. "Sit here, Buffalo Dreamer."

Buffalo Dreamer obliged, moving to sit down beside him. She let out a little scream when he quickly put an arm around her breasts and pushed her all the way down onto the blanket. "Sometimes you are so weary at night that I decide I should leave you alone," he said, hovering over her. "I think today is a good day to take my pleasure in you."

Buffalo Dreamer giggled, reaching up to playfully push at him. "It is also *my* pleasure, but I remind you, dear husband, that we have had much time during the long, cold winter to indulge our desire. You act as though it has been many months since we enjoyed this."

"Two nights is too long for me."

Buffalo Dreamer felt a surge of the wild passion only this man could stir in her. She traced her fingers over the firm lines of his lips as he unlaced her tunic at the shoulders. She arched her body so he could pull the dress down and off, and she lay there naked beneath him. He quickly removed his leggings and breechcloth, and Buffalo Dreamer touched his hardened penis, stroking its soft skin.

"The first very warm day plays with my emotions," he told her, moving between her legs. "It makes me more hungry for my woman."

"Then you should satisfy your appetite," she replied, toying with his nipples. She gladly opened herself to him, and he entered her quickly and eagerly. Buffalo Dreamer gloried in the pleasure of feeling him inside of her. United this way, she felt she took strength from him, shared in his mystical powers. Lying here on Mother Earth seemed to bring them together with the whole universe. She could look up at the clouds and remember her vision when she was a young girl of dancing on the stars.

She arched upward, groaning with pleasure at the way he rubbed himself against her, bringing excitement to every part of her body until she gasped in an exotic climax that made her want to touch him, taste him. He leaned closer, as though sensing her need, and she licked at the salt on the warm skin of his muscular arms and shoulders, tasting her way up to his neck, enjoying the smell of him, finding his mouth. Rising Eagle returned the need to taste, touching her tongue with his own as he drove himself deeper in sweet rhythm.

How happy it made Buffalo Dreamer to know that she still pleased him; each time they mated, it brought another chance that his life would again grow in her womb, another child for Rising Eagle, another link in the constant circle of life, death, and new life.

He moved his hands under her hips, pounding wildly until she felt his life pulse into her. He groaned with his own pleasure before rolling away and resting at her side. Both of them lay there naked under the warm sun. Beyond the trees and over a rise lay their winter camp, where men, women, and children were busying themselves with preparations to move to another location in yet another quest to find the sacred animal that sustained them.

"Hey, you two!" a woman shouted from the trees behind them.

Buffalo Dreamer recognized her mother's voice. Both she and Rising Eagle looked toward the trees.

"Quit frolicking naked like young lovers!" Tall Woman laughed.

Buffalo Dreamer grasped her tunic and held it in front of her, giggling to herself.

"Come back to camp!" Tall Woman yelled. "White men are coming!"

Tall Woman turned and left, and Rising Eagle quickly rose and tied on his breechcloth and leggings, while Buffalo Dreamer slipped on her tunic and wrapped the blanket around her waist.

"Again the white man comes right into our camp," Rising Eagle complained with a frown.

Buffalo Dreamer picked up the basket she had been using to gather plants, and together they hurried into the thick stand of trees toward camp, Buffalo Dreamer irritated at the fact that these new intruders had interrupted what had been a lovely, peaceful day. She hoped these *wasicus* would not bring the trouble their last visitors had brought. She followed Rising Eagle to their camp, which lay nestled along a creek that ran between two hills covered with pine. Wind In Grass had chosen a good site for winter camp. The valley had provided shelter from the northern winds over winter, as well as plenty of wood for fires, and drinking water from the creek.

When they reached the main camp, all the children and dogs were heading toward the north end of the village.

"Wasicus!" someone shouted to them.

Many Horses hurried up to Rising Eagle. "The runners say these white men are different. They are not traders. They are seeking a road to places where the sun sets."

Buffalo Dreamer noticed how the past winter had aged Many Horses. The extreme cold and harsh weather had been hard on both children and old ones, and at fifty-eight summers, Many Horses was beginning to display the signs of an old man, walking a little slower, his face showing pains that he would not openly admit to suffering.

"Again white men walk into our camp as though they have the right," Rising Eagle answered. "Not one of our natural enemies would do this, and we have not yet decided if the *wasicu* are friend or enemy. I do not like the way they come here, as though they belong wherever the Oglala belong."

The huge Oglala village was spread out so far that it took several minutes to walk to the meeting place, where old Runs With The Deer stood facing the white men waiting there. Barking dogs ran about as though frenzied, and as the elders gathered, children followed behind them, squealing with excitement.

When she and Rising Eagle came closer, Buffalo Dreamer could tell by the looks on the white men's faces that most of them felt nervous and intimidated, not sure of what to expect.

Indeed that is how they should *feel,* she thought. The newcomers carried canoes packed with supplies and a few strange-looking instruments Buffalo Dreamer had never seen before. Several horses were led by the men, and they, too, were loaded with supplies. Many of the men sported the usual beards Buffalo Dreamer had come to expect on white men, but even the bearded ones seemed cleaner than any white men she had encountered at other times.

As the more important Oglala men gathered closer to the visitors, the crowd quieted and women hushed their children. One of the white men stepped forward, as though he was the leader of the others. His hair was neatly cropped, and his beard and mustache were trimmed and combed. Buffalo Dreamer guessed him to be perhaps twenty-five or thirty summers in age, and he had a pleasant, though wary, look in his eyes. All the same, one thing about him made her gasp and step back. This movement by their holy woman made the others take more notice.

Women retreated a little, pulling their children with them, and those warriors gathered closest to the visitors tensed.

"What is it?" Rising Eagle asked Buffalo Dreamer.

"His coat! He wears a blue coat! It is like the coats in my dreams! It is a bad omen, Rising Eagle!"

The white men looked confused. One of them, wearing buckskins and looking more grizzled than the others, said something to them, apparently interpreting Buffalo Dreamer's words. The man in the blue coat looked at Rising Eagle then, asking him why the woman beside him was afraid of "Monsieur Fremont's" blue coat.

"It is a bad sign," Rising Eagle told him in the Sioux tongue, and gesturing with his hands. "My wife has had dreams about men in blue coats."

The interpreter spoke to Monsieur Fremont and the man answered. The interpreter then spoke not just to Rising Eagle, but turned and gestured to all of the people as he explained: "Monsieur Fremont comes to you as a friend. He is searching for a good road west, to the land of the setting sun, because his Great White Father in the land to the east wishes to know how far it is from the big waters where he lives to the big waters that lie far beyond the western mountains. Some of the white men who live in the east wish to go to these far places."

"Through *Lakota* land!" Rising Eagle exclaimed.

The translator smiled; *a rather patronizing smile*, Buffalo Dreamer thought.

"You need not worry, friend," the interpreter replied for Fremont. "We come here only to bring gifts, in return for your permission to continue passing through Lakota land. We wish you to send runners farther west to tell others we come in peace and that we only search for a way beyond the mountains."

"That means *more* white men would come through our land," Bold Fox spoke up. He stepped forward, scowling.

The interpreter explained the words to his leader, who sat down, motioning for the Lakota men to do the same. He said something, and the interpreter told Rising Eagle that Monsieur Fremont wished to powwow peacefully. "He would like to smoke the pipe with you, as a sign of his friendship," the man told Rising Eagle. "He has gifts for your women, and he will explain about the path west that we wish to explore."

The man in the blue coat shouted something in his language to the other men, and those carrying canoes set them down. All the men began rummaging in their gear, retrieving bright cloth, ribbons, mirrors, and tobacco. A few Lakota men gave their wives and daughters permission to approach the white men and accept gifts, and Looking Horse told Tall Woman to get him and Rising Eagle some tobacco.

Buffalo Dreamer remained standing behind Rising Eagle, who sat down warily in a circle with the other *Nacas* and Shirt Wearers, crossing his legs and resting his elbows on his knees. She could not deny the worry and alarm the white leader's blue coat caused her, and she hoped the *wasicus* planned to leave quickly.

She watched as Runs With The Deer took his pipe from the young boy who carried it for him and filled it with sweet grass. Using a twig from the fire around which the Lakota and the white men had chosen to sit, he lit the pipe, puffing it quietly for a moment before pointing it toward the spirits above, then toward Mother Earth. He smoked it once again, then handed it to his brother, Bold Fox, who sat to his left. Bold Fox smoked it, then handed it to his brother-in-law, Many Horses, who passed it on to Rising Eagle.

More Oglala men smoked, handing the pipe then to the white man in the blue coat. He smoked the pipe in the same way he had seen the Oglala men smoke it, then handed it to his interpreter. When the pipe came back around to Runs With The Deer, he smoked it once more, then offered it again to the heavens before handing it back to the young boy.

The leader of the white men leaned forward with a serious but friendly look. Using his interpreter, he explained his presence to Rising Eagle and the others, while many more Oglala listened intently.

"I am called John Charles Fremont. I am a lieutenant in the army of the United States, a land of many, many thousands of white men east of the great river where now sits Fort Pierre. My army is much like your warriors, chosen to protect my people, and also to map new roads to the west. As I fulfill this mission, I have been ordered to explain to all the Lakota—as well as to Crow and Blackfoot, Shoshoni, and other tribes with whom I might come in contact—that we are only passing through your land to go on to other places. Anyone who comes after me will also be only passing through. This is a promise I make to you."

Rising Eagle looked over at Runs With The Deer. "Even if they are only passing through, they will need to hunt game to eat, game that belongs to us," he told his uncle. "And we have seen how dirty and wasteful some of the *wasicus* were at Fort Pierre, throwing their slop and filth onto the ground wherever they chose. Surely the others are the same."

The elders nodded.

"It will not be that way," Fremont explained after Rising Eagle's words were translated. "My people will respect the land, and most will bring their own supplies from the east so that they do not have to kill much game. I make you a promise that we only seek permission to journey through Lakota lands on our way west. There is nothing within your land that we want." He threw out his hands. "Look at how big your land is! Surely there is plenty of room for a few hundred of my people to pass through at times in the warm summers. And I have seen one of your buffalo herds. It was so big I could not see an end to it. You cannot tell me that is not plenty for all of us, and plenty more left over. You have nothing to fear from allowing us to pass through your land, I assure you."

The elders studied him quietly.

"And what if we say you cannot come through?" Rising Eagle asked.

Fremont shrugged. "Some of my people are very determined to get to the ocean beyond your mountains. It is a great body of water, bigger than you could ever imagine. A man can travel on it by boat for months and see no land. We have a great desire to see this ocean, and to see what the land is like along its shores. I assure you, once we get beyond the mountains, you will not see us again even if we return. We will probably return by ship, or by another route, so as to do more exploring on the way back."

Looking Horse rubbed at his jaw in thought before speaking. "Will all those thousands of white men in the land of the east try to come through our land?"

Fremont laughed. "Mercy, no! Just a few of us. The land to the east is a beautiful place. We have great cities, where many thousands of my people live, far more in numbers than the Oglala. Our way of life is unlike anything you have ever seen or experienced, and most of my people prefer to stay right where they are."

Rising Eagle straightened. "I am called Rising Eagle, and I tell you true, John Charles Fremont, that we will not take it lightly if you lie to us about only passing through our land."

Fremont faced him squarely. "I am not a liar, Rising Eagle. I truly come in peace, and I respectfully ask your permission to pass through Lakota lands." He turned to take something from one of his men, then handed it out to Rising Eagle. "Here. Take this bag of tobacco. It is some of the finest we grow in the States. It is grown in a place called Virginia."

Rising Eagle took the pouch and opened it, sniffing the contents. He smiled. "It has a good smell."

Fremont laughed. "Of course it does! A man of any race appreciates a good sniff of tobacco."

Rising Eagle passed the pouch among the others, and they all nodded with approval when they smelled it.

"We want three bags of your tobacco," Bold Fox told Fremont. "And our women will keep the things they have taken. Then you can pass through."

Fremont looked pleased. "Will you send runners to alert more of your people, so that they do not delay us?"

Rising Eagle turned to discuss the matter with the others, and Buffalo Dreamer kept her eye on John Charles Fremont and that blue coat he wore. The coat gave her a bad feeling, but at least he was the only man wearing one. If she saw many of those coats, then she would be more alarmed. One man could do no harm.

"You may pass through," Rising Eagle consented. "But your men must respect Mother Earth and all the two-leggeds and winged ones she embraces."

Fremont nodded. "Agreed." He rose then. "You see? I took very little of your time. My men and I must be getting on now. We have to cover as much ground by daylight as is possible." He bowed to the elders, then turned to Buffalo Dreamer. "Be assured that I bring you no harm. You need not fear my blue coat."

Buffalo Dreamer did not reply. She turned and walked away, and for the next several minutes most of the Oglala gathered around those who had accepted gifts, looking over the fine things that had been collected from the white man. Buffalo Dreamer turned after moving farther away, and she watched the white men pick up their canoes and check the ropes on the supply horses. Bold Fox and Runs With The Deer ordered two of their younger scouts to go to the next Lakota camp and inform the people of the coming of the *wasicus* and their intentions. Along the way, they would help show the white men the right path. From the next camp, new runners would do the same, taking the white men to yet another Lakota camp and so on, until the white men had left Lakota country.

Preparations were made, and the scouts packed supplies. Many of the Oglala followed the *wasicus* away from camp and westward. Amid the commotion, Rising Eagle came to find Buffalo Dreamer.

"You still do not trust them," he said. "Nor do I."

Buffalo Dreamer met his gaze. "Good. I feared that you might. There are only a few of them, but I worry when he

speaks of how many more there are in the land to the east."
She shivered, pulling the blanket up around her shoulders.
Suddenly the air felt colder again. The frolicking and lovemaking she had shared earlier that day with Rising Eagle
were spoiled now.

"I would not be so concerned had I not seen that blue
coat with the gold buttons," she explained. "It is just as in
my dream."

Their gazes held, and Rising Eagle straightened, a
haughty look coming over his face. "Let more men come
wearing the blue coats. They will be in Lakota lands,
where they do not belong. They will find out that it is not
a safe place for them to be. In your dream, we rode the
blue coats into the ground and they became a pool of
blood. Remember that, Buffalo Dreamer."

Buffalo Dreamer nodded, but she could not shake her
uneasiness. She felt that there was still something unfin-
ished about her dreams, and she suspected the Oglala certainly had not seen the last of these white men who were
"just passing through."

CHAPTER THIRTEEN

FLORENCE STEPPED OUTSIDE the log cabin she shared with Abel at Fort John. The North Platte River flowed softly nearby, shallow at this time of year. She breathed deeply, enjoying the pleasant day, as well as her surroundings. She was much happier here than back east at Fort Pierre. Here, she was in the heart of buffalo country, the very area where the Oglala sometimes hunted both buffalo and wild horses.

Abel had been right about this place being a rest stop for emigrants, but even he had underestimated just how many whites now made their way west. Their numbers surprised Florence, and also alarmed her. She knew better than anyone how much the intrusion of these *wasicus* would upset the Lakota.

Sometimes part of her ached to be living with her people again, and she dearly longed to see Rising Eagle, to find out if Little Wolf was alive; but so far, few Lakota had bothered to come around the fort, and those who did were mostly Brule and Blackfoot. The Oglala and Hunkpapa, always the more cautious and suspicious among the Lakota, stayed away. She could only pray that someday Rising Eagle and his clan would come here and that her son would be with them. Little Wolf, or whatever the Oglala called him now, would be ten years old.

She sighed, putting a hand to her belly. After all the men she had slept with, and during the three years of her marriage to Abel, she had never again conceived. She concluded that she probably never would, and she was certain it was because of her heavy drinking. She was being punished for her past sins, and rightfully so. God could not have chosen a better punishment, for she dearly wanted another child to hold to her bosom, to love and care for the way she should have done for Little Wolf. Apparently that would never be.

Abel had accepted what seemed inevitable. As usual, he did not complain, but she knew he would have liked at least one child to call his own. Unlike a Lakota man, he would not take another wife just so he could have descendants. Such things did not seem to be as important to white men as it was to Lakota men. Perhaps that was because there were so many hundreds of thousands of white men in the East. They did not worry so much about their race surviving, not the way the Lakota worried. Life was much harder for the Lakota.

Continuing the circle of life was vital, but whites seemed less concerned. In fact, more than once while living here, she had witnessed something unthinkable: Among the emigrants who stopped at Fort John to restock their supplies and make repairs, she had seen parents strike their children. This was unheard-of among the Lakota, and to witness such a thing had shocked her. Abel tried to explain that this was the form of discipline some white parents used, and she had gently but firmly told him that she would never strike a child of her own, nor would she allow him to treat a child that way.

Not that it mattered. There would be no children for them. The thought broke her heart. She studied the surrounding mountains. At least she had this beautiful land. She felt more at home here, but she did miss the Black Hills. *Paha-Sapa* held a certain magic like no other place. There the spirit of the Lakota would live forever.

She saw Abel walking toward her then. He'd been helping with the construction of a small log church at the post. When he came closer, she could see that he looked sweaty and tired. She walked out to greet him and relieved him of the suitcoat he carried in one hand. He seldom removed his jacket, but the weather was warm enough today that hard work in the hot sun forced a man to remove extra layers of clothing. She found it interesting if not humorous that white men would not remove their shirts the way Lakota men did. White people in general had a far different outlook on nakedness than the Lakota, who wore clothing more for protecting their skin and private parts than because of modesty. The naked body was as much a part of nature as an unclothed animal was, but men like Abel could not understand that way of thinking. When they made love, it was always after dark, and always under a blanket. She smiled inwardly at what a far cry that was from the way Rising Eagle made love. She often had to chastise herself for still sometimes thinking about him that way.

"You look tired, Abel. Come in and rest. I will make you some lunch."

"I'll eat," he agreed, "but I don't dare lie down or I'll not get up for hours. I have a lot of help today, so I want to keep going." He walked with her into the cabin, where Florence had soup and coffee warming on a wood-burning stove. He sat down with a sigh, and she felt his eyes on her as she poured him some coffee. When she turned to set it on the table, she saw that he seemed concerned about something.

"What is it, my husband?"

Abel shrugged. "I'm not sure if it's anything to worry about or not. Maybe *you* would know."

Florence raised her eyebrows in curiosity and sat down across from him. "What would I know more about than you?"

He picked up his coffee. "The army. Bluecoats, as I've heard some of the Indians refer to them."

"What about them?"

Abel sipped his coffee before continuing. "The men helping me said the government will definitely turn this place into an army post. I guess there has been some trouble with Indians harassing some of the wagon trains, stealing some of their horses, trying to trade with them, things like that. The emigrants are complaining and want some protection. How do you think the Lakota would feel about the army coming out here?"

Florence thought for a moment, then snickered. "I would ask the men in the army how *they* would feel about coming out here and getting into problems with the *Lakota*. I can tell you who would come out on the wrong end. The white man's army cannot compare to Lakota warriors."

"The white men have better weapons."

"I suspect they are not as brave, as willing to give up their lives for their cause. They certainy could not be as good at sneaking up on the enemy. Remember, to the Lakota, this is *their* land and *their* game. They will do anything necessary to protect it. I am not surprised there has already been trouble."

Abel wiped sweat from his forehead with the back of his arm. "That's what I'm afraid of." He studied her for a moment. "What if things got really bad, and your people started fighting with mine? Where would your sympathies lie?"

Florence smiled wryly. "Why do you ask such a question? Do you think I would turn on you and slit your throat in the night?"

Abel finally grinned. "*Would* you?"

Florence laughed lightly. "I should say I do not know and let you worry." She grasped his hand. "I am a Christian now, Abel, and I love you. I would never turn on a man who has done so much for me. I am more white than Indian now. You know that."

He squeezed her hand. "I know that. I'm just teasing you. But the possibility of soldiers coming out here does concern me. I hope it doesn't lead to anything disastrous."

She nodded. "So do I. I can only tell you that I know your government has been promising that the emigrants will come *through* Indian lands, but that they will not settle there. I suspect the Lakota do not even like the whites coming through, because they leave behind garbage and dead animals. They dirty the water and shoot game the Lakota need for survival. Right now there are not so many emigrants, so it probably will not be much of a problem. But if more come, and the Lakota see that they do not respect Mother Earth and her creatures, there *will* be trouble, I am afraid, especially if soldiers come with their long guns and try to stop the Lakota from doing whatever they wish to do."

"Then we must pray that things don't get worse," Abel said somberly. "For the sake of my people and yours."

"I agree. I will do what I can and talk to the Lakota who do come here about keeping the peace."

"Thank you, Florence. And I'm sorry you haven't found your son. Perhaps one day you will. I'm hoping for that, and also I hope one day to meet Rising Eagle."

Florence leaned back in her chair. "I think he would probably like to meet you, too. I want him to know that I have changed, and that my new husband is a kind man, nothing like John Dundee."

Abel smiled again. "From what you have told me about Rising Eagle, he could be useful in keeping the peace, if we could find him and convince him to cooperate with our government."

Florence chuckled. "Oh, no. No one tells Rising Eagle what to do. He decides for himself, and then he acts on his decisions; but he *will* keep any promises he makes. The important thing is that your government, and your people, keep *their* promises. There are few things a Lakota man hates more than liars."

"Except for men who steal their wives and horses."

Florence laughed harder then. "Yes, except for that." She squeezed his hand in return and got up, going to the stove and dipping some soup from a pan into a china bowl. She loved china, so beautiful and delicate compared to the plain wooden bowls she once used; it seemed strange to be Lakota and yet live the way she did now. "I hope the soldiers do not come," she said, sobering. She turned and set the bowl of soup in front of Abel.

Abel rubbed his eyes. "Actually, I hope the same thing. I am afraid my government has a way of inventing trouble where none exists." He rose. "I'm going outside to wash at the pump before I eat."

He walked out, and Florence stared at the bowl of soup. How awkward things would be if there were to be trouble between the Lakota and the whites. Most of all, she feared for her son, if he was still alive. She knew firsthand how rapidly things were already beginning to change in this land that once belonged only to her people, this land into which only a few years ago, hardly any *wasicus* ventured.

JULY 1843

Moon When the Cherries Are Ripe

CHAPTER FOURTEEN

"SO, THIS IS the way the white man keeps his promises." Rising Eagle gazed at the string of wagons that stood unmoving in the distance. From the bluff where he and Standing Rock sat astride their horses, he counted eight wagons, most of them the larger ones used for transporting supplies the white men needed. That much he'd learned over the past year since John Charles Fremont had visited his camp, although he could not imagine why the *wasicus* needed so many things in order to live. What the Lakota needed, they carried on a few horses pulling travois.

With the freight wagons were two smaller, canvas-topped wagons. Standing Rock told him he had seen a white woman along, which was why he'd reported the wagons to the rest of Rising Eagle's camp. Having a woman along could only mean family and settling, and the wagons had remained in one place for four days now. These travelers were definitely not just passing through Lakota country.

"More white man's supplies," Standing Rock spoke aloud. "I thought they might be going to that new fort west of this place, the one called Fort John, but they have not moved for days. If they do not plan to settle in our hunting grounds, why do they not keep going? And why did the white men build that fort anyway? Is it to supply those who will come here to settle instead of traveling on?"

"I am wondering the same," Rising Eagle told him, anger building in his soul. "Look what happened at Fort Pierre. It, too, was once a trading post, and now it has become a large settlement for white men and their families. We cannot allow the same thing to happen here. Soon we will see their wooden houses, maybe even the noisy fire-boats coming down our rivers, belching their black smoke and dirtying the sweet waters of Mother Earth. It seems the white men are like ants, busily scurrying about, forever carrying more food and supplies to their new homes. This is not what John Fremont said would happen."

Standing Rock nodded, sweat glistening on his dark skin from the heat of midday. "I do not understand why they build all those fires. They are bigger than cook fires, as though they are burning some of their own possessions. Why would they do such a thing?"

Rising Eagle shook his head as he studied the scene below. "Perhaps they know we have settled our hunting camp just on the other side of this bluff. Perhaps they are planning something we know nothing about, thinking that if they stay here long enough, we will leave."

"That explorer, John Fremont, said those who traveled through our land would not hunt our game. But these surely will need to hunt if they stay much longer."

Rising Eagle sneered. "Already we can see that white men lie. I think we should go back and get more warriors. We will ride down there and give the *wasicus* a good scare, chase them off our land! They promised only to pass through. We will make sure that is what they do."

"I agree! I for one will ride with you, my cousin." Standing Rock turned away from the bluff's edge and rode his horse back toward camp.

Rising Eagle did the same, heading his painted roan gelding down the sandy bluff to the Oglala camp below. This land south and west of the Black Hills was made up mostly of great sand hills and vast stretches of open grass-land, a favorite hunting ground, even though it was closer to the land of the Shoshoni. Sometimes even the Pawnee hunted here, though none were welcome.

The only tribe welcome here were the Shihennas, who also resented the intrusion of the white man. It was they who had first told the Lakota about the new fort built west of here, right in the midst of prime hunting grounds that both tribes now shared.

Rising Eagle raised his lance and shouted a war whoop as he rode into camp, signaling other men that if they chose, they should prepare for possible fighting.

"The white man's wagons still sit far out in the valley beyond the sandhill! Standing Rock and I go there to make them leave! Who will join us?" Rising Eagle announced as he rode his horse throughout the camp. Standing Rock did the same, both men stirring up the others to come with them. Rising Eagle charged his horse to his and Buffalo Dreamer's tepee, where he slid off his mount and greeted his wife. "We go to chase away the white traders who still have not left their camp on the other side of the bluff. I will take my war shield in case it is needed, and my long gun."

Buffalo Dreamer touched his arm. "Do not trust them, Rising Eagle. I have been uneasy ever since seeing John Fremont in his blue coat."

She ducked inside the tepee to retrieve his war shield and gun, and Rising Eagle's heart swelled with pride at the sight of the baby in the papoose she wore on her back. Buffalo Dreamer had presented him with another son six moons ago, born during the Moon of Blizzard Winds, while their tepee sat buried beneath snow in winter camp deep in the Black Hills. His new son was named Kicker because he had kicked his poor mother's ribs so often while still in her womb that she'd had trouble sleeping and eating.

Another son for Rising Eagle! It made him very happy. Now he had three sons, one destined to be a great horseman and surely a great warrior, another destined to be a healer. His beautiful little daughter was five summers in age now, and looking more like her mother every day.

Buffalo Dreamer brought the war shield and gun to her husband. "Remember that they will also have the long guns."

"There are many of us. They will run from us, and then

we will take what we want from their supplies. I will bring you some of their fine things, food and cloth and blankets."

Pretty Feather ran to her mother then, with several other young Oglala girls at her side. They had been practicing building their own small tepees. Pretty Feather's long black hair hung in wet strings due to the heat of the day. "Can I go with you, Father?" she asked.

Rising Eagle's heart warmed every time he looked upon his beautiful little girl. Although he prized his sons highly, he held a special place in his heart for Pretty Feather, who had a way of getting anything she wanted from her father. But not this time.

"A warrior does not take his daughter into danger," he told her. "Stay here with your mother and brothers. Help your mother take care of Kicker. I will bring you something special from the white men's supplies."

Pretty Feather grinned and clapped her hands. "I will be waiting with *Uncheedah*."

Buffalo Dreamer walked closer as Rising Eagle mounted his horse in one swift leap. When she handed him his war shield and gun, he slipped the shield over his left arm and shoved the long gun into its boot. He nodded to her, then rode off to join the gathering of other men, including his uncles and cousins. They headed out at a hard ride. The weather had been very hot, with no breeze. Scouts had found no buffalo for weeks, and they all believed that was because the whites, with their rattling wagons and herds of cattle and horses, had scared the buffalo off, not to mention those they had killed for their own food.

With nothing to do but wait for more scouts to return with news of where to hunt, Rising Eagle and the other men had been bored. They had planned to soon join the Shihenna for a communal Sun Dance. It promised to be a huge gathering, a time for extravagant feasting and celebrating, and also for holding high council with the Shihenna to discuss what should be done about the white man and his lies. If the Oglala could chase away those *wasicus* who camped only a few miles away, it would be a good story to tell—one more success at making sure no whites settled in prime hunting territory.

CHAPTER FIFTEEN

RISING EAGLE AND his followers approached the wagon train from the west end of the massive bluff that separated the Oglala camp from the white men's wagons. Seven of the wagons sat parked in a circle, an eighth one sitting apart from the others. Two fires burned outside the circle, and Rising Eagle noticed remnants of clothes and blankets. He halted his horse, and others rode up beside him.

"Why would anyone burn up their own supplies?" Rising Eagle said quietly to Arrow Runner.

Arrow Runner shook his head. "It is indeed strange. But they are a strange people, with strange ways."

"I see no sign that any of those below want to fight us. They are at least twenty strong, but no one moves."

"Perhaps they are only afraid and are hiding," Standing Rock suggested.

Rising Eagle felt an odd foreboding. "Perhaps. Then again, perhaps it is some kind of trick."

All of them drew cautiously closer and circled side by side around the wagons. After a few minutes of silence, only one white man finally emerged from inside one of the wagons. He showed no weapon, but rather, held his hands in the air as though surrendering.

"Are these *wasicus* really such cowards?" Rising Eagle muttered.

"There could be many more hiding in the wagons," Many Horses warned his nephew.

Rising Eagle urged his horse even closer.

"Be careful, my brother," Arrow Runner cautioned.

As Rising Eagle approached, the man holding his hands in the air backed away. Suddenly he began waving Rising Eagle off, motioning for him to leave.

Rising Eagle frowned in confusion. *Surely there are several more white men with this one. Why do none of them show any resistance? Does this man think that simply by waving me off, the Oglala will leave? How ridiculous! And how foolish!* He sneered at the man and began prancing his horse back and forth in front of him, then rode around the whole circle of wagons, taunting whomever might be inside to come out and stand up for themselves, but no one showed, nor was there any sight of the woman seen with them earlier. He shouted several war cries, charging over a wagon tongue and into the middle of the camp. Still no one made any resistance. The one man who had instantly surrendered stood cowering next to one of the wagons.

Rising Eagle rode close to him and shouted. "What do you fear? Where are all your men? Do you try to *trick* me?"

He felt repulsed when the man knelt and covered his head with his hands. He rode back to the others then, feeling only contempt for these *wasicus*. "They must all be afraid," he declared. "The one who came out to surrender bent down and covered his head, as though a frightened child. He makes it seem as if we are welcome to take anything we want."

"Then I say we do take whatever we want, from *all* of the wagons!" Arrow Runner offered. "And if they are such cowards, they deserve to die. What kind of men refuse to protect what is their own?"

"Maybe there is something special in the wagons," Many Horses said. "Maybe they wish to hide it from us."

"All the more reason to *fight!*" Arrow Runner exclaimed.

Rising Eagle shook his head. "I have no use for such an enemy. Why count coup on someone who will not fight back? It brings no honor, and requires no bravery."

"Then let us go and take what we will," Arrow Runner replied. "We can take blankets, cloth, and beads and cook pots for our women. Some can stay here and watch while others go back for the women and bring them here with travois. These cowards apparently will let us take anything we want. We will raid *all* the wagons!"

Several others shouted their agreement.

"If we raid their wagons and take what we want, it will teach them a good lesson," Wind In Grass added. "And their horses appear to be fine and strong. We will take them, too. Maybe then these men will tell others to stay out of our land."

Olute shifted and whinnied. Rising Eagle studied the scene a moment longer, an inner voice telling him to stay away. "I say we leave them. I have no use for these cowards, or for anything they have. I have changed my mind about attacking them."

"And I say we go and take what we want," Arrow Runner argued.

Rising Eagle turned his horse and looked at the rest of them. "No Oglala man tells another what to do. I can only tell you I do not trust what I see. I choose not to take anything from the wagons. Each of you can do as he wishes."

The younger warriors began yipping and shouting eagerly, some ordering others to go and get some of their women to come and gather whatever supplies they decided to take.

"First we must make sure there is no danger," Arrow Runner told the rest. "We will go and look in the wagons for men and weapons, then take their horses and supplies."

More shouts of excitement filled the air. Some of the warriors charged away, back to camp to bring their women; the rest gave out calls of attack and rode down to the wagons, Arrow Runner in the lead.

Rising Eagle stayed put, his uncles, Runs With The Deer, Many Horses, and Bold Fox beside him.

"I trust your judgment, my nephew," Bold Fox told him. "I, too, choose not to attack, but the younger ones, they are restless for something to do."

"I wanted to frighten those white men away," Rising

Eagle answered, "but they have already given up in some other way. I could see it in the face of the man who came out to surrender. They do not want to be here, yet they do not leave. It makes no sense."

They watched the other warriors ransack the larger supply wagon that sat away from the others. They threw out sacks of flour, bolts of cloth, pots and pans, clothing, brown bottles.

"Firewater!" Rising Eagle grumbled. "I think that is what is in those bottles. The young men must not drink it. I will warn them." He moved a little closer as Arrow Runner and others circled the rest of the wagons, beginning to release horses tied at the rear of them.

Arrow Runner leaped from his horse and climbed inside one of the wagons, then almost instantly climbed back out, running to his mount as though frightened. Rising Eagle came alert, making ready to ride down and help his brother-in-law.

Arrow Runner took his long gun from its boot and fired it into the air, arresting the attention of the others. "Sickness!" he screamed. "Terrible sickness! Faces covered with red spots! Vomit! Fever! The smell of death! Get away! Get away!"

"*White* man's sickness," Rising Eagle growled. He rode forward. "Kill them all! Kill all the white men, the woman, too. Burn the wagons! Burn everything!" he yelled. "That is why they light the fires—to kill the sickness!"

He rode down on the man who had come out to surrender. The man screamed and cringed, and Rising Eagle rammed a lance into his back. Fear mixed with excitement spread throughout the rest of the warriors. Some grabbed blankets and a few supplies and rode away, others grabbed burning wood and clothing from the fires and threw them inside the wagons. Rising Eagle joined them, then halted his horse and stared in wonder at a man who was trying to climb out of a burning wagon. His face was red with fever and covered with darker red spots. He was naked but for the blanket to which he clung.

To Rising Eagle, the only way to stop these men from spreading their strange sickness was to kill them. He took an arrow from its quiver at his back and his bow from where it hung at the side of his horse. He raised the bow and positioned the arrow. The man faced him and spread his arms, as though asking to die. Rising Eagle obliged him, sending the arrow into his heart. The man crumpled over, and immediately the scene around Rising Eagle became pure chaos. More white men emerged from the burning wagons, only to be shot down or bludgeoned. He heard a woman's scream, and a young warrior came out of the wagon carrying a fresh scalp of long red hair. Other young warriors circled the wagons on galloping horses, shouting threats to the white men.

"Die!"

"Do not ever come to our land again!"

"This is how you pay for coming into our land!"

"*Wakan-Tanka* is punishing you for daring to come here!"

More shots were fired, and the screams of the white men added to the noise. All the wagons were soon engulfed in flames, black smoke billowing skyward. The extra wagon filled with supplies was also set on fire. The Oglala warriors quickly gathered the supplies they had taken from it, carrying them away from the flames; soon the women would come to collect them.

The air became filled with acrid smoke, and with shrill cries of victory, the warriors expressing their joy at seeing the failure of the white man to survive in their country. There would be stories to tell over fires tonight about the strange happenings here today, and the terrible look of the sick white men. There was also much bounty to be shared by all.

Arrow Runner rode up to Rising Eagle, his eyes still wide with surprise. "You should have seen them, my brother. It was a terrible sight. The smell!" He crinkled his nose and spat. "These white men are very weak." He held up something gold and glittering that hung from a gold chain. "The sick man gave this to me. Look!" He popped it open. "It opens, and inside, it makes a ticking sound." He held it to his ear, then out to Rising Eagle again.

Rising Eagle took it and also listened for a moment. He handed it back, scowling. "Something makes me uneasy about all of this. Maybe it is not good to get close to these sick white men."

Arrow Runner shrugged. "We cannot catch their sickness. We are too strong." He held up his golden prize and whirled his horse to watch the wagons burn. "When others come and find these wagons and bodies, they will think twice about daring to travel through our land and kill our game. And they will be afraid to stop anywhere for too long!" He gave out another yell and rode back to find those who had gone to get the women.

Rising Eagle turned to his uncles. "I think we should keep the women away."

Bold Fox nodded. "I agree. But each man decides for himself. I for one will go and tell Running Elk Woman not to come here." He rode off, and Rising Eagle followed. After several minutes of riding, they came upon a throng of Oglala—men, women, and children—all headed for the site to collect more bounty left lying on the ground, and to round up the white man's horses.

Rising Eagle rode back and forth in front of them, holding up his lance. "*Hiya! Hiya!* Go back! Stay away from the white man's wagons. *Niksapa hantans ecanu kte!* Be wise, my brothers and sisters! Do not go there!"

Many of them stopped, but some of the younger warriors who had taken part in the raid, including Arrow Runner, began riding among them, shouting about their victory and urging them to go and see, and to collect the fine goods they had taken from the wagons before burning them.

Rising Eagle noted doubt in the eyes of many of his people. What was planned to simply be a venture of threats and curiosity had become one of confusion and destruction. A few of those coming from camp began arguing over whether to go or not go. After all, Rising Eagle was a holy man. He had seen the Feathered One. His visions held great power, as did his intuition. Others could not see the harm in going to look at the destruction and gathering perfectly fine trade goods for free.

Rising Eagle headed toward Buffalo Dreamer, who carried Kicker in his papoose. Spirit Walker and Brave Horse walked beside her, as did Tall Woman, leading little Pretty Feather by the hand. Rising Eagle dismounted, seeing the concern in Buffalo Dreamer's eyes at his warning to stay away.

"There is a bad sickness there," he told his wife and mother-in-law. He looked around. "Where is Looking Horse?"

"My father stayed behind to help guard the camp," Buffalo Dreamer answered.

"Good. He is wise. I want all of you to go back. Keep the children away from there." He turned to his sister. "Stay away, Many Robes Woman."

"But my husband wants me to go!"

"Arrow Runner is not in the mood to listen to me right now. He is full of victory and excitement. But I think it is unwise to go there."

Many Robes Woman looked toward where Arrow Runner rode in circles, shouting for them to come and see. She looked back at Rising Eagle. "You are my brother, but he is my husband."

Rising Eagle sighed and looked away. "Do what you will, then."

Many Robes Woman hesitated for a moment longer, then left, leading a horse pulling a travois. Her sons, Little Beaver and Fox Running, walked beside her.

Rising Eagle closed his eyes. "Do you see, Buffalo Dreamer? The *wasicus* are only passing through our land, and already they cause trouble and arguing among our people." He turned and shoved his still-bloody lance into the leather loops that held it to the side of his gear. "Go back to camp. I am going to find a place to be alone. I must pray about this."

Buffalo Dreamer touched his arm. "I will also pray."

She turned and left him, and Rising Eagle watched her walk back to camp, while many others went on and were nearly out of sight. The heavy feeling in Rising Eagle's heart, and the black premonition of some kind of doom to come, would not leave him.

CHAPTER SIXTEEN

BUFFALO DREAMER WALKED to the stream where Rising Eagle had gone to lie in the water and cool his fever. Never had she experienced such agony and despair. Somehow, even though only two or three of the Oglala who attacked the wagon train had actually touched any of the white men there, close to half of the three hundred or so who were a part of the hunting camp suffered with the hideous spotted disease. Many—including Arrow Runner—had already died. Many Robes Woman suffered as much from grief as she did from the ugly sickness that she, too, had contracted.

Buffalo Dreamer could remember when Arrow Runner had courted Rising Eagle's sister, how happy the two had been, even happier when Many Robes Woman gave birth to two sons. Now both Little Beaver and Fox Running lay near death from the disease.

Tall Woman also suffered, and Buffalo Dreamer hardly knew where to turn. So many loved ones needed her. Rising Eagle, Many Robes Woman and her children, her mother . . . and her own youngest son and daughter. Pretty Feather lay in terrible sickness, as did young Kicker. Old Moon Painter prayed over them now. She had sat with them herself for the past four days, hardly sleeping, praying constantly, yet fearing that this time her prayers would not be strong enough to save them. Her arms were scabbed from cuts in blood offerings made to *Wakan-Tanka* during her prayers to the Great Spirit to save her husband and children from the ugliest sickness she had ever seen.

Nothing like this had ever happened to Rising Eagle's Oglala clan, or to any of the others in the camp. Except for bouts of hunger in the dead of winter, and cases of old age and pneumonia, rampant sickness throughout a camp of this size was unheard-of until now.

She struggled just to walk, weak from her blood sacrifices and days of fasting and prayer; yet for some reason, she had not taken ill, and so far, Spirit Walker and Brave Horse were well. Years ago, when she had thought Rising Eagle would die of battle wounds, she'd cut off her hair, a symbol of sacrifice to *Wakan-Tanka* for his aid. Now, because of this new horror, she had again sliced a knife through her hair, hoping that a second such sacrifice would again save loved ones.

Others were here at the stream, trying to cool themselves, searching for relief from raging fevers. Feeling almost dazed with hunger and weariness, Buffalo Dreamer continued searching for Rising Eagle. She was loath to leave the children, but this, too, was important. Moon Painter's wife, Crow Chasing Woman, tended them for the moment, while Moon Painter continued his prayer songs for the people. In spite of their seemingly ancient years in age, neither Crow Chasing Woman nor Moon Painter had become ill, but many other old ones were already dead, and most who remained alive were horribly ill.

Buffalo Dreamer approached a man lying facedown, thinking he might be Rising Eagle. She could not see his face. She touched him, and only then realized he was dead. She gasped and pulled her hand away, walking around to look closer at him.

"No!" she gasped. It was Chasing Antelope, an honored elder and good friend to Rising Eagle . . . and Arrow Runner's father. Arrow Runner had been his and Making Clay Woman's only son. Now Making Clay Woman had also lost her husband, and she, too, was sick. Buffalo Dreamer closed her eyes and took a deep breath, fighting tears of rage and desperation as she staggered along the flat, sandy river, calling Rising Eagle's name. No one answered.

"Do not let him be dead!" she pleaded. A proud man like Rising Eagle should not have to die this way. How could this be? She and Rising Eagle had always been so blessed. Rising Eagle's prayers had even had the power to heal Spirit Walker in a most miraculous way. If only they were closer to Medicine Mountain. They could go to the top and pray again at the Medicine Wheel, where one seemed to be standing at the center of the universe. Surely there the Feathered One himself would come and heal them.

She moved past men and women who were vomiting, others who simply lay groaning and holding their heads. Others lay in the water because of fiery fevers. All of them were covered with ugly red spots, and one rolled in the grass trying to scratch himself.

"Rising Eagle!" she called again.

"Go away!" someone growled in a raspy voice. "I am full of evil spirits!"

The voice came from the midst of thick underbrush ahead of her. She heard a groan, then sounds of vomiting.

"Surely there is something I can do for you, my husband. I have been praying—"

"There is nothing!" he barked before she finished. "If I survive this . . . I will *kill* every white man who steps in my path!"

Buffalo Dreamer heard the terrible hatred in his voice. "And you *will* survive, Rising Eagle, for you are a holy man, one with great powers."

"Not enough to keep . . . the white man's evil power of disease from attacking me . . . without even *touching* me! I did not even . . . fight with them by hand. I feel . . . *shamed!*"

Buffalo Dreamer felt her heart breaking into pieces. "You will get better again, my husband, and it will be a sign that you are stronger than the white man's disease that tries to kill you. You must fight in a different way now. But fight you must!"

He groaned again. "My head . . . of all the wounds . . .

and Sun Dances . . . I have suffered . . . I can hardly bear the pain . . . the fever."

"I wish I could help you, my husband." Buffalo Dreamer choked back more tears. "It is worse for the children. They are so small and helpless." She could hear Rising Eagle thrashing around for a moment, but he did not show himself. She heard him vomit again.

"The . . . children," he finally spoke up. "All of them?"

Buffalo Dreamer held her stomach in agony. "The baby, and Pretty Feather. Brave Horse and Spirit Walker are still well, but you already know that Arrow Runner died. Your sister is sick, as are both of her sons. And my mother. And so many others. My father is still well, but . . . in coming here, I found one man dead. It was . . . Chasing Antelope."

"Noooo!" he groaned.

"I am sorry, Rising Eagle. I have prayed and offered blood. I have shorn my hair. I have asked the spirit of the white buffalo to save our children and those who remain. I am weak from hunger, but I do not have the disease. I wish I could do more, but I am at a loss to know what it could be. The white buffalo told me that as long as I kept its robe, we would be safe and prosper. Because of this, I have told Brave Horse and Spirit Walker to always sleep on the white robe. I am hoping that it will protect them."

"This sickness is *evil!*" Rising Eagle groaned. "Do not allow anyone who is sick . . . to touch the white robe, or it will . . . lose its power."

He broke down into weeping, and Buffalo Dreamer felt as though her heart was being torn from her body. For loss and illness to be so devastating as to make someone like Rising Eagle weep was monumental. At the moment, no man had better reason to hate the coming of whites into Indian lands. She wondered if this was happening to other Lakota tribes, or perhaps to the Shihenna.

More vomiting. Oh, how she ached for him!

Finally he spoke again. "Perhaps . . . the white buffalo . . . was speaking only of plenty of food . . . and victory in battle. Perhaps the sacred beast did not know of the power . . . of the white man's diseases. I can fight any man . . . with any weapon . . . outhunt any man . . . outride him. I fear . . . nothing . . . Buffalo Dreamer. But this is something I cannot see . . . I cannot touch. Yet it gets into . . . a man's blood . . . into his *guts!*"

"Then you must be strong from the inside, my husband, strong in spirit, not just in physical and mental strength. This is something you must fight in a new way, and your weapon is nothing more than desire, a fierce desire to conquer this evil enemy."

For a moment, she heard only silence. Then he spoke again. "And you? You are well?"

"I am well. The spirit of the sacred buffalo is at least strong enough to keep me well so that I can tend to my sick children and my husband and my mother. But I feel guilty that my prayers could not protect my family from this terrible thing."

"You cannot blame yourself. This is . . . new to us."

"Then we will fight it together. Let me touch you, Rising Eagle."

"No!"

"Then let me give you something." She untied her medicine bag from her waist belt. Reaching inside the small pouch, she removed some of the white hairs she had saved since the sacred white buffalo first appeared to her when she was only ten summers in age. "Take these buffalo hairs. Perhaps they will help somehow."

"There is nothing to help."

"We cannot give up hope, my husband. We cannot let this evil defeat us. Come out and take the sacred hairs of the white buffalo."

She heard more rustling. "Do not look at me," he demanded.

"I promise not to." Buffalo Dreamer cast her eyes down, longing to look at him, to hold him, to comfort him in some way.

He took the hairs from her hand, and she noticed that the palm of his hand was red with fever.

"Go now," he told her, pain in his voice. "I will . . . come to you when I am well."

She took hope in his words. He was at least not giving up.

"When this is over," he continued, "we must go to Medicine Mountain. It is there I get my strength, and there that I receive my greatest visions, the wisdom I need for whatever is to come."

Tears fell from Buffalo Dreamer's eyes. "Yes. It is there we truly became one, there our first blood son was conceived, and there that Spirit Walker was healed."

Rising Eagle moved behind the brush again, and Buffalo Dreamer slowly turned away, heading back to camp, agonizing over having to leave him there alone. Before she reached camp, she fell to her knees and wept, for her husband, for her children, for the Oglala. A new, invisible enemy had come upon them, brought by the white man. What was this power the *wasicus* had, that they could kill without even touching a person?

CHAPTER SEVENTEEN

THE SOUNDS OF wailing and keening filled the air, rising to the very heavens. Buffalo Dreamer's own lamentations mixed with those of other grief-stricken mothers, wives, and daughters. Pretty Feather, only five summers in age, and her six-month-old baby brother lay wrapped together atop a small scaffold. Buffalo Dreamer's two youngest children had died within an hour of each other.

Her hair was now a shaggy array of dark shocks from having been chopped off even shorter out of grief. Feeling removed from reality, Buffalo Dreamer managed to tie the children's medicine bags to the scaffold. Sewn into the shape of turtles, the little leather pouches carried the children's umbilical cords in what had been intended for the beginning of their own personal medicine bags. Buffalo Dreamer also tied little moccasins to the scaffold, and beside the children there lay a little leather rattle that had been Kicker's, and a straw doll that had belonged to Pretty Feather. It was important that those who died took with them items that were dear to them, as well as necessities for life in the hereafter. The bodies were wrapped in several buffalo robes for warmth, and cradles were placed beneath the scaffold to indicate that those lying there were children.

Buffalo Dreamer's grief was made even more unbearable by the fact that the dead body of her own mother lay nearby on a scaffold. Her father sat beneath the scaffold singing a song of sorrow for both his wife and his grandchildren but Buffalo Dreamer, numb from the inconsolable loss of loved ones, could neither sing nor pray. She could only cry, at the same time wondering where so many tears came from.

Arrow Runner, his father Chasing Antelope, and his sons Little Beaver and Makes Fist—all of them gone. Arrow Runner's mother, Making Clay Woman, nearly bled to death letting blood in her grief over so much loss. Even now she lay unconscious in Moon Painter's tepee, where the old medicine man prayed over her.

Rising Eagle's cousin, Sweet Root Woman, was also gone. She left behind a husband, the highly honored scout Wind In Grass, and two sons, eight-summers-old Wolf's Foot and six-summers-old Little Bear. Her mother, Yellow Turtle Woman, who had been almost like a mother to Buffalo Dreamer in the years when she first came to live among the Oglala, had also died. Losing her was nearly as painful to Buffalo Dreamer as losing her own mother.

This place, in a narrow valley of yellow grass south of the Oglala camp, had become an Oglala burial ground in the two weeks since the encounter with the wagon train. Out of a hunting camp of approximately three hundred Oglala, one hundred twenty were dead, and many others bore white scars: pockmarks on their faces and bodies where scabs had been scratched or rubbed off in frantic itching.

Buffalo Dreamer took solace only in the fact that Brave Horse and Spirit Walker lived, as did Rising Eagle. But upon finding out about the deaths of his two youngest children, her husband had gone even farther away to be alone. Buffalo Dreamer ached to have someone with whom she could share this immeasurable grief, but all those closest to her were gone, and Many Robes Woman's own grief kept her in a near coma.

Soon they would have to move on, get back to hunting buffalo in order to store food to feed those who had survived this horror. She would have to leave her little girl and her baby, lying here together . . . yet alone. And her mother. Dear Mother.

This was a grief that would never truly go away. Her only comfort was that her mother was now with *Uncheedah*, Walks Slowly, the precious grandmother who had taught Buffalo Dreamer everything about how to be an honorable and respectable young woman. Buffalo Dreamer knew that together her mother and grandmother would love and take care of Pretty Feather and Kicker. They were all in a place where there would be no sickness, no hunger, no cold. There they waited now for her own arrival, watched over by the Feathered One. Perhaps he would decide to come to earth soon, bringing with him all the Lakota ancestors, to take control of the Lakota lands and make sure no more whites came here with their filth and their dreaded diseases.

She lay down in the grass beneath her children's scaffold and wept deep, engulfing tears that tore at her soul. Never had she felt so alone. Never had she felt so helpless, for always she had counted on her own holiness, the powers of her prayers. It seemed that she had suddenly lost that power. She was sure it had something to do with the white man who had come wearing the blue coat with the gold buttons. Since then, it had been difficult to locate a herd of buffalo big enough to provide a good hunt. Now this terrible disease had fallen upon them. She could only be thankful now that her two eldest sons had survived. It seemed that the disease had run its course, since no new cases had arisen over the last several days. Once the dead were properly buried, the people would have to move on, get away from this place and never return. How hideous that the wasicus were literally chasing them out of their own land, a beautiful area that had been perfect for making a hunting camp.

Buffalo Dreamer felt weak and spent, suddenly realizing that she did not have the strength to rise. Nor did she *want* to rise. Too much had been lost. Right now Brave Horse and Spirit Walker were out riding with Yellow Turtle Woman's eldest son, Standing Rock, whose way of dealing with the grief of the loss of his mother and sister was to get on a horse and feel the wind in his face. He knew Buffalo Dreamer would need this time alone, and so he had taken his second cousins with him. At twenty-five summers, Standing Rock was now a respected young man known for his riding skills. He was helping train Brave Horse and Spirit Walker in the warrior way, and he and Brave Horse got along famously through their mutual love of horses.

Buffalo Dreamer longed to hold her baby again, to feel him suckle at her breast. Her arms felt so empty. She wept until her stomach and neck muscles hurt, and she wondered if she, too, should just lie here and die. Her thighs and arms bore long, scabbed cuts from her ceremonies of bloodletting for her dead children, and she felt she had no strength left.

"Buffalo Dreamer."

The words were spoken behind her in a hoarse voice. Wearily, she turned over onto her back, and she could not help crying out at how Rising Eagle looked. *He's gaunt! So haggard and hollow-eyed!* On his face there were tiny white scars, not the compelling scars of physical battle that only added to his fine, handsome looks, but scars of another kind of battle . . . with a disease that had left permanent, pitted marks on him. His arms and legs bore several slashes in recognition of his own grief, as well as more of the pitted scars.

He reached down for her, and she took his hand, glad to know he had enough strength left to pull her to her feet. *Oh, such anger and hatred and sorrow in his eyes!*

"The others will move on soon, to make a new camp for the hunt," he told her, "but you and I are going to Medicine Mountain. We will not again know strength and peace until we go there." His voice was strained, bearing none of its usual strength. "You will bring the white buffalo robe. It saved our two older sons, and the white buffalo hairs saved me. We must take our most sacred objects to the mountain, and there we will learn what we must do about the coming of the white man."

The words were spoken in cold command. He was a changed man. She hated what the coming of just a few white men had already done to her family. What if more came? Would she ever again know the proud, strong, happy Rising Eagle she had wed?

"It is a long journey. You are not yet fully recovered."

"And you are spent from grief," he replied, "but there is a need in both of us, a need to go to the place where we first discovered the center of our being. I must regain my strength and my pride, for there is one thing of which I am certain. Until my dying day, I will fight the coming of the wasicus into our land. I will kill them until there are none left to kill. I will claim their women and take their children, burn their wagons, steal their horses and livestock and all their supplies. I will make sure they no longer *want* to come here!" He stepped closer. "And I will give you another child of our own, another baby to hold in your arms and soothe your heart. The marks on my face are a sign that I have won another victory over the *wasicus,* for their disease did not kill me. But it killed two of my children, and for that, I will *never* forgive or forget!"

Buffalo Dreamer leaned gently against his chest. "When will we go?"

"Tomorrow."

She drew in her breath. "I cannot bear leaving my baby and my little girl all alone here . . . and my mother."

"It must be done. They are in a better place. Now it is up to us to protect the children who are left behind to face this new enemy. Tonight we will sleep as best we can. Tomorrow we go."

She turned away. "I will sleep here, near my children." She sat down on the white buffalo robe. To her great relief, Rising Eagle sat down beside her.

"I will stay here with you."

She turned to him, unable to control renewed grief. She

fell into his welcoming arms, and although it was close to forbidden for a Lakota man to show emotion in front of others, he held her, stroking her hair. Amid her own tears she heard a choking sound, and she knew that he also wept.

AUGUST 1843

Drying-Up Moon

CHAPTER EIGHTEEN

THE RAGE AND hatred that burned in Rising Eagle's soul now could not compare to any rage Buffalo Dreamer had ever seen in her warrior husband. Warring among tribes was as old as the earth itself, with a sense of respect among warriors for even the enemy. But this new enemy did not deserve respect, and he showed no respect in return. This new enemy could kill from a distance with its long guns. It could even kill when not in sight, without even touching a man, without letting blood. It counted no coup. It cared not for women and children and old ones. It attacked whomever it wanted, whenever it wanted, invading land that belonged to others. This new enemy required a new way of fighting, a new kind of strength and cleverness to compete with it.

Rising Eagle intended to find that strength and cleverness at the top of Medicine Mountain. Some of the Oglala moved on to join other clans in search of buffalo, but what was left of Rising Eagle's clan, many of them still weak, agreed to go with Rising Eagle to the mountains of the bighorn sheep. They all knew the path, for the Oglala were as familiar with this vast and beautiful country as with the backs of their own hands. Every rock and forest, every mountain, every stream was an oft-used landmark. They knew all the places where grass grew in abundance and where it was scarce, where to find turnips, where to find clay for paints, where to find the flowers used for making the colors, or for food and medicine, and where the game was usually most abundant.

Buffalo Dreamer's heart felt as heavy as stone. Her husband's anger made him unreachable and her own suffering over the loss of her baby and her little girl found no place to turn for comfort, for even her mother was gone, as well as Yellow Turtle Woman, her best friend. She could not forget the sight of the platform she'd had to leave behind, where her babies lay wrapped together forever.

Rising Eagle's countenance remained dark and grim, and a determination not to be outdone by this new enemy made him distant and sullen, a man concentrated on finding answers. Two other clans joined them along the way, one Oglala, the other Hunkpapa. A clan of Shihenna also decided to accompany them, and the *Nacas* among them agreed to first hold a Sun Dance at the foot of Medicine Mountain, after which Rising Eagle and Buffalo Dreamer would go to the top and make further blood sacrifices at the sacred stone Medicine Wheel, where they would pray for answers to the new challenge the *wasicu* brought to them. Buffalo Dreamer also wanted answers; but no answer could bring back her children, her mother, her friends, her sister-in-law's husband and children.

The journey itself—putting up with the mean heat of the Drying-Up Moon, making camp every night, sleeping sometimes inside a tepee, sometimes simply under the stars—all helped keep Buffalo Dreamer too busy and weary to dwell on her loss, but the deep ache was always present and she felt that it would probably never go away. She knew it was the same for Rising Eagle.

The loss seemed to bring a new maturity to Brave Horse and Spirit Walker, who rode directly behind their parents. They did not partake of their usual playfulness, such as racing their horses and playing warrior. Instead, they remained solemn, realizing that something grave had taken place and seeming to understand that it was time to think about how they would handle these new challenges when they, too, became honored men like their father. After all, the sons of a man as important as Rising Eagle were expected to follow in his footsteps.

They traveled along the wide, flat river they had followed for decades on this journey from the buffalo plains and sandy hills of the country south of the Black Hills into the more lush, rolling hills to the west. After three weeks of travel, they left the sandy river and headed north, passing through wild canyons and deep forests, country in which Buffalo Dreamer hoped no white man would ever place his feet.

From there, the land gracefully descended over smatterings of rocks and outcroppings into a magnificent plain of deep green studded with more wild rock formations. There one could see for miles, and in the distance was the low, purplish line Buffalo Dreamer knew were the Bighorn Mountains, looking small now, but soon to become high and challenging. At this place, Rising Eagle halted Olute and stared quietly for several minutes.

"It would seem this land should be so big that it would be impossible to cross paths with the white man," he said rather absently.

"Perhaps that is the way it will be," Buffalo Dreamer answered, her heart aching with a wish that she was right. "It should not be so hard to avoid them."

Rising Eagle turned to her. There was that black rage in his eyes again. It frightened even Buffalo Dreamer. Every night her husband went off alone to sing his songs of mourning and to pray. He had barely touched her or spoken to her since their one night together beneath the burial platform of their children.

"I will make sure *they* want to avoid *us*."

Buffalo Dreamer studied the pitted white scars on her husband's face. The new marks did not destroy his handsome looks after all. There were not so many of them, now that a few weeks had passed since his illness. Some had disappeared, but it was obvious that others would remain for life, his mark of victory over death. "I will pray and sing with you at Medicine Mountain, my husband, and then perhaps our desire to rid our land of the *wasicus* will be realized. Or perhaps one of us will have a vision that tells us what we must do."

He nodded, looking again across the vast expanse of peaceful green earth ahead. "This is ours, Buffalo Dreamer. This land belongs to us, and to our children and our children's children. We fight enemy tribes over good hunting grounds, yet we do not mind that they share this land with us. They treat it the same as we do, with honor. They, too, worship the buffalo and find their sustenance from the sacred beast given to us by *Wakan-Tanka*. But the white man has no respect for such things, or for his enemy." He met her gaze again. "He will *learn* to respect us."

Buffalo Dreamer felt a swell of hope. "I am sure that he will, my husband. If nothing else, he will learn to respect the warrior Rising Eagle."

For the first time since the horrible sickness and the death of their children, she noticed a tiny hint of a smile at the corner of Rising Eagle's lips. "I can promise you that. I can also promise that you will bear more children to help fill your empty arms and your sorrowing heart."

He rode forward, and Buffalo Dreamer followed, her spirit a tiny bit lighter. Rising Eagle had a purpose, one that would give him new energy and new life.

CHAPTER NINETEEN

THE DANCE ARBOR resounded with rhythmic drumming and singing, Lakota and Shihenna alike sharing in the spiritual celebration of the Sun Dance.

Buffalo Dreamer could not take her eyes from Rising Eagle, feeling his pain as he leaned back, allowing the skewers under his skin to pull against his weight, stretching the skin of his already-scarred breasts and increasing the flow of blood from the wounds. He blew almost constantly on the bone whistle given to him many years ago by Runs With The Deer for his first sacrifice. Blowing the whistle was a way to keep from crying out with the pain. At times, the singing and drumming were nearly drowned out by the sound of those whistles.

> *See me here, Great One.*
> *I beg your blessings on my people.*
> *I offer my blood to you.*
> *See me here, Great One.*
> *I seek all good things for us.*
> *See me here, Great One.*

The singers, men and women alike, repeated their song over and over, some of the women also dancing in a circle, nicking their arms and legs in a blood sacrifice. Tears streamed down Rising Eagle's face, and Buffalo Dreamer knew it was not because of his pain. The tears were for his dead children, and for his shame. Skewers had also been pierced through the calves of his legs, with buffalo skulls tied to them. Dragging the skulls as he danced around the sacred pole caused more pain and bloodletting, but he bore his suffering willingly, and with pride. This sacrifice would make his prayers on Medicine Mountain stronger.

Buffalo Dreamer in turn felt her own pride soar watching him, and she loved him all the more for what he was doing now. It actually soothed her heart. On either side of her sat Brave Horse and Spirit Walker, both boys swaying to the songs. When she looked at them, she saw their pride, too, sparkling in their eyes as they watched their father. Brave Horse met her gaze then, and she noticed his dark eyes were misty with tears.

"One day I will be the one suffering the Sun Dance," he told his mother.

Buffalo Dreamer saw a young Rising Eagle in his face. "Yes, you will, son. It will be hard for me to watch, but I will watch with pride."

Brave Horse looked back at his father. "I hope I can be as great a man as my father."

"You will be, Brave Horse. Because Rising Eagle is such an honored warrior and *Naca,* you will follow in his footsteps and take his place someday."

Spirit Walker spoke up. "I wish to be a healer, not a warrior," he said. "Will my father be as proud of me for this?"

Buffalo Dreamer put a hand on his shoulder, gazing into his sky-blue eyes and noticing how the summer sun had lightly bleached out strands of his brown hair. "Of course he will be, Spirit Walker. You were yourself miraculously healed, and so you are very special, a gift from the Feathered One. It is good that you study healing with old Moon Painter. That is as it should be, and what your father expects."

"But I helped pray with Moon Painter over my young brother and sister, and they both died. My powers are still very weak. Even Moon Painter could not save my sister and brother, but I fear my prayers will always be weak because I carry white blood."

The singing and drumming grew to faster, louder proportions as they spoke, and they nearly had to yell to be heard.

"When Rising Eagle and I go to meditate at the top of Medicine Mountain, we will find the answer to what has happened," she told Spirit Walker. "You should not doubt your powers, or those of Moon Painter and your father. Your mother, Fall Leaf Woman, gave you to us so that you could be raised as an Oglala, and once you were blessed and healed in your father's arms at the top of Medicine Mountain, you *became* Oglala. No one thinks of you anymore as having white blood, Spirit Walker. Your Lakota blood is much stronger, and the Feathered One thinks you are special, and so you should think that way of yourself, too. Pray to always use your gifts for the good of the people. That is what your father prays for now."

One of the younger dancers, who was making his first sacrifice, crumpled to the ground then, when the skewers tore out of his breasts. When his whistle fell from his mouth, he began crying and singing a special prayer, lost in his own vision trance.

Rising Eagle continued dancing. As was custom, his back had been painted by Moon Painter with a drawing of an eagle, his animal mentor. His hands and feet were properly painted red. Blue stripes, a symbol of the sky, were painted across his shoulders and chest. Another blue stripe decorated his forehead. He wore a long, red kilt, as well as armbands and ankle bands of rabbit fur. A fur necklace graced his throat, and he carried a spray of sage in his right hand, with more sage on his head in the form of a wreath.

To her right, an altar had been prepared, facing the sacred pole. A buffalo skull sat propped on the altar, and before it, a fire made of buffalo chips kept sweet grass burning, creating a purifying incense. Earlier, everyone had smoked a pipe that was lit and passed around by Moon Painter, as a symbol of harmony among all those present.

The day of sacrificial dancing grew long, and outside shadows from nearby trees began to loom across the dance lodge. New babies, whose wailing had earlier filled the air when their ears were pierced, had finally quieted. By allowing their ears to be pierced, their parents vowed to raise them faithfully in the Lakota way. Brave Horse's and Spirit Walker's ears had been double-pierced long ago, and now rawhide strips were tied through them from which hung small sun catchers decorated with quills and feathers, gifts from some of the women.

Both boys closed their eyes and joined in with the singing, and Buffalo Dreamer, too, closed her eyes, quietly singing her own personal prayer song amid the much louder singing taking place all around. Her face was painted with white prayer stripes, and she wore a bleached doeskin dress, one her old grandmother had made for her years ago. She always felt closer to her *uncheedah* when she wore it.

> *Grandmother, hold my baby to your breast.*
> *Grandmother, touch my daughter's hair and make her smile.*
> *Grandmother, watch them play.*
> *Hold them close, as you once held me.*

The singing warmed her heart. She felt stronger, more confident in knowing that her little ones now lived somewhere on a star, in that wonderful land where all their ancestors rested in peace with the Feathered One. She looked forward to her and Rising Eagle's trip to Medicine Mountain, where they would stand on top of the universe . . . and feel the power of the heavens.

CHAPTER TWENTY

IN SPITE OF his weakness from the illness, and then his sacrifice at the Sun Dance, Rising Eagle made the climb up Medicine Mountain by foot, taking only Buffalo Dreamer with him. Just as with the last time he had come here to pray, Moon Painter and his uncle, Runs With The Deer, had been there before him to prepare the sacred fire and to hang amulets from properly positioned poles at the north, south, east, and west points of the sacred Medicine Wheel. This ensured that the surrounding area would remain pure, untouched by evil spirits.

Rising Eagle had decided to drink only broth while healing from the Sun Dance. He refused to eat anything solid, and he told Buffalo Dreamer to do the same. Although she had not been sick during the time of the hideous plague, Rising Eagle knew she remained frail from exhaustion and despair. Their journey here, the rigors of the Sun Dance celebration, and the climb to the top of Medicine Mountain had seriously weakened his wife. He was himself barely able to walk when they reached the Medicine Wheel. Still, only by being drained of strength, and totally purified through the Sun Dance and its preceding purification ceremony, could he hope to be blessed by *Wakan-Tanka*.

He wore a breastplate of bone hairpipes and a breechcloth, nothing more. Buffalo Dreamer carried his sacred pipe for him, and he in turn carried her white buffalo robe because of its weight, an added burden to the difficult climb to this place.

"Before we enter the sacred circle, you must paint the

white prayer color on my face and shoulders," Rising Eagle told Buffalo Dreamer when they went to stand at the edge of the circle of stones. He spread out the robe and sat down, his heart heavy when he saw the sadness in Buffalo Dreamer's eyes as she took her place across from him. She wore a plain, tanned-deerskin tunic, and her straggly hair hung at various lengths . . . yet still she was beautiful. He was glad her perfect complexion had not been marred by the white man's disease.

Obediently, she opened a pouch she had brought with her at Rising Eagle's instruction. Inside was the white clay they found in only one area along the wide, sandy river to the south. She had saved it, keeping it moist. She dipped her fingers into the pouch, moving a little closer to her husband and slowly smearing the clay across his cheeks in white stripes, then across his forehead, one wide stripe down his nose, two more stripes down over his chin. Her touch awakened something Rising Eagle had not felt in the nearly two months since the death of their children. His weakness and shame, his uncertainty about how Buffalo Dreamer felt about the pits in his face, and his determination to remain completely cleansed and purified, had kept him from looking at Buffalo Dreamer with desire; yet he knew that soon they must join their bodies again.

He closed his eyes. "Your touch comforts me," he told her.

She began painting stripes across his chest, from right to left. "And it comforts me to touch you," she answered. "It has been too long since we touched, Rising Eagle."

Their gazes held, and he sensed that she, too, was feeling the tiny sparks of desire that both knew still lay somewhere deep inside, beyond the loss, beyond the shame.

Buffalo Dreamer rose and moved behind him, painting more stripes across his upper shoulders. He reached over his shoulder and took hold of her free hand.

"You should sit with me at the center of the circle. We will pray together all night, as we did those years ago. We will find answers, and somehow we will be happy again.

Come around and sit down so that I can paint you with my prayer color."

He kept hold of her hand as she came around and sat before him again. Then he picked up the pouch and dipped his fingers into the wet clay. He gently painted two stripes on her face, across one cheek, over her nose and to the other side.

"You are as beautiful as the day I took you for my wife."

He enjoyed seeing her slight smile at his remark.

"And you are as handsome as that day, *more* handsome, because you bear scars from fighting to save me from the Crow, and from the grizzly bear you killed in order to win my hand. I know that you worry over the marks left on your face by the disease, but I see them as only another battle scar, a different kind of battle, but another battle you have won."

He closed his eyes. "But my prayers were not strong enough to save my son and my daughter."

She grasped his wrists. "That is because it took all of your spiritual and physical powers to ward off the disease. There was nothing left for our son and daughter. I am the one who should have been able to save them, yet in spite of being filled with the spirit of the Sacred White, my prayers also were not strong enough. It is good that I pray with you now."

Rising Eagle got to his feet, pulling her up with him. "Take up my prayer pipe and bring it. I will bring the robe. We will sit on it together, smoke the pipe together, pray together. And when I am stronger, Buffalo Dreamer, we will mate again. I will give you another son or daughter to hold to your breast."

Tears spilled down her cheeks, and he leaned down to lick them. "You will not again cry over the loss of a child." He picked up the robe and walked with it to the center of the sacred stone circle, where he spread it out beside the sacred fire there prepared by Moon Painter and Runs With The Deer, who were now descending the mountain so that he and Buffalo Dreamer could be alone. He added sweet grass to the hot coals as Buffalo Dreamer closed the pouch of clay and joined him at the circle's center. Both sat down on the robe, and Rising Eagle breathed deeply of the smoke from the sacred sweet grass. He wafted it over his face, then gently blew it over Buffalo Dreamer. Then he lit his prayer pipe.

"I did not tell you," he said, "of the vision I had while suffering the Sun Dance."

He drew deeply on the pipe, then again blew smoke over Buffalo Dreamer before raising the pipe in the four directions of the earth. He lowered the pipe and gazed at his wife.

"I saw a young Lakota warrior whose skin was much lighter than that of most Lakota men. His hair was also lighter, like Spirit Walker's but it was wavy, not straight. This young man painted himself and his horse with white spots, like hail. He rode against many white men wearing blue coats, just as you dreamed. He led many Oglala and Shihenna into battle, and they circled the soldiers until they became a pool of blood, just as you dreamed. I feel there is more I must know about this dream, and I still must know why my prayers did not save me and my children from the white man's dreaded disease. That is why I have come here to the top of the world. I must know who the man with the white spots is and what happens after the soldiers become a pool of blood. In this way, our people will know what is to come and can prepare for it."

"The fact that you saw the same vision as I means we are forever bonded, Rising Eagle," Buffalo Dreamer told him. "This is not the first time we have shared a vision. We have both seen a great herd of buffalo come toward us from out of the heavens. Whatever happens, we will experience it together, just as we sit here now and pray and fast together."

Rising Eagle handed her the pipe. "Breathe deeply of the sacred smoke, my wife. Then we will stay here and fast and sing for as long as it takes to know what we must know, to suffer what we must suffer. We are still weak, but here, high on this sacred mountain, we will find our strength."

Buffalo Dreamer pulled deeply on the prayer pipe, blowing the smoke into Rising Eagle's face then, so that its sacred powers might fill him. She handed back the pipe. "I will stay here with you for as long as it takes."

Rising Eagle laid the pipe across his knees, and he began his prayer song.

For two full days and one full night, man and wife sat singing and praying. Rising Eagle neither ate nor drank, waiting for the vision he was sure would come. Now it seemed that the world below spun around him. Somewhere nearby, he could hear Buffalo Dreamer also singing a prayer song; yet he could no longer see her. He saw only spinning clouds that changed colors, then grew dark when the sun set. The clouds floated away and left a black sky filled with bright stars. They, too, began spinning around him until he felt almost sickeningly dizzy.

He keeled over. In his mind it seemed he was falling down a steep cliff, yet he did not feel stones and gravel beat against his body. He felt only softness. Part of him realized that he lay on the white buffalo robe, but his starved, confused mind could not quite bring him to full reality.

Then, across the night sky, he saw him again, the young warrior with brown, wavy hair and white spots painted on his chest and shoulders. This time a bolt of lightning was painted on one side of his face. The stars began exploding—white, fiery streaks flying toward the rider as though being fired from the white man's long guns. Rising Eagle struggled to his feet as the rider continued to gallop daringly among the stars, as though taunting them. He shouted war cries, his long hair flying, his lance raised, his dark eyes sparkling. It was the same man Rising Eagle had seen in his Sun Dance vision, the one who had led the Oglala against the white men in blue coats. He had returned!

Back and forth he rode, and voices from out of the night shouted his name: *Ta-sunko-witko! Ta-sunko-witko!*

Crazy Horse. They called him Crazy Horse. He made one more dash across the stars, and from the other direction there came another horse, this one unpainted. It carried heavy gear that Rising Eagle had never seen before, and on its back rode a white man, wearing a blue coat. He held forth a long gun, and at the end of it there was attached a pointed saber. He charged Crazy Horse, and to Rising Eagle's horror, the white man's saber landed deep into Crazy Horse's side.

Instantly, Crazy Horse melted into a pool of blood that dripped from his horse as it vanished into the stars. The man in the blue coat held up his saber in victory, but then a hoard of Oglala warriors emerged from the stars and surrounded him. They attacked him and sent him falling away from the stars. Then they looked upward, raising their arms as though in glorious worship, and from the heavens a gigantic Being, part man and part eagle, descended into their presence.

The Feathered One! For the third time, Rising Eagle came into the presence of the Great Spirit, the sacred eagle that was his spiritual guide, the Being who ruled in that place where all Lakota went after death.

"Speak to me, *Wakan-Tanka,*" he begged. "Who is this warrior the white man killed with his saber? What does this mean?"

The Oglala surrounding the Being parted, and Rising Eagle realized they were those who had left their earthly life. His heart beat with joy when he saw Buffalo Dreamer's mother, who stood holding Kicker in her arms, Pretty Feather at her side. His children were whole and beautiful and looked happy. Beside them stood Arrow Runner and his children, as well as Yellow Turtle Woman, and Buffalo Dreamer's old grandmother. All those he had known who had died were there. All looked healthy and happy, and they were smiling.

The feathered Being moved closer, holding out his arms. *"The one called Crazy Horse already lives among the Oglala,"* he told Rising Eagle. *"He is but a baby now, and his father, too, is called Crazy Horse. One day when the child becomes a man, he will ride among the Oglala as one of their greatest leaders. Though your bones will be older then, my son, you will ride at his side against many white men in blue coats. All of them will die at your hands, the greatest victory the Oglala will ever know. Yet one day thereafter, Crazy Horse will die by a white soldier's sword, as will you, Rising Eagle."*

Rising Eagle fell to his knees. "Then there is no hope."

The Being shook his head. *"I did not say there was no hope. I tell you now, Rising Eagle, as I told you before, you must beware of the white men in blue coats. They lie, steal, and kill. They have no honor, no respect for Mother Earth. Yet in the end, the Oglala will defeat them. For hard as these* wasicus *try, they will never own Paha-Sapa. The Black Hills will forever belong to the Lakota."*

Rising Eagle felt enshrouded in a white glow, sharing it only with the Feathered One. The Being told him, *"You did not fail your people. You survived the worst weapon of the white man, his invisible disease. Your children were taken only so that you will always remember the strange weapons of the white man. Never forget that it is the power of your prayers that healed Spirit Walker. Even when you die by the soldier's sword, you will have won, for the white men will learn that nothing they do against the Oglala can make the people weak enough to give up their land. One day the white man will destroy himself, and the Lakota will be left to take what has always belonged to them. You will yourself find victory in death. Never again think that you have lost your powers or your honor. This cannot happen, for I have chosen to allow you to set your gaze on me. This I afford only to the greatest among the Oglala."*

The Feathered One reached out, and Rising Eagle daringly did the same. He touched the tips of the Being's fingers and felt a white-hot heat move through him, bringing a sensation of new strength. The Feathered One drew back, whirling into a dizzying cloud of sparkling white streaks mixed with fire. He rose into the heavens then and became the brightest star in the black sky.

Rising Eagle stared at the star until he felt his legs give out.

CHAPTER TWENTY-ONE

MORNING BROKE WARM and sunny. Buffalo Dreamer, too weak to sit up, opened her eyes to see her husband dancing around the outside of the stone Medicine Wheel. He whirled and stepped high, singing out in great celebration, showing no signs of weakness from all he had been through over the last few weeks.

Buffalo Dreamer felt as though her eyes were playing tricks on her, for although still underweight, Rising Eagle appeared as strong as before he'd become sick, and he showed no signs of defeat and sorrow. His song was one of joy.

> *See me here?*
> *My heart is happy!*
> *See me here?*
> *I am a warrior!*
> *Victory is mine!*
> *See me here?*
> *My heart is happy!*
> *I am a warrior!*

Buffalo Dreamer could not restrain a smile of curiosity and pleasure at seeing her husband looking so much stronger, his spirit lighter. He danced around the entire circle once more before noticing he was being watched. When he met her gaze, he raised one arm and let out a piercing war whoop that Buffalo Dreamer did not doubt could be heard throughout the surrounding mountains. He actually laughed after that as he walked toward her.

"This is a good place!" he told her. "*Our* place! Here we came together in marriage. Here we conceived our first child."

He came closer and leaned down, and to Buffalo Dreamer's astonishment, he picked her up in his arms as though he felt no weakness at all. "Here our son was healed, and here we will again conceive a child, Buffalo Dreamer." He bent his head and licked at her mouth. "It is time to give you another baby to fill your empty arms, my wife."

Buffalo Dreamer frowned, managing enough strength to raise her hand and touch his face. "Rising Eagle, how can you be so strong as to carry me, strong enough to mate? And what has brought you such happiness?"

He took a deep breath, total confidence in his handsome dark eyes. "Because I am a *warrior!* Another will come after me who is even greater, and together we will ride against the white man's soldiers who wear the blue coats. They are the ones you saw in your dreams, Buffalo Dreamer. *Soldiers!* They will come against us, but they will know only defeat. One day they will suffer in a battle that will be spoken of by both white men and the Lakota throughout all time. And *I* will be a part of that battle. I can hardly wait! And even when one day I die by the white man's sword, I will know only victory. The Lakota will *never* lose *Paha-Sapa*. The Black Hills are ours *forever!*"

Buffalo Dreamer's heart was filled with both joy for his happiness and newfound confidence, and sadness over his prediction that he would die by the white man's sword. "Who has told you these things?" she asked, barely able to speak above a whisper.

He bent down to grip the white buffalo robe in one hand and drag it with him as he carried Buffalo Dreamer away from the stone circle. "Once again the Feathered One came into my presence," he told her. He walked to a grassy area and set her on her feet, then spread out the buffalo robe. He again took hold of her and gently laid her on the robe. He untied the leather cords at the shoulders of her tunic and pulled the dress down over her body, exposing her nakedness. She had no strength to help him, or to object. He leaned close then, speaking softly in her ear. "I saw them, Buffalo Dreamer, your mother and our children."

Buffalo Dreamer sucked in her breath. "You *saw* them?"

"*All* of them! Your grandmother, Arrow Runner, Yellow Turtle Woman, my nephews, my mother and father, our children, all of them! They were with the Feathered One, and they looked happy and well. And I saw the warrior who painted himself with white spots. He is called *Ta-sunko-witko*."

"Crazy Horse?"

"The Feathered One told me that already he lives among the Lakota, hardly more than a baby. He said that one day I would ride with him against many blue-coated soldiers. The man I saw was perhaps thirty summers or more. Do you see what that means? We have many more years together, Buffalo Dreamer, and we will know many victories before the soldier's sword finally ends my life. I will die a warrior's death, not the humiliating death of the white man's disease. I have been victorious over everything the white man has sent against me, and I will continue to be victorious for many years to come. I will die an honorable death, and my name will be spoken by white men and Lakota alike for many years after that! All our victories now will ensure that the Black Hills will forever belong to the *Lakota!*"

He leaned down and rubbed his cheek against hers.

"All that we have suffered, Buffalo Dreamer, was only to teach us how strong we truly are. It was to prepare us against the white man's weapons. We have no greater enemy now than the white man. The Crow, the Shoshoni, the Pawnee . . . all pale by comparison."

Buffalo Dreamer's eyes teared. "My own happiness

comes from knowing my children are happy and well with my mother, in that beautiful place where the Feathered One takes them."

"Someday you and I will go there. You will hold your children again. Until then, I will give you more children to hold here on earth. And our sons and daughters will know days of victory and bounty. They will ride into battles about which they can tell their own children and grandchildren. Our descendants will always have stories to tell about Rising Eagle and Buffalo Dreamer. This I know. We will live forever through our children, Buffalo Dreamer, and through their spoken words."

A tear slipped down the side of Buffalo Dreamer's face. She reached up and pushed some of Rising Eagle's straight black hair behind his ear. "In spite of all the sorrow we have known, I have never known such happiness as I feel now, Rising Eagle, seeing you this way, knowing my children are well and happy. The Feathered One has made you strong again, and because of that, your seed will be strong. Plant yourself deep, my husband, and give me another child. During my own prayers and singing, I also had a dream. You and I sat together at the center of the Medicine Wheel. It began to lift away, carrying us with it. It whirled skyward, into the stars." She traced slender fingers over his lips. "And so I know that when you do leave this earth . . . for that heavenly place . . . I will go with you. Until then, I will always have children and grandchildren around me."

She moved her legs around the outside of Rising Eagle's legs. "I am so weak, Rising Eagle. I can barely move, yet I am anxious to hold another baby to my breast."

Rising Eagle reached down to untie his breechcloth. Weak and starved as they were, an inner, spiritual strength allowed them the energy for mating, for it was something that must be done, that their visions might be fulfilled. Buffalo Dreamer's breath caught when her husband penetrated her womanliness, his hard shaft pushing deep.

Still light-headed from her ordeal, Buffalo Dreamer felt as though all this was happening in yet another dream. Perhaps it was, for never had she felt such peace and happiness. Never had mating with this man held so much hope and joy, even more than that first time when he had taken her here at the top of this majestic mountain. His talk of victory and of many more years of sharing their love brought visions of wonderful times to come. She lay on the sacred white buffalo robe, the precious robe that boded good things for the Oglala—as long as it remained in her possession.

She was too spent to move. She let Rising Eagle take her on his own. He moved gently, in a sweet rhythm that comforted her. His life spilled into her in the heavy throbbing of his climax, and he continued to mate with her for several more seconds before finally relaxing and pulling her close. They lay there quietly for a moment before he finally spoke.

"We must go below and drink water and eat."

"Yes," she whispered.

"Are you strong enough to walk down?"

"I am not sure. You might have to help me."

Rising Eagle rubbed his nose against her cheek. "I love you, Buffalo Dreamer. I thought that I had failed you, but now I know I did not. Back when the Crow stole you away all those years ago, I thought I had failed you then. But now I know it has all been a test. Everything that has happened was a test to make us stronger. Each time, we both dreamed and heard predictions of the future. Each time, we learned to love each other even more. Together we will lead the Oglala into victory and prosperity. And together we will know victory even in death."

Buffalo Dreamer rose up and gently kissed the still-puffy scars at his breasts, where he had pulled against the skewers inserted there during the Sun Dance. "I have never been more proud of you, Rising Eagle."

He ran a hand through her cropped hair. "Nor I of you. Soon your hair will once more fall over your shoulders, and you will never have to cut it again in sorrow. I promise you."

She smiled through tears. "I believe you."

They lay there side by side, gathering strength to walk down the steep pathway to the waiting Oglala below. "How soon do you think they will come, Rising Eagle?"

He reached over and grasped her hand. "They are already here."

"I mean in bigger numbers. From all we have learned in our dreams and visions, we know that surely many more *wasicus* will come."

He squeezed her hand. "Soon, I think, while most of our children are still young. But I am ready for them." He raised up on one elbow. "And I promise you this. One day the white man will speak the name of Rising Eagle with great fear."

Buffalo Dreamer did not doubt his prediction.

PART THREE

Promises

Brothers! I have listened to many talks from our Great Father. When he first came over the wide waters, he was but a little man . . . he begged for a little land to light his fire on . . . but when the white man had warmed himself before the Indians' fire, and filled himself with their hominy, he became very large. With a step he bestrode the mountains, and his feet covered the plains and the valleys. His hand grasped the eastern and the western seas, and his head rested on the moon. Then he became our Great Father. He loved his red children, and he said, "Get a little farther, lest I tread on thee. . . ."

Brothers, I have listened to a great many talks from our Great Father. But they always began and ended in this: "Get a little farther; you are too near me."

—SPECKLED SNAKE, A CREEK INDIAN, 1829, JUST BEFORE THE INFAMOUS FORCED EXIT OF CREEKS, CHICKASAWS, CHEROKEES, CHOCKTAWS, AND SEMINOLES TO INDIAN TERRITORY, IN WHAT IS NOW KNOWN AS THE TRAIL OF TEARS.

JUNE 1845

Moon of Making Fat

CHAPTER TWENTY-TWO

RISING EAGLE CHARGED Olute back and forth in front of the wagon train he had caught traveling through prime buffalo country. Eighty Oglala warriors, all primed for attack, sat in a line facing the wagons. They shouted war cries, enjoying the fact that the *wasicus* had begun circling their wagons, obviously preparing for a fight. And they would get one!

"Do you see me?" Rising Eagle taunted his enemy. "I am Rising Eagle! Do you know my name?"

He saw a puff of smoke, heard the crack of a long gun, but he rode too fast for the aim to be good.

"You do not belong here!" he screamed. "I will show you what happens to those who come here unwanted!"

He laughed, as did several of the other warriors. The *wasicus* were afraid! Rising Eagle could *smell* their fear, and he relished it. He could tell that there was no sickness among this group of travelers. They kept moving every day, and they did not burn their belongings. Besides, he no longer feared their sickness; he had conquered their new weapon. Nothing could stop him now, and nothing could quell his hatred.

He continued parading and taunting them, holding his lance high, daring the white travelers to stop him. He knew they could not understand the exact words he shouted, but they surely knew by his actions what his intentions were.

"Do you see me? Be afraid, white man! When I am through with you, your brothers and sisters will never dare come here! They will never kill our buffalo and our deer!

They will no longer make our water dirty! They will be afraid to bring their *women* here!"

He and the young warriors who gladly rode with him had successfully attacked a supply train last summer, killing two of the wagon drivers, one of them by slow torture. That was a moment of great satisfaction for him and others who had lost loved ones to the spotted disease. After all, many Oglala had also died a slow, tortuous death by the white man's sickness, including his own innocent son and daughter. It was only right that whites should also die slowly.

"Soon all *wasicus* will know my name!" he taunted. "Fire your long guns, white man! Your bullets cannot hit Rising Eagle!"

In that first attack, several miles south of the Black Hills, two drivers had escaped by riding fast on spare horses, but they'd left behind two wagons full of food, cloth, tools, pots and pans, a host of bounty that many Oglala now enjoyed. They'd also left behind several horses that Rising Eagle's people now used for packhorses. Perhaps the wagons that lay before him now would yield even more useful items. If the white men were going to continue their stupidity in daring to ride into Oglala country, daring to again bring their deadly diseases that killed small children and shamed grown men, they would suffer for it. This was the only way to stop them. If enough of them died and enough horses and supplies were stolen, enough wagons burned, maybe then they would understand how dangerous it was to come here.

Rising Eagle turned and faced his followers, one of whom was Wind In Grass. Since his wife and mother-in-law had both died from the white man's disease, Wind In Grass also felt a need for vengeance. He had since taken Rising Eagle's widowed sister for a wife, and he and Rising Eagle had become closer, for Wind In Grass was nearly the same age as Rising Eagle, and was an honored Shirt Wearer. Recently, Many Robes Woman had given birth to a son by her new husband, helping heal her heart from the loss of her own two children. Little Foot was only six moons old, and finally Rising Eagle had seen smiles on his sister's face again.

Also among the warriors was his cousin, Bear Dancing, now twenty-six summers in age. Bear Dancing was in his prime, ready and eager to follow his mentor against this new enemy with white skin and hairy face.

Most of the other warriors who followed Rising Eagle were also young and eager, although several older *Nacas* joined him as well. They, too, had lost wives, children, grandchildren, nieces and nephews to the hated disease. Yellow Turtle Woman's husband, Many Horses, was here, proudly wearing his full war bonnet decorated with eighty eagle feathers. Rising Eagle rode close to him, thinking how strong and virile his aunt's husband still looked, in spite of his sixty-one summers.

"What do you say, Many Horses? Are you ready to attack our enemy and chase him out of buffalo country?"

Many Horses nodded, his weathered skin crinkling around his eyes as he squinted against the sun. Rising Eagle saw the distant tears in those eyes. "I am ready to kill those who killed my beloved wife, the mother of my children, and who killed my beautiful daughter, Sweet Root Woman."

Rising Eagle turned Olute, raised his lance and gave out another shrieking war cry, then kicked the horse into a full gallop. More war whoops filled the air as Many Horses, Standing Rock, Bear Dancing, Wind In Grass, and the others followed, screaming their war cries, raising bows and arrows, lances, some of them aiming long guns as they charged the wagon train.

Rising Eagle never felt more determined, even when going to war against the Lakotas' ancient enemies. He felt bullets singing past him, but he did not fear them. He was *Naca*. He had again seen the Feathered One, who promised he would live many more years. Not only that, but he would die by the sword, not by the long gun. And Buffalo Dreamer still possessed the robe of the sacred white buffalo. Nothing could harm him.

Already he saw three white men lying dead, two with arrows in their chests, one with an arrow in his neck. He raised his own bow, aiming at a kneeling man who had his long gun pointed right at him. Apparently something was wrong with the gun, however, because suddenly the man began frantically trying to reload it, then rose when Rising Eagle charged closer.

The man's eyes widened, and he raised his gun as though to swing it at Rising Eagle; but Rising Eagle let go of his arrow, striking the man in his lower left side. He was perfectly aware that an arrow in that location would not kill the *wasicu* instantly. It would take him a while to die, and rightly so. He *should* suffer slowly!

With a chilling war whoop, he charged Olute over the wagon tongue and the white man he'd just wounded. He rode down another man, slamming his war club into the man's skull, delighting in the crushing sound of the bone caving in. That would teach him to stay in the land of the rising sun!

The warriors swarmed around the wagon train, some hitting the white men with war clubs, then touching them to count coup. It was important to count coup against an enemy who could kill them from afar. To be able to get this close and touch them would bring them great honor when they told their stories of battle around campfires and before the *Naca Ominicia*.

Olute whirled in a circle as Rising Eagle leaped from the animal's back to walk up to the man he had clubbed. He kicked him onto his back to see that he was still alive, then grinned with satisfaction. This one, too, would suffer. He whipped his coup stick from where it was stuck into his belt and he touched the man with it, then let out another war cry.

He turned to walk back to the man he'd shot with an arrow, who now lay writhing on the ground, screaming with pain. A young woman crawled out from under the nearby wagon and went to him, weeping uncontrollably. Rising Eagle walked up to her and grabbed her by her hair, jerking her away. She screamed in terror. The man on the ground began yelling, "No! No!" Rising Eagle did not understand the word, but he certainly understood the way it was said, the pleading look in the man's eyes.

So, he thought, *this woman must belong to him.* In Rising Eagle's world, one sure way to humiliate an enemy was to steal his horses, his women, and his children. If stealing the white men's horses and supplies was not enough to deter more *wasicus* from coming into this land, perhaps stealing their women and children would teach them a final lesson. It was one way to find out just what these white men valued most.

He kept a tight grip on the knot of hair at the back of the woman's head and dragged her, kicking and screaming, to a wagon wheel, making sure they remained in full view of the wounded white man. He guessed the man must be her husband. That was good. It was important that the *wasicu* see this, so he could tell other white men about it and warn them to stay away.

Grabbing a piece of slender rope hanging on the side of the wagon, Rising Eagle used it to tie the woman's wrists to the wheel, keeping a knee planted in her midsection so that it was difficult for her to move, or even to breathe. Once her wrists were secured, and while the white man still shouted in pleading tones, Rising Eagle pushed up the woman's skirts. To his surprise, she wore many layers of cloth under the dress, something no Lakota woman ever wore. Irritated with the cumbersome clothing, he used his knife to begin slicing away layer after layer, astonished that white women dressed so swathed, even when it was this hot. How foolish!

The woman begged and pleaded just like her husband was doing, but Rising Eagle paid no heed, except to think of how ashamed her husband must be to see the way she behaved, screaming and weeping as she was. No Lakota woman would carry on like this. Yes, she would fight, but she would not cry like a child. Any Lakota woman taken by the enemy would expect this, for it was all part of shaming the enemy. When Buffalo Dreamer had been stolen by the Crow, she'd managed to cleverly find a way to kill the Crow warrior who intended to claim her for his own, even though she knew it would mean her own death. If not for the intervention of a thundering herd of buffalo that destroyed the Crow camp but left Buffalo Dreamer alive, she might be dead now, or still a slave to some other Crow man.

Rising Eagle sat on the white woman's ankles and angrily ripped away at her clothing, while all around him the other Lakota warriors began raiding the wagons for any useful blankets and supplies they could find. He would not look for such things today. He would take Buffalo Dreamer the best reward of all; a woman to be her slave, to help her haul wood and clean skins and aid with other duties. After all, Buffalo Dreamer had given him another son, Little Turtle, who was over one summer in age already. The boy was healthy and active and still feeding at his mother's breast, and Buffalo Dreamer needed help with her chores.

He slit his knife through something the woman wore to cover her private places, still wondering at all the clothing, some kind of stockings on her legs, hard shoes, more layers over her chest.

Now the woman no longer even fought him. She simply continued to scream and weep. He slit his knife through the bodice of her dress, tearing it away, frustrated at something stiff and hard she wore underneath, slicing at that, too. It was as tight as rawhide shrunken by water and sun. When he slid his knife along the ties at the front of it, it literally popped open. He ripped it away, looking in wonder at her white skin and pink nipples. *What do white men find attractive about these pale, cowardly women?* He could hardly find enough about her to desire in order to do what he must. His only incentive was to shame her husband, and so he did, pulling aside his breechcloth and ramming himself inside of her. She screamed and cried even more, as though he were skinning her alive.

In seconds, it was over. He cleaned himself with a piece of her dress and adjusted his breechcloth, then ripped away the rest of her clothing while she lay limp and weeping. He began to wonder if she would be of any use to Buffalo Dreamer at all. He would take her back with him, and if she proved to be more bother than she was worth, he would give her back to her people.

He turned to look at her husband, who was screaming and obviously cursing at him. He grinned, holding his chin proudly. Yes, he had rightfully shamed the man. He had shown him what would happen if white men continued to come here and try to kill the Lakota with their long guns and their invisible evil spirits that crept into a man's blood and killed him slowly and quietly.

He knelt down to cut the ties that held the woman to the wagon wheel. That was when he noticed her, a young girl crouched under the wagon, staring at him with big blue eyes that showed a mixture of terror and curiosity. He left the woman for a moment and crawled under the wagon. The man screamed even louder, and Rising Eagle realized that this child must belong to him.

He smiled at the girl, who just stared back at him, her blond hair hanging in strings about her shoulders. He guessed her to be perhaps ten summers in age, and even at that young age, she showed more courage than either of her parents had. Yes, this girl understood. She was not the sniffling coward her mother was. And she was still young enough to be taught the Lakota way. Children this age adapted well. And even though Buffalo Dreamer now had a new child to hold in her arms, she still missed her daughter.

What a prize! He would take this girl to Buffalo Dreamer, and she could raise her as her own. At the same time, the girl was big enough to help with chores. He reached out, admiring the child's courage when she took his hand and let him help pull her out from under the wagon. Rising Eagle felt excitement at his find. Stealing this girl away would be the ultimate warning and humiliation for her father. He would leave the man alive, so that he could tell his story to others, warning his white brothers to stay out of Lakota country or they could lose their women and little ones.

He urged the child to her feet, studying her wide blue eyes and tousled yellow hair. He sensed her terror, even though she put on a brave front. To help keep her from being too frightened, he finished cutting away the ties that held her mother to the wagon wheel, thinking the woman would put her arms around her daughter and comfort her. Instead, the woman just curled up, still weeping. Her behavior disgusted him, and he considered not bothering with her at all. Still, for the sake of the child, he should take the mother along, at least for a while, until the child became accustomed to her new people.

He called to Olute. The well-trained animal trotted closer, and Rising Eagle dragged the white woman away from the wagon wheel, lifted her and tossed her over the horse belly-down. He curled his lip at the sight of her white rump, wondering if these people had any appreciation for the sun, which gave life to anyone who basked in its light. He walked to the wagon, taking from the back of it a blanket left behind by the other warriors. He walked back and threw it over the naked woman.

All the while, the woman's daughter stared, standing stiff and unyielding, as though in a trance. Rising Eagle walked over and smiled down at her, then picked her up and set her on Olute behind her mother. She did not resist. He leaped onto the horse behind mother and daughter, and Wind In Grass rode up to him then, leading two fine-looking horses stolen from the small herd that had accompanied the wagon train.

"What do you have there, my brother?" Wind In Grass asked.

Rising Eagle laughed. "A white woman. I think the

young one is her daughter. I will keep them. The woman can help Buffalo Dreamer with chores, and the daughter can help soothe my wife's heart. Buffalo Dreamer can raise her as her own. The woman's husband is wounded, but he is alive. We will let him live, so that he can tell his brothers never to come here again!"

Wind In Grass let out a war whoop of victory. "Now we can go hunt buffalo. We have given the white man enough warning."

Rising Eagle nodded. "I ask to use one of your horses to tie the woman to it. I do not wish to tire my best horse because of so much weight."

Wind In Grass agreed. He brought up one of the stolen horses beside Rising Eagle and maneuvered the woman's body off Olute and onto the other horse. He dismounted and tucked the blanket around her, then reached into his parfleche and took out a long piece of red ribbon he had stolen for Many Robes Woman. He used it to tie the woman's wrists and ankles together under the horse.

Rising Eagle noticed that the woman no longer wept but was completely quiet. Good. He could not stand a cowardly, sniffling woman who had no pride and no courage.

Wind In Grass rode off with another cry of victory, leading the stolen horses, the woman bouncing on the back of one of them. Rising Eagle reached past the little girl in front of him, taking up the ropes around Olute's neck and using one arm to hold the child tight against him, giving her a reassuring hug. He hoped she understood that she would not be harmed. She was prize bounty, a new daughter for Buffalo Dreamer.

He rode off with the others. He would keep the white woman until she was no longer useful. Then he would throw her away. But the little girl he would keep forever. She would become Lakota!

SEPTEMBER 1845

Moon When the Calves Grow Hair

CHAPTER TWENTY-THREE

"SHE IS USELESS! All she does is cower and weep," Buffalo Dreamer complained to her sister-in-law. "I would die before I behaved that way in front of my captor and his wife or wives. And the woman has no idea of how to properly scrape a hide or how to stretch it to dry."

Many Robes Woman giggled. "I do not understand how white men put up with such women. They are pale and weak and have no courage. The daughter is much braver than the mother. Already she plays with the other young girls and is learning how to bead and quill."

Both women worked vigorously as they talked, scraping fresh buffalo hides from a recent, very successful hunt. Buffalo Dreamer glanced at the white woman, who knelt next to them doing her best to scrape another hide but working much too slowly, her mouth squiggled in obvious disdain for such a chore. She kept stopping to wipe her hands on the nearby grass, and occasionally she sniffled from the almost constant tears she had displayed since her capture nearly three months ago. The scrapes and bruises she had suffered during her capture and from the beating she had taken from the Lakota women when she was first brought to camp had healed, and no one had touched her since; but she continued to cower at the very approach of any man or woman.

They learned that the white woman was called Mary, and Rising Eagle spoke with her every chance possible, making her tell him the English words for anything he pointed to. He intended to keep her only long enough to learn some of the white man's language from her. Other than that, he had no need of her. He had used her to properly humiliate her husband, and that was that. The pale, whimpering thing annoyed him.

In contrast to her mother, the young girl, whom Buffalo Dreamer guessed to be around ten or eleven summers in age, was a pleasure. Named Yellow Bonnet for her yellow hair, the child was quite amiable. She learned easily and willingly, and she seemed more curious than afraid. She had adapted well to the Lakota way of life, and Buffalo Dreamer enjoyed letting her help with Little Turtle.

"My husband cannot get rid of the white woman soon enough," she told Many Robes Woman. "She irritates me with her constant tears. When I was captured by the Crow, I never cried in front of the man who chose to try to claim me. I stood right up to him, and if I had not found that knife with which I stabbed him in the heart, I would have allowed him to take me without so much as a frown. I would never have let him break me into the sniveling coward this woman is."

Many Robes Woman shrugged. "I enjoyed beating her with my stick. It made me feel better about losing my beloved Arrow Runner and my two sons. It is a pain that will never truly leave me, and anyone with white skin should suffer the same. I hope the woman's husband has died from his wounds." She wiped sweat from her brow with a chubby hand. "I only wish to never lose Wind In Grass the way I lost Arrow Runner. I am learning to love my new husband, but we both know I will never take the place of Sweet Root Woman for him, and he can never replace Arrow Runner for me. But he holds me close at night and—"

She hesitated, glancing at Buffalo Dreamer and chuckling lightly. "You know. He is very good under the robes."

Both women laughed then, and Buffalo Dreamer felt desire welling deep in her loins. Because it was dangerous for a woman to have her babies too close together, she and Rising Eagle had not mated for the past several months, not since Little Turtle's birth the past autumn. "You had better be careful, Many Robes Woman. Already you have your new son, as well as Wind In Grass's two motherless sons. With no mother of your own, your burden is great, but if you enjoy your husband under the robes too often, there will be yet another child to feed at your breast."

Many Robes Woman smiled. "I do not mind. Wind In Grass speaks of taking the widow White Moon for a second wife to help me. She can have no children of her own, so she would be a good helpmate."

"Hmmmph," Buffalo Dreamer grunted. "I thought *I* had a helpmate when Rising Eagle brought the white woman, but she is more work than help. And if we keep having such good hunts as this one, we will not be able to keep up with so many hides to stretch and tan, and so much meat to cure. I wish my mother was still with me."

She sat back on her heels and looked around the camp. In every direction, women were scraping and stretching hides. Many fires burned, giving off smoke to cure the strips of meat that hung over them. A good buffalo hunt meant a lot of hard work, and depending on what they would be used for, hides were treated in many different ways. The one Buffalo Dreamer worked on now would be scraped of all its hair and used for new tunics. Others would keep their hair and be used for robes and warm clothing and winter moccasins. Some would be cured and cut into rawhide strips for tying supplies onto horses and travois, and some meat would be mixed with berries and pounded into pemmican.

It pleased her to see such a large, peaceful camp. Things seemed more in order again. No more whites had come through this part of the country, south of the Black Hills. Maybe Rising Eagle's last attack had had the effect he'd intended and they would be relieved of the pesky white emigrants.

"I miss my grandmother also," she told Many Robes Woman with a deep sigh. "It hurts to know that Yellow Bonnet and any other daughters I might bear will not have a grandmother to turn to. I learned so much from my *uncheedah*, and I will always remember that last night I slept in her arms before I married Rising Eagle."

"Running Elk Woman will help you raise Yellow Bonnet, and any daughters you have by my brother," Many Robes Woman answered her. "She is the wife of Bold Fox, brother to Rising Eagle's dead father. It is her responsibility to take over for your mother and for Yellow Turtle Woman now that they are gone."

Buffalo Dreamer nodded. "Yes, but she tires easily." She noticed Rising Eagle riding toward her then on Olute. At the same time, a commotion arose toward the northern edge of the large camp. She stood up when Rising Eagle came closer and slid down from his horse. Mary cowered and looked away as he approached, and Buffalo Dreamer could not imagine why she was afraid of him. Rising Eagle had not laid a hand on her since bringing her to camp. *And look at what a muscled, handsome man he is! Mary should feel honored to have been claimed by such a respected Lakota leader. The silly woman has no idea of how lucky she is to belong to Rising Eagle.*

"White men come," Rising Eagle reported. "They are not like the others. They dress like us, and they speak our tongue. They say they come in peace."

Buffalo Dreamer shaded her eyes against the afternoon sun. "Do you think you can trust them?"

"I do not know. Our scouts say they show bravery unlike any we have seen in other *wasicus*, and they see respect in their eyes. They wish to smoke the pipe with us and talk about trading something for the white woman and her daughter."

"Her daughter! I have grown attached to Yellow Bonnet. I do not want her to go!"

Rising Eagle nodded. "I do not intend to trade her, but you are anxious to get rid of the woman, and so am I. Perhaps I have kept her long enough to teach her people a lesson. Maybe these men will promise that their people will now stay out of Lakota country. Keep the woman here until I send for her. I do not want these white men to see her until I find out what they have to offer for her. I came to get my pipe."

He ducked inside the tepee Buffalo Dreamer had erected nearby. She followed, watching him take his prayer pipe from the wooden frame she had tied together in a tripod on which she hung his war shield and set his prayer pipe whenever they were not being used.

"Be careful, my husband."

"These men come humbly, as they should. And they are far outnumbered. They do not even carry the long guns, a signal that they come in peace. I will speak with them." He turned and ducked outside, and Buffalo Dreamer followed.

"Do the white men have a leader? Is it the one called John Fremont, who visited us before?"

"No." Rising Eagle leaped back onto Olute. "This one calls himself Thomas Fitzpatrick, a strange name. One of the Shihenna women who lives among us said that her people call him Broken Hand, because he has a crippled hand." He turned and rode off toward several more warriors who were gathering.

"Broken Hand," Buffalo Dreamer repeated in her own tongue. She hoped this one was honest.

CHAPTER TWENTY-FOUR

RISING EAGLE TOOK his prayer pipe from Broken Hand, who had smoked it reverently and offered it to the four directions. This man understood the Lakota way, and Rising Eagle respected him for that, taking hope that maybe this particular white man spoke with a true tongue.

He smoked the pipe again himself, the first and last to smoke it. It had been handed around the circle of *Nacas*, who had gathered to hear what Broken Hand had to say. In a mixture of his own tongue and sign language, Rising Eagle began the conversation.

"Our scouts say you are called Thomas, but our Shihenna friends who live among us call you Broken Hand."

He studied Fitzpatrick closely as the man nodded in reply. He appeared rugged and experienced, and he wore fringed buckskins, just like a Lakota man. His gray hair fell to his shoulders in gentle waves, and his face was clean-shaven. His blue eyes sparkled with goodwill and honesty.

"It is true that some call me Broken Hand," he answered, holding out his crippled hand. "This is because of an accident with a small gun, which works much like the long guns you know." He allowed the Lakota men present to study the crippled hand for a moment. "I wish to speak to the one called Rising Eagle," Broken Hand said then.

Rising Eagle set his pipe across his folded legs. "I am Rising Eagle. Do your people know of me?"

Broken Hand nodded again. "Yes. You shouted your name to a white man you had wounded. He repeated it to those who found him."

Rising Eagle grinned and nodded. "Good. Now your people will know whom to fear when they come through Lakota land. Already they know to stay away or they will die and their women and children will become Lakota. This has been the way of our people since the beginning of time. It is something that is understood by us and by our enemies, a lesson the white man is just beginning to learn."

Broken Hand rubbed his forehead as though perplexed. Rising Eagle smiled at the gesture, enjoying the fact that he had the upper hand in this matter. Broken Hand sighed deeply before answering.

"You took this man's wife and daughter."

Rising Eagle nodded. "I claimed them for myself. But the woman is not of much use. All she does is cry, and she knows nothing about the duties of a Lakota woman. She is weak and stupid. She does not even know how to scrape and tan a buffalo hide."

Broken Hand paused, as though contemplating his next words. "Is the woman in this camp?"

"She is."

"Will you trade her and the girl to me? I have brought long guns. Her husband's last words before he died were to ask me to try to find them and bring them back to his people."

Rising Eagle looked around at the other *Nacas* in his circle. His uncles, Bold Fox and Runs With The Deer, nodded their agreement. Rising Eagle cast an arrogant look at Broken Hand, deciding that it would not be wise to ever agree to anything a white man wanted.

"I will give you the woman, but not the daughter. She is now *my* daughter, and she has helped heal my wife's sorrow over losing two of our children to the white man's disease—" he pointed to the pockmarks on his face "—the same disease that left its white marks on me. It is the white man's invisible weapon, and I have vowed that he must suffer for using such a cruel way to try to kill the Lakota."

Broken Hand shook his head. "I can't give you all the

long guns I have brought unless I get the woman *and* her daughter."

Rising Eagle almost laughed. "I will remind you that there are many of us and only a few of you. We could take the long guns whether you want to give them to us or not."

"I came to trade, not to make war. Ten guns for both woman and child, five if I can have only the woman."

Rising Eagle shrugged. "Then five guns it is. You cannot have the girl."

Broken Hand turned to the four buckskin-clad men with him. They stood behind him, hanging onto their horses' bridles and to the two packhorses they had brought with them. One of them smelled so bad that Rising Eagle caught his scent from across the circle of men. They all looked stronger and more able than most white men Rising Eagle had seen, and in spite of their unkempt hair and beards and yellow, rotted teeth, they at least held a look of respect and friendliness in their eyes. Broken Hand spoke with them for a moment before moving his gaze back to Rising Eagle to speak in the Lakota tongue.

"I wish to speak with the woman before we make a decision."

Rising Eagle nodded, then motioned to a young Lakota boy who stood in the crowd that surrounded the council. "Go and tell Buffalo Dreamer to bring the white woman," he told him.

The boy grinned and scampered off, and Rising Eagle again aimed his attention at Broken Hand. "White men like you have lived and hunted here for many winters. You understand and respect the Lakota and their ways. But these new whites who come, they bring diseases, and they know nothing about how to treat Mother Earth. I took the white woman to teach them a lesson. I hope that her husband is going back to where he came from."

"Her husband died of his wounds, but you can be sure that news of your attack and the taking of his wife and daughter will make its way back to the land in the east, where many more white men live. They will hear of it, and they will give much more thought to coming into Lakota country."

Rising Eagle felt great satisfaction at the words.

"I must warn you though, Rising Eagle, that there is talk in a place called Washington, where the Great White Father of our people lives, that a fort will be established in the middle of your prime hunting grounds. A *fort,* not a trading post. Our Great White Father will fill this fort with his soldiers. So far, this is still just talk, but if you keep attacking the wagon trains of whites who come through here, it will certainly become real. You would be better to leave the travelers alone, or you will only cause our government to send soldiers to protect them. I must have your promise that you will stop this raiding and killing."

Rising Eagle thought for a moment, glancing at one of the other white men, who stood leaning on his long gun. Again he determined that he would not bargain with these men, even if they spoke true.

"I do not fear the white man's soldiers. I promise nothing, not if you cannot promise in return that no more white men will come into this land."

Broken Hand stroked his chin as he answered. "I cannot promise that."

"Then I cannot promise I will not kill more of them and steal more of their women and children. But I see that you are sincere about hoping for peace. I will wait a while and see if the white man continues to only travel through our land and not stay here."

"I am glad you will wait."

The white woman, wearing an Indian tunic and moccasins, her blond hair greased and braided down her back, approached then, Buffalo Dreamer on one side of her, Running Elk Woman on the other. Her eyes lit up at the sight of white men, and she gasped with relief as she insultingly ran right through the circle of Lakota elders and grasped Broken Hand's arm. There was no doubt in Rising Eagle's mind that she was pleading with the man to take her away with him. He waited while they talked for several minutes, angry with her for having dashed through the gathering of *Nacas,* showing no respect for these most honored men. Lakota women knew they must always sit behind their men in such gatherings, but in all these moons, this woman had learned nothing of such observances.

The only thing that made him glad about having taken the white woman was that now he actually understood some of what was being said between her and Broken Hand. After a few minutes of conversation, he noticed an odd look of surprise on Broken Hand's face, and then it seemed the man was almost arguing with the woman. Rising Eagle glanced at Buffalo Dreamer, who stood behind him, as anxious as he to learn the outcome of this confrontation. She raised an eyebrow, telling Rising Eagle again, this time with her eyes, that she, too, would like to see the white woman gone. Buffalo Dreamer had complained about her practically every night since he'd brought her back from the raid.

Broken Hand stepped forward, pushing the woman behind him. "This woman's name is Mary Higgins," he told them. "She tells me that if she can go back without the child, she will agree to it."

Rising Eagle glanced at Buffalo Dreamer again. He could see that she was as surprised as he that the woman would give up her daughter so easily. He looked at Bold Fox, and the man shrugged in amazement. Rising Eagle turned his attention again to Broken Hand, glad for the response, but confused. He rose to face the man in reply. "What kind of mother would so easily leave her child behind?"

"She tells me the child belonged to her husband, not to her. He left no other family, so there is no place to send the girl, whose white name is Miriam. Her real mother died two summers past, and this woman states that she has no feelings for her as a daughter. She wishes to go back to her own family in the East and never return to this place. She tells me the little girl is happy here. Is this true?"

Rising Eagle nodded, still rather dumbfounded at the revelation. What kind of woman did not love her own husband's child? No Lakota woman would deliberately abandon a child to the enemy. "Even now she is off playing with Lakota children. She is well and happy. I will raise her as my own, protect and care for her. One day she will become a proper Lakota woman and bear Lakota children."

Broken Hand smoothed his hair back from his forehead. "I think it is wrong to leave the child here, but I don't know what else to do. The woman wants to go home. I will take her to Fort John first. I do this only because I am aware of other cases where white children were adopted into native families and lived to be old and happy. But I warn you, Rising Eagle, you must not do this again. There are many, many more white men in the East, and many soldiers. You will know peace only if you desist from attacking the white travelers who come through this land."

Rising Eagle stepped closer. "The white man will know no peace until he stops coming through prime buffalo country. He is our *enemy*."

"He is *not* your enemy. He wishes only to use your land for travel, and surely you realize that very few come here."

Rising Eagle dropped his arms to his sides, his gaze turning to a glare. "I only know that my son and my daughter were killed by the same disease that left these marks on my face and shamed me with its evil spirits. This I cannot forget—*ever!*"

Broken Hand faced him eye to eye. "Once you have had the disease, which the white man calls smallpox, you can never get it again. And those who were exposed to it and never got it should also not have to worry."

"That does nothing for those who died from it!"

Broken Hand lowered his head and nodded. "I understand." He turned to the men with him and barked an order. The men started untying blanket-wrapped bundles from their horses. "I will make you one more offer, Rising Eagle. Five guns for the white woman, the other five for a promise that you will not raid more wagon trains."

Rising Eagle shook his head. "All ten guns for the woman. I make no other promises. And since the woman agrees to leave the child here, there is nothing else to talk about."

Broken Hand put his hands on his hips and slowly smiled. "For having little contact with my people, you seem to have already learned much about how to trade wisely."

"My wish is that my name will often be on the lips of your people, as a Lakota leader they fear."

Broken Hand just shook his head, then turned back to his men and shouted another order. Two of them stepped forward, laying all ten long guns at the center of the circle of elders. Another brought forward leather bags of black powder and lead balls.

Rising Eagle raised his chin proudly as the men helped the white woman onto one of their horses. He felt quite pleased with the bargain he'd made: all ten long guns for one useless white woman. These men had no conception of the true value of anything.

Broken Hand walked closer and put out his hand in what Rising Eagle perceived as a token of friendship. He grasped the man's wrist, and Broken Hand grasped his in return. "I am honored to meet you, Rising Eagle," he said. "I hope we can always meet as friends. My government has made me an Indian agent. I will visit your people whenever there is news to tell you. I want to help keep the peace between the Lakota and my people. I assure you that the white man does not use his diseases to kill the Lakota. The same disease kills them, too. If they could stop it, they would. However you think the white man gave this disease to you, it was not a trick. If you believe this, perhaps you can forgive my people for your loss. I speak the truth, Rising Eagle."

Rising Eagle studied the man's eyes and he saw and felt his sincerity. "I believe you, Broken Hand. But already I am learning that few white men can be trusted. You I trust. When you come into my camp again, no harm will come to you. I will have scouts and runners spread the word that you are welcome in any Lakota camp."

Broken Hand let go of his wrist. "Thank you." He gestured a good-bye and Rising Eagle nodded, then watched the agent mount his sturdy horse. The white woman cast Rising Eagle a look of disdain before hanging her head as she left with the white scouts.

"Good riddance!" Buffalo Dreamer spat. She looked up at Rising Eagle. "Will you attack again if more *wasicus* come through buffalo country?"

He watched Broken Hand ride away. "I will wait and see how true Broken Hand's words are and if he is really our friend—or our enemy." He looked down at his wife. "For now we have ten more long guns. Someday perhaps every Lakota man will own one of the white man's weapons. Then the *wasicu* will fear us even more. And now, Buffalo Dreamer, Yellow Bonnet is your daughter . . . forever."

OCTOBER 1845

Moon of the Changing Seasons

CHAPTER TWENTY-FIVE

FLORENCE LAID OUT some clothes for Mary Higgins, her emotions running in circles at the sight of her, wearing a Lakota woman's tunic, her blond hair braided down her back, her light skin burned a reddish brown.

Broken Hand had said she'd been the captive of Rising Eagle! That meant he was alive. She had feared the worst after hearing about the smallpox epidemic that had ravaged many Lakota bands. And since Mary had been Rising Eagle's captive, perhaps she had seen her son. Broken Hand claimed he had seen no young boy her son's age with missing fingers and toes; but then he'd told her that Mary had been in a very large Oglala camp and that he had spoken with only a few of the older men. It was very possible that her son had been elsewhere in camp with the others.

Little Wolf would be almost twelve years old now. If anyone had seen him, it would be Mary . . . unless the boy had died from the smallpox, or perhaps died at a younger age.

"Mrs. Higgins?" She faced the woman, who sat in a rocker in the corner of the small bedroom of her and Abel Kingsley's three-room frame house, built for them by the traders who ran Fort John. It had more room than the log cabin, and it had real wood floors.

Mary had said little other than "Thank you" when Abel offered his home as a place for her to stay while she recovered from her "ordeal" with the Lakota. Broken Hand had arrived earlier that afternoon with the woman in tow, and

Florence could not help the way her heart leaped when she heard where Mary was found.

The woman had barely raised her head since her arrival, apparently feeling shame. Florence thought of how different she would feel if she were a "captive" of Rising Eagle. She would like nothing better, even now, after being married to Abel for five years and after becoming, in most ways, a white woman.

Mary did not look up or reply right away when Florence spoke her name. "Is there anything more I can do to help you?" Florence asked then. "We do not have all the comforts here you might be used to back East, but there is fresh water in the pitcher I have set out for you, along with a bowl and some towels for washing. The clothes here on the bed should fit. We are about the same size, and—"

Mary suddenly looked up at her, her eyes flashing contempt. "You're *Indian!*"

Florence felt her old Lakota pride begin welling up inside. She raised her chin slightly. "Yes. I am Oglala, the same as the people who held you. But I have not lived among them for many years. I am married to Preacher Kingsley now."

Mary looked her over disdainfully. "I never would have agreed to stay here if I'd known you were his wife. I thought perhaps you were simply his housekeeper. Why would a fine Christian white man marry an *Indian* squaw?"

Florence flinched at the term "squaw." The way whites used the word, her people would consider it a grave insult to their honorable women. She suddenly lost any pity she had for Mary Higgins. "That is a question for my *husband* to answer."

Mary looked away. "When I was first taken to Rising Eagle's camp, his squaw gave me one of her tunics to wear, a *Lakota* woman's clothes! Now another *Lakota* woman gives me *her* clothes to wear! Are there any *white* women around here whose clothes I might borrow, and with whom I might stay until I can go home?"

Florence kept her new Christian faith in mind as she struggled with her anger. If she still lived with the Oglala, she might have beaten this woman with sticks and fists when she was first brought to camp. All prisoners suffered such treatment, to ensure they understood their lowly place among the Lakota women. She folded her arms and fought an urge to spit back something insulting.

"If that is what you wish."

"It is. And when I leave this place, I never want to see another Indian the rest of my life!" Her eyes teared and she looked away again. "The only problem is that I can't leave here, not for at least another six months. It makes me sick. *Sick!*"

Florence frowned. "Why are you not able to go back to your people right away?"

Mary began wringing her hands, and it was obvious to Florence that her next words came with great difficulty. "That man . . . the one called Rising Eagle." She spoke the next words in a near growl, through gritted teeth. "He . . . *raped* me!" She covered her face with her hands and broke into tears. "It was hideous and humiliating! My husband lay there wounded and tortured, unable to help me!"

How strange, Florence thought. *She thinks it was such a terrible thing, yet if I had one wish, it would be to lie with Rising Eagle again.* She loved Abel Kingsley, but she had never experienced the true passion for him she had always held for Rising Eagle.

"A Lakota man does not know the meaning of rape," she explained. "There is no such thing among my people. Unlike many white men, Indian men do not do such things for their own evil pleasure. All Rising Eagle did was claim you as his property, stealing you from a people he probably believes are his enemy. When the Lakota raid an enemy camp, besides horses and meat and robes, they sometimes take women and children. It is their way of humiliating the enemy warriors."

Mary looked back at her, hatred spitting from her eyes.

"Well then, my poor husband was certainly *humiliated!* And now he's . . . dead." She wept again, and Florence could understand that part of her sorrow.

"I am sorry." She allowed the woman several minutes of crying, then walked to a dresser and opened a drawer to take out a neatly folded handkerchief. She handed it to Mary. "You have not said why what happened to you means that you must stay here through the winter."

Mary shivered and blew her nose, then wiped at her blue eyes. "Can't you guess?" She choked back a sob. "I can't go back East and give birth to an *Indian* baby! I don't intend for *any*one there to ever know what happened to me. I would be shamed forever. No other man would ever touch me; my own family would shun me!"

Florence's heart pounded faster. "An *Indian* baby? You carry Rising Eagle's child?"

Mary groaned. "It makes me want to vomit!"

A stunned Florence sat down on the rope-spring bed. "How . . . how do you know it is not your husband's child?"

The woman grasped her stomach and hung her head. "I just know, that's all. Since my last . . . time . . . my husband and I had not—" She shivered again. "The hard life of traveling out here by wagon does not leave a woman the time or the energy for such frivolous chores."

She thinks pleasing her husband in the night is a frivolous chore?

"You wish to stay here then until the child is born?"

"I have no choice."

Florence frowned. "And you intend to abandon your own baby?"

Mary met her gaze again, her upper lip curling into a sneer. "I could never have feelings for a child of rape, especially when it will have *Indian* blood! I noticed plenty of lazy, drunken Indians around this trading post when we arrived. Let one of *them* have it!"

She looked away again, and Florence could not help wanting to shout with joy. *This woman carries Rising Eagle's child! And she doesn't want it!* Always Florence had longed to have another child to replace the one she had given away to the Lakota, but she had never again conceived. And more than anything else, she would have wanted that child to be fathered by Rising Eagle. Now here was this woman who carried his seed! What better way to still feel close to Rising Eagle and to soothe her own empty heart than by raising Rising Eagle's child?

This would take much thought, and a good deal of conversation—and possible argument—with Abel. He might be a little jealous, for he was aware of how she had always felt about Rising Eagle, though he had never met him.

For the moment, she quelled the urge to tell Mary that she would gladly take the baby herself. She would have to talk to Abel first. And she did not want to get too excited yet, in case the woman should change her mind.

"Are you sure this is what you want?"

"Of course I'm sure!" Mary snapped. "Why do you ask such a thing?"

Florence rose and walked to look out the window at a trader's wagon passing by. "Because I know the emptiness of giving up a child."

Mary sniffed. "I will feel no such emptiness giving up *this* one!"

Florence sighed. "Is that why you left your husband's daughter with the Lakota? You are afraid she will tell your people what happened?" She turned to face the woman again. "You wish to hide all of this? What will you tell your family?"

Mary put her head in her hands. "That my husband and stepdaughter died in a drowning accident. I can go back and return to the comfortable life I had there, be with my mother again, my sisters. I never wanted to come out here in the first place. I miss my family terribly. The raid was almost . . . almost a blessing." Her voice broke and she wept again.

Florence shook her head. "Your husband was killed. You call that a blessing?"

Mary blew her nose again. "I hated him for bringing me

out to this godforsaken place. And it's his fault I suffered that horrid rape and life among the Lakota. Right now I feel void of *all* feelings."

Florence walked closer. "I must ask you something. I want to know if there was a boy living with Rising Eagle and his wife. He would be about twelve years in age. Actually, there would be *two* boys about that age living with them. They probably have other children by now, but one of the boys, he would be Rising Eagle's son. The other—" She felt the never-ending tug at her heart at the memory of giving her tiny deformed baby to Rising Eagle to raise. "The other is almost the same age. He was . . . mine. I will not explain why I gave him to Rising Eagle, but—"

"You *know* Rising Eagle?"

Only too well. I loved him. "Yes. And my son, he had fingers and toes missing. He was small and weak. He may still be smaller than other children his age. I need to know if you saw such a boy, with deformed hands and feet. His father was white. My son might have lighter skin and hair than the others, and his eyes are blue."

She watched Mary's forehead wrinkle in thought, and to her disappointment, the woman shook her head. "No. There were two young boys about that age, and one did have blue eyes. I supposed he was simply the child of another of Rising Eagle's rape of some poor, helpless, innocent white woman. The boy I saw was not deformed. He had all his fingers and toes, so he could not have been your son."

Florence's heart fell. Her poor little son must have died after all, if not of the smallpox, then maybe not long after Rising Eagle took him—the child had been so small and sick. Even after all these years, it still hurt to think that her little boy no longer lived. A lump rose in her throat.

"I see," she said, wondering who the boy with the blue eyes could be. "Thank you for telling me." She walked to the door. "I will see if I can find you some clothes belonging to a white woman." She looked down at her own neat gingham dress, and for a moment she longed to wear only a tunic again, to be free of stays and slips and hard shoes. She loved Abel and believed in the Christian way now, but so much talk of Rising Eagle brought back painful memories.

Her clothing, the way she lived now, the way she wore her hair, her new religion, her work with Abel to bring Christianity to the Indians who hung around the fort—none of it could change the fact that from the marrow of her bones to her nearly black eyes and her dark skin, she was still Lakota, and she would never feel shame because of it.

MARCH 1846

When the Geese Return from the
South Moon

CHAPTER TWENTY-SIX

MIRIAM STOOD BESIDE Spirit Walker, watching the horse races. What a strange, exciting, wonderful new world this was among the Lakota. She was learning their language, and in return, she taught her new brothers English words.

Everything with these people was an adventure, which had quickly helped ease her terror when first captured. She had never known a day of abuse. Everyone treated her in a friendly way, and her new mother and father actually seemed to love her like their own.

Today the Oglala celebrated the first truly warm day of spring, after a hard, freezing winter and weeks of being confined to warm tepee fires. She enjoyed helping care for Little Turtle, a chunky baby boy whom Buffalo Dreamer doted on. She was surprised at how much attention Indian women paid to their babies, keeping the little ones with them almost constantly, most of the time in cradleboards they wore on their backs. Lakota children seemed to have almost complete freedom. There were no strict rules for them, and they were never whipped for wetting themselves, or forced to sit for hours in prayer, or chided for laughing. The smallest children ran naked in hot weather and no one seemed to think it was wrong. There were no rules for eating or dressing, no hard shoes to wear, no dishes to wash. Unlike the stepmother who had abandoned her to the Lakota, Buffalo Dreamer never looked at her as though she were bad or unwanted, nor did she ever strike her. Miriam had never seen anyone hit a child of any age. Before being captured by Rising Eagle, she hardly knew a day that she didn't have a bruise from her father's belt or her stepmother's "training stick."

Today Brave Horse raced his father's swiftest horse, Wind. He charged past, just ahead of the rest of the thundering horses, all of them ridden by young boys. Rising Eagle raised his fist and yelled out in happy victory when his son passed the goal marker in first place. The whole camp of at least two thousand Oglala was happy. A good hunt last fall had produced enough meat to last the entire winter. Miriam had heard that they would soon pick up camp and migrate from their homeland in the Black Hills and head south and west again for more buffalo hunts and to trade with the Shihenna.

She turned to Spirit Walker, who held a young raccoon he'd found wounded by a predator. He'd spent the last two days praying over the animal, packing its wounds with moss and waving the smoke from sweet grass over the creature, more of the healing techniques he was learning from old Moon Painter.

Moon Painter looked a thousand years old to Miriam. She had never seen anyone so wrinkled, but watching him was fascinating, and Spirit Walker truly did seem to have learned from him the ability to heal. She reached over to pet the baby raccoon.

"Is he all right now?"

Spirit Walker stroked the animal's head. "He is well. Grandfather thinks I should send him out into the wild, but maybe I will keep him."

Several men and women gathered around Brave Horse after he won the race, and Spirit Walker headed toward them. "Come on!" he told Miriam. "Let's see what the elders give Brave Horse for winning the race."

Miriam ran with him to the place where all the young boys who had raced their horses were being congratulated as well as teased by relatives. There was so much good-natured humor and laughing among these people.

The Lakota were her family now. They called her Yellow Bonnet because of her yellow hair. She could not quite think of herself yet by that name, but she did not mind it. This place was her home now, where she felt free and happy and loved. And life here was so different, not at all terrible as she had imagined the West when she still lived in the East and heard stories about the "savage" Indians.

Strangely, on the day of the Indian attack on her father's wagon train, she'd felt no fear when Rising Eagle held out his hand to her, in spite of watching him club a man to death and tie up her stepmother and rip off her clothes. She'd felt sorry for her wounded father, and a deep sorrow at learning he'd died, even though the man had been brutally strict with her. But when she'd looked into Rising Eagle's eyes on the day of the raid, she saw something there that told her child's heart she could trust him.

Now she watched Rising Eagle, the proud father, strut and brag about how well his son could ride.

"He could win a race against *you,* Rising Eagle!" Bold Fox told him.

Rising Eagle laughed. "I think he could!"

Rising Eagle's pride in both of his sons was evident, for he also liked to brag about how one day Spirit Walker would be a great healer. Miriam knew now that Spirit Walker was adopted, just like she was. Seeing how much he was loved made her feel more confident about her own place in Rising Eagle's family. He and Buffalo Dreamer seemed to consider her their daughter.

Brave Horse grinned with embarrassment at all the attention, but great pride shone in his eyes. He accepted a prayer pipe from Bold Fox, and Rising Eagle took from around his own neck a string of eagle claws. He placed it around Brave Horse's neck, and the boy looked up at his father in near tears.

"Thank you, *Ate,*" he said. He leaped onto Wind's back again, raising his fist and letting out a war whoop of victory.

"I am going to play kick ball," Miriam told Spirit Walker. "Come watch us!"

She ran off to join a group of young girls playing the

game, and she screamed and laughed when she collided with two other girls trying to kick the grass-stuffed leather ball at the same time. She and another girl fell together, and she laughed so hard that her stomach hurt.

Yes, she loved this new life. It was full of adventure, and she felt more wanted here than she had felt with her father and stepmother. She hoped no one ever came for her now. She had no desire to return to the white man's world.

APRIL 1846

Moon of the Birth of Calves

CHAPTER TWENTY-SEVEN

FLORENCE TRIED TO explain to Helen Myers that birthing would be much easier for Mary if she would squat on her knees rather than lie on her back; but Mary refused to give birth like a "heathen," and Helen barely understood anything Florence tried to tell her. An immigrant fresh from Germany, Helen understood only a little English, but at least she had given birth to a child of her own. They did not need to fully understand each other verbally, for the needs of a woman having a baby were universally understood by all women who'd been through it.

Mary's screams filled the grounds of the trading post, and Florence did not doubt they were louder than necessary because of Mary's disgust at having to suffer this pain for a child fathered by a Lakota man. The woman lay in her own bed, in the one-room dwelling added onto the back of Hans Myers's trading store, an establishment built by Hans not long after his arrival at the post. He had appeared with three wagons filled with supplies from New York City, intending to start a wonderful new life in America. The man was convinced that many more people would be coming west over the next several years, and he intended to become the richest trader along what some were beginning to call the "Oregon Trail," which went right past Fort John.

Florence did not know much about the place called Oregon, or why so many whites were determined to leave their homeland to go there. She only cared about the fact that Mary Higgins was giving birth to a child fathered by Rising Eagle. Her heart pounded with anticipation. This would be *her* child! Abel had agreed that she could keep it and raise it if Mary truly wanted to give it up.

Again she urged Mary to get to her knees.

"Don't touch me!" the woman shouted. "I never want to be touched by an Indian again!"

She screamed the words, and Florence thought: *What a hypocrite this woman is! She claims to be Christian, and Christians are supposed to love all people.* Yet Mary Higgins had not loved her own stepdaughter enough to plead with Rising Eagle for her. She held no respect at all for any Lakota or any other native, and she loathed the baby she gave birth to now. How could any mother hate a child of her own blood, no matter who the father was?

Florence was swiftly learning that white Christians spoke in two tongues, one of love and one of hate, one of truth and one of lies; they showed open, forgiving hearts, yet were capable of being ruthless, according to what suited them. So far, Abel was the only white person she knew who fit the description of what she had learned a true Christian should be.

"It's coming! It's coming!" Mary screamed. "I feel it!"

The woman's water had broken hours earlier, but her labor had been difficult. Florence checked under the blanket over Mary's bent knees to see the head appearing.

Helen Myers began carrying on excitedly in German and became almost useless. Florence tried to explain to her that she must grab the scissors and get ready to cut the cord, and a flustered Helen, only twenty-one herself and still nursing a year-old baby, began searching frantically for scissors that lay right next to her on a bed stand.

In spite of a very warm March, this April day was unusually cold, and a cloudy sky had even produced some light snow. The small room Mary called home was chilly, but Mary sweated profusely from the hard work of giving birth. The baby was coming fast now, and Florence laid yet another clean towel under Mary. Helen finally grabbed the scissors and stood shaking while Florence helped pull the baby into its new world. In spite of the bloody membrane enshrouding it, she could already see a shock of straight black hair, as well as a ruddy, red color to the baby's skin. Yes, the child was all Lakota, and when it was finally fully birthed, she could also see that it was a boy.

A son for Rising Eagle! He would be so proud if he knew. In that moment, she forgot about Mary. She could not think of anything but the baby. Quickly she had Helen cut the cord, and she wrapped the baby in a towel. She told Mary to lie still and let Helen help with the afterbirth.

Smiling with joy, she picked up the baby and hurried with him to a table prepared with a blanket and a basin of warm water. With her finger, she carefully but quickly dug the membrane from inside and around the baby's mouth and cleaned his nose, then laid him on his belly, pounding his back lightly until he coughed and choked, then let out a squeal of objection, followed by a deep breath and his first real cry of anger at being thrust into the cold world outside his mother's womb.

It was a fine, healthy cry! Would Rising Eagle father a weak, sickly child? Never. This was at least an eight-pound baby, she was sure, and as she proceeded to clean him up, she was thrilled to see that he was perfect in every way. In her whole life, she had never known such joy! She tied off the umbilical cord with a piece of ribbon, then washed the child again. She smeared his tender new skin with the soft cream white people used, and to which she had herself grown accustomed to using. She wrapped him in a clean blanket then, and through it all, he continued squalling, demanding already to be fed. If only her own breasts were capable of producing milk . . .

She carried him to the bed to see that most of the afterbirth had been expelled. She laid the squalling boy in a waiting cradle Abel had made, then wrapped the afterbirth in the towel under Mary, taking it away and setting it near the door. She was certain that neither woman would understand if they knew she intended to keep the afterbirth rather than throw it out the way she'd learned white women did. The Lakota in her heart told her she must put it in a leather bag and hang it somewhere high, where it would be protected from evil spirits. All her Christian teaching could not change her belief that certain rituals must always be adhered to, for surely Jehovah was the same as *Wakan-Tanka*. He expected certain Lakota ceremonies to be celebrated.

Helen was washing Mary, who still lay groaning from her ordeal.

"Your new son needs to feed at your breast," Florence told Mary. "I will help you learn how to—"

"I will not put that bastard to my breast!" Mary interrupted. "His father disgraced me beyond endurance. He killed my husband and planted his heathen seed inside of me. Take the baby away. I don't even want to *look* at him!"

Florence took the child from the cradle and held him close. "But he needs—"

"I don't care *what* he needs! You said you wanted him for yourself. *You* find a way to feed him. I intend to wrap my breasts tight and let the milk dry up. And as soon as I am able, I am going home." She began to cry. "Home! No one there will ever know the truth, because I will never tell them. As far as I am concerned, my husband and his daughter died, and that baby never existed."

Florence stepped back. "What a sad, lonely woman you will be for the rest of your life," she told Mary. "I feel sorry for you." She walked out, picking up the towel that held the child's afterbirth. Let Helen finish with Mary and with cleaning up. At last she had a baby to hold and love. At last she had a part of Rising Eagle that would be hers forever! She would do whatever it took to keep the boy alive, using goat's milk or cow's milk, honey and water. He was strong, for he was fathered by Rising Eagle. He would survive.

She hurried to her own little frame home, setting down the towel by the door before going inside to find Abel sitting in a chair next to the fireplace, reading his Bible.

"Abel!" Florence exclaimed. "It's a boy! We have a son to raise!"

Abel smiled, rising and coming over to see the child in Florence's arms. The baby still fussed, but he was not squalling as hard as earlier.

Abel smiled. "He looks strong, Florence. Very healthy."

"He could be no other way, being fathered by Rising Eagle." She met her husband's gentle brown eyes, seeing just a hint of hurt. "I am sorry. I only meant—"

"It's all right. I will love him as my own, Florence. I am glad you finally have a child to hold and love. But I am a little worried for you."

Florence patted the baby's bottom. "What worries you?"

Abel sighed. "The fact that Rising Eagle *is* the baby's father. You have explained to me how Lakota men feel about such things. What if he finds out about this son of his? He might come after him, wanting to take him and raise him as Lakota. And you, my dear, would never be able to give him up. I could lose both of you to your native people, because I already know that wherever that baby goes, so will you go."

Florence blinked in thought, looking down at the baby. "I did not think of that." She met his gaze again. "I will never leave you, Abel. And Rising Eagle will never try to take this child from me. We must both pray about this. I gave up my own child to the Lakota. I will never give this one away. My first child had no father to love and guide him. This one does. My first child was abused by his father and other whites. This one will not be treated so, for you will love him, and others will respect that."

Abel smiled sympathetically. He reached out and put an arm around Florence and the baby. "Then we will pray that either Rising Eagle never finds out about the boy or that if he does, he will understand that this child belongs to us and should be raised by us."

Florence leaned down and kissed the baby's soft, warm cheek. "Yes. Surely he will understand." *But it would be better,* she thought, *if he never knows.*

AUGUST 1848

Summer Moon

CHAPTER TWENTY-EIGHT

RHYTHMIC DRUMMING FILLED the warm summer air, as did the voices of men and women who sang songs in hope of virtue, beauty, and many children for the young white girl named Yellow Bonnet, who two weeks earlier had experienced her first menstrual flow. At thirteen summers, the daughter of Rising Eagle and Buffalo Dreamer was budding into womanhood, and it was time to celebrate *Isnati awicalowan,* the puberty rite.

Inside the tepee erected specifically for Yellow Bonnet's new status, Buffalo Dreamer stressed to her daughter the importance of virtue, truthfulness, and chastity. No man should touch her intimately before marriage, for then she would disgrace her father and mother, and lose her chance of marrying in honor.

As Buffalo Dreamer explained all that and more, Yellow Bonnet sat cross-legged between a sacred altar, erected by Moon Painter, and a central tepee fire. On the altar Moon Painter had placed a buffalo skull, a prayer pipe, prayer wands decorated with eagle feathers, a bowl, and sweet grass. Rising Eagle had asked the old man to conduct the ritual, for only a respected, sacred man could perform the ceremony.

Moon Painter wore a buffalo headdress, and a buffalo tail was attached to his back. Several men and women of high respect, including Wind In Grass, Bear Dancing, Bold Fox, Standing Rock, and their wives, as well as Runs With The Deer and Many Horses, were invited to sit inside the special tepee erected by Buffalo Dreamer and several of her women friends. Only adults were allowed, for Yellow Bonnet was young and beautiful, already appearing older than thirteen summers. She could no longer run and play with the young boys or teenage men. She could not even be alone with her older brothers, because they were not blood related. From now on, she must be in the company of other women whenever she left the tepee. It would be at least two more summers before Rising Eagle would consider her of a marriageable age, and Buffalo Dreamer knew he would ask a very high price for his sunny-haired, blue-eyed daughter.

Moon Painter drew on his sacred pipe and blew smoke into the ear and nasal orifices of the buffalo skull. He then painted the forehead of the skull with a vertical red stripe. Then he instructed Yellow Bonnet to be as industrious as a spider, as cheerful as a bird, and as wise and quiet as a turtle. For this, she would one day bear many children.

His advice was followed by singing inside the tepee, and Moon Painter danced toward Yellow Bonnet, lowering his head like a bull buffalo and telling her she was now a cow and must be wary of evil influences. He placed in front of her the bowl, filled with water and chokecherries, and instructed her to drink from it like a buffalo. She glanced at Buffalo Dreamer, who nodded that this is what she should do, and the girl bent down and drank from the bowl, smiling when she raised her head again and wiped at the water that dripped down her chin.

Moon Painter instructed her then to remove her tunic and place it over the buffalo skull. Yellow Bonnet obeyed, covering her breasts with her arms as she sat back down and bent her legs to the side, an indication that from now on, she must always sit like a proper, virtuous woman, rather than bending her knees out and crossing her legs in the way men and children sat. Buffalo Dreamer placed a white tunic over her head then, a beautifully quilled dress she had made for the girl for just this occasion. Moon painter announced that the girl's old tunic was to be given to a needy woman, who had already been chosen by

Rising Eagle. The woman then entered the tepee and took the dress. This was a sign that Yellow Bonnet would always be generous of heart to other women.

Moon Painter painted the girl's forehead red, then traced a red line through the part in her hair. Buffalo Dreamer pulled the girl's hair around and over the front of her shoulders, another indication that she was now a woman. Girl children wore their hair braided down their backs. Women usually wore theirs in two tails draped over the front of their shoulders and wrapped with fur, or with quilled or beaded leather ties.

Now Yellow Bonnet was a woman. Those inside the tepee sang songs of joy and celebration, and Buffalo Dreamer walked outside with Yellow Bonnet, taking her over to where a side of deer hung sizzling and dripping over an open fire. It was time for the expected feast, conducted by the initiated woman's family.

Buffalo Dreamer gladly began carving pieces of meat for all who came to partake of the meal she had provided. After Pretty Feather died, she thought she would never have a moment like this with a daughter. But now she *did* have a daughter, and she enjoyed doing these things for her, just as her own mother had helped with her puberty rites.

As always, the thought of her mother brought a quick pain to her heart, for she would miss her and her old grandmother forever. Women came up and congratulated Yellow Bonnet, many bringing gifts that would be useful to her as a women: blankets, quills and beads, cook pots, ribbon and cloth, deerskins, and buffalo hides to be used to one day construct her own tepee, one she would share with a husband. Some of the women teased her about taking a husband and spending time "under the robes" with him, asking her if there were any young men among them for whom she already had an eye. They warned her to be careful not to be alone with him, lest he steal her heart and her virtue.

The feasting and celebrating continued well past sunset, and Buffalo Dreamer thought of how good life had become once more. She and Rising Eagle could smile. They had a daughter again, and Brave Horse, a strong, fast-growing young man, was fourteen summers, already showing the makings of a true warrior. Spirit Walker, their beloved adopted son, was only a few moons older, not as strong and wild as Brave Horse, but a young man with a kind heart and a true and honorable desire to help and to heal. Little Turtle was three summers now, healthy and playful, as daring as his big brothers had been at his age.

Though she had not yet told Rising Eagle, Buffalo Dreamer celebrated the fact that she was quite certain she carried yet another child. She thanked *Wakan-Tanka* every day that she was able to have more children to help her heart heal over the loss of her sweet Pretty Feather and Little Kicker.

The side of deer she'd furnished for the feast was stripped to the bone by nightfall, and by then, the singing and dancing had dwindled to a circle of elders and the more experienced warriors, who sat around a central campfire telling stories. Many couples and families, their bellies full and their bodies weary from hours of dancing and singing, had retired to their dwellings, and most of the children slept. Brave Horse and Spirit Walker sat near the circle of men, listening to the stories, and Little Turtle slept soundly beside his brothers. Since Buffalo Dreamer was expected to stay near the meat she served until it was finished, Yellow Bonnet was told to go and sleep in Running Elk Woman's tepee, for now she must never sleep alone, not even inside her own family's tepee unless Buffalo Dreamer or Rising Eagle, or both, were there to guard her. Running Elk Woman was now the girl's mentor and *uncheedah* and Yellow Bonnet would be spending more time with her.

"You did well with your feast," came a man's voice from out of the darkness behind her.

Buffalo Dreamer smiled. "I thought you were over at the campfire telling stories, my husband," she replied, recognizing Rising Eagle's voice. "Or should I say stretching the truth?"

Rising Eagle laughed lightly. "I never stretch the truth. You know that."

"There is not a Lakota man living who does not stretch the truth. And why did you leave the bragging fest?"

"Being with my wife sounded more entertaining to me," he answered, putting his hands on her shoulders.

"Oh? And how can that be more entertaining?" she teased, turning from the cook fire that had dwindled to just a few glowing embers. She let out a little scream and laughed when Rising Eagle lifted her, nuzzling her breasts. She breathed deeply as he moved his arms under her bottom and carried her out of the light of the campfire.

"It is always more enjoyable to join with my wife than to sit around listening to stories."

Buffalo Dreamer wrapped her arms around his head and kissed his hair. "And you do not want to again tell the story of how you fought the biggest humpback bear ever created, just to win my hand?"

"I still carry the scars from that fight, all to claim a haughty Brule woman who did not even want me." He lowered her, grasping the hem of her tunic as he did so. When her feet touched the ground, her dress was already lifted to her waist.

"I do not feel sorry for those scars, my husband. You wear them with joy and pride, and you use them to brag about your bravery."

He chuckled, then knelt to his knees in the high grass. He licked at her thighs, and at the crevasses where her legs met the most sacred womanly part of her body. "It is *you* who make me brave," he told her softly.

Buffalo Dreamer ran her fingers through his hair and loosened it from the tie that held it in a tail. He shook it off as he pulled her down into the grass.

"I am supposed to stay with the meat," she said.

"There is none left," he reminded her.

Buffalo Dreamer laughed. "I have news for you, my husband. Now is a good time to tell you." She leaned up and licked his lips. "Yet another of your seeds has sprouted in my womb. I have been waiting to be sure before I told you."

Rising Eagle was silent for a moment, then leaned down to brush her cheek with his own. "Again you bless me with a new life. You have made sure that I will live forever through my sons and daughters."

He licked at her mouth, and Buffalo Dreamer felt his joy. It made her heart swell with pleasure and pride, and a sudden, sweet desire to be one with him, just as she knew he wanted the same with her. She ran her fingers over his muscled arms as he reached down to untie his breechcloth and toss it aside.

"I want you, Buffalo Dreamer. My heart sings tonight."

"As does mine. Take your pleasure, Rising Eagle, just as I take pleasure in feeling your life pulse within me."

He bent lower to lick at her belly. She opened her legs, and he licked her inner thighs, bringing forth the hungering, aching need to feel him inside of her. He moved upward, licking her belly again while he caressed her most private place. Soon came the deep, thrilling grip at her insides drawing her husband to her, and in the next moment, Rising Eagle surged into her with such fullness that she gasped in pleasure, glad that after all the children she had borne him, she could still feel this glorious mating with this much ecstasy. In women's quilling circles, and during the long hours of skinning and tanning hides after a hunt, some women joked about finding it difficult to please their husbands after having had several children, laughing at the fact that no man could fill what a child's body had passed through. Buffalo Dreamer still had not sensed that any such problem existed for her and Rising Eagle.

He rolled onto his back, pulling her with him so that she mounted him. She grasped the hem of her tunic and pulled it up and over her head so that she sat naked atop her husband in the bright moonlight. She threw back her head, and Rising Eagle reached up so she could grasp his hands to support herself while he thrust himself upward and she rode him in rhythmic motions as though riding a horse.

For several minutes they enjoyed the sweet ecstasy of mating under the stars, while in the distance, old men laughed and bragged over campfire stories. Buffalo Dreamer groaned then when her husband's manpart swelled even bigger just before his life spilled forth inside of her. She squeezed his strong hands, feeling like the most beautiful, most blessed of all Lakota women.

Life had renewed itself again. The fear of a bigger invasion of white men into their hunting lands had been eased. They still lived as free and prosperous Lakota people, still roaming and hunting wherever they chose, taking their bounty home to the sacred Black Hills, the land the Feathered One had told Rising Eagle they must never give up.

Right now Buffalo Dreamer could not imagine how and why their right to *Paha-Sapa* should ever be tested. After all, even the whites who did come through this big land on their way to the land of the setting sun almost never ventured into the sacred Black Hills. That was one place that did not seem to interest the *wasicus*, and that was good. It would always be the Lakota's best refuge.

"Brave Horse has decided that next summer he will seek his first vision," Rising Eagle told her then. "He will be fifteen summers, and already he is the size of most who are seventeen." He rolled her onto her back in the thick grass. "My eldest son is almost a man. And he has asked me, his own father, to help him with his vision quest. This is my greatest honor. I thought he would ask Bold Fox, for he has been grandfather and mentor to Brave Horse for many years now."

Buffalo Dreamer ran her fingers over his finely etched lips. "You are the first love of his heart, the one he most wants to please with pride. He knows what it would mean to you to be the one to lead him in his first search for a vision that will guide him for the rest of his life."

"I have asked Bold Fox to help, out of respect for the fine way he has trained our son."

"That was a good thing to do." Buffalo Dreamer felt her husband's penis begin to grow hard again.

"He will carry on the way of the Lakota, as will his children, and their children." Rising Eagle was starting to move rhythmically now. "The circle of life never ends, my wife—not here, not with our children or their children. No enemy can stop it, not even the *wasicus*."

Buffalo Dreamer closed her eyes and drew in her breath as she arched up to greet him in more lovemaking. This was the way life should be: sweet, free, blessed with good hunts . . . and many children.

MARCH 1849

Windy Moon

CHAPTER TWENTY-NINE

A LOUD CLAP of thunder shook the earth, and to Buffalo Dreamer, it seemed that the mighty crash matched the screams that welled up from her deepest being. This was her fifth birth, and for most women, each succeeding birth was usually a little easier than the last. It had been that way for her . . . until this child.

Her labor had lasted all day and into the night, and now white lightning from a rare early spring storm lit the tepee in sporadic, ripping flashes, each one followed by another clap of thunder. Was it all some kind of sign, or was the Thunder God simply giving his blessing upon yet another child for Rising Eagle?

At last she felt the baby begin to emerge, and with sweat pouring over her naked body, she screamed to Running Elk Woman and Many Robes Woman that they should finally prepare to cut the cord and clean the baby. A quilled, yellow, turtle-shaped amulet lay nearby. It would be tied to the baby's cradle, and once the child's umbilical cord fell off, it would be sewn inside the amulet. Her baby would wear it at all times for the first few years of its life to keep evil spirits away.

Many Robes Woman positioned a clean square of deerskin under Buffalo Dreamer, and after several more minutes, the baby finally dropped onto the hide. Many Robes Woman cut the cord and wrapped the baby in the skin, and Running Elk Woman then split the end of the cord still attached to the afterbirth, in the belief that doing so would cause the afterbirth to be expelled quickly.

Buffalo Dreamer screamed when the older woman massaged her belly to help rid it of all the membrane still within her. Something felt different—as though something had torn inside of her. It was nothing she could explain to anyone else, just a feeling she had that all was not right.

Running Elk Woman helped clean her, then packed her with cattail down stuffed into the thin membrane of a buffalo bladder, designed to absorb the bleeding until it finally stopped.

"You have another daughter!" Many Robes Woman told her. She sat bent over the kicking, squalling baby, who lay on a blanket while Many Robes Woman cleaned her.

"A daughter," Buffalo Dreamer repeated. Her heart swelled with love and happiness, and now she knew that all the agony had been worth the effort. She looked at Yellow Bonnet, who had watched the birth with fascination. "You have a sister, Yellow Bonnet!" Buffalo Dreamer told her in a weak voice. "You can . . . help me care for her."

Yellow Bonnet smiled with joy at the words. "I will practice for when I have my own babies," she told Buffalo Dreamer. "What will you name her?"

Running Elk Woman wiped Buffalo Dreamer's body down with dampened sweet grass, taking away the perspiration and making her skin smell fresh and clean. Another loud clap of thunder made them all jump, and the baby cried harder.

"I do not know yet. I will speak with Rising Eagle about it, and he must in turn discuss it with Runs With The Deer and Bold Fox," Buffalo Dreamer answered Yellow Bonnet. "I think perhaps 'Little Storm' would be fitting."

Yellow Bonnet giggled. "That is a good name."

Buffalo Dreamer sat up so that Running Elk Woman could slip a clean tunic over her.

"I hope I have many children," Yellow Bonnet said.

Buffalo Dreamer lay back on a clean bed of robes, feeling very weak and a little light-headed. "I am sure that you will."

She rubbed her stomach, still feeling a strange pain inside that she could not quite explain. "Go and tell Rising Eagle I must speak to him," she told Yellow Bonnet.

Many Robes Woman laid Little Storm beside her mother then, and Running Elk Woman gathered up the afterbirth in a small piece of deerskin. "I will go and find a high place for this," she said. She left the tepee, and Many Robes Woman frowned at Buffalo Dreamer. "You sound worried," she told her.

Buffalo Dreamer smiled at her sister-in-law. "I just want to speak to your brother about a name," she said, feeling bad for lying. Many Robes Woman was prone to fretting easily, and she did not want to alarm her. The woman smiled, telling her she would find Rising Eagle. Moments after she left, Rising Eagle ducked inside the tepee, all smiles, his skin dripping from a hard rain.

"We have another daughter!" he said, taking up a piece of soft deerskin to wipe the extra water from himself. "It is just as you wished." He moved closer then and knelt down to pull away the deerskin that swaddled the infant. She lay writhing slightly, making only little squealing sounds now.

"She is going to be a good baby, I can tell," Buffalo Dreamer told him. "I wish to name her Little Storm."

Rising Eagle nodded. "I will speak to my uncles. We will have a feast to celebrate our new daughter, and there we will announce her name," he said, still staring at the tiny girl and smiling.

Buffalo Dreamer smiled sadly and placed a hand on his arm. "Rising Eagle."

He turned his attention to her, losing his smile at the look of concern in her eyes. "What is it?"

"Are you sure you are not disappointed that she is not a boy?"

He touched the baby's cheek. "You needed another daughter to further heal your loss of Pretty Feather. And I already have three sons, Buffalo Dreamer. I am not disappointed."

"I am glad, for I must tell you I . . . felt something . . . a kind of tearing inside when she was born. Something feels different. My heart tells me I will never bear another child."

He lost his smile completely, reaching out and touching her cheek. "How can you know this?"

Tears welled in her eyes. "I cannot explain it. It is just something I know. One day we might discover I was wrong, but I do not want you to be disappointed, mating with me and thinking you are planting yet another seed, only to never have that seed become life."

He frowned as he gently wiped away a tear that slipped down the side of her face. "Then we will mate simply for the pleasure of it," he told her. "Is that not a good reason?"

Buffalo Dreamer could not help smiling through her tears, just then realizing that the storm outside had subsided. "It is a very good reason, my husband." Thunder still rolled in the distance. She prayed she was wrong about her suspicions, but instinct told her she was right. "I love you, Rising Eagle. I wanted to give you still more children before my body became too old for childbearing."

He continued to stroke her cheek. "You gave me five sons and daughters, and you took in and loved two more. It is the fault of the white man that we lost two of our own, but *Wakan-Tanka* has given you another son and daughter to take their place. You have pleased me greatly, Buffalo Dreamer, in every way."

"Will you keep your promise of not taking another wife in order to bear more children?"

He sat back on his heels and took her hand. "A promise is a promise. You know I am a man of my word." He squeezed her hand. "I am afraid I must leave soon for a few days, Buffalo Dreamer. Before darkness fell, while you were deep in childbirth, a runner came from the Shihenna to the south. He told us there is something we must go and see for ourselves."

Buffalo Dreamer drew her baby closer, alarmed at the sudden look of dark anger that had come into her husband's eyes. "What is it?"

"The runner told us something of great worry. He said

that white men have been moving through their land, the best buffalo country that we share with the Shihenna. He told us that this time there are so many it would be useless to try to attack them."

Buffalo Dreamer gasped. "Surely there could not be that many!"

"This man says it is so. He says there are so many of them in their white-topped wagons that the line stretches as far as the eye can see in either direction. They all take the same path. They seem to be in a great hurry to get to the land of the setting sun, and they leave behind the graves of their dead, some so shallow that wolves dig them up. They even leave behind large objects made of wood, some good for sitting in. They also leave behind spoiled food and dead horses, and their animals are grazing on grass meant for the buffalo."

Buffalo Dreamer rested her head back against the robes and closed her eyes. "Then it has begun. There is only one thing left we have not seen. When we do, we will know our time of peace may be coming to an end."

"What is that?"

Buffalo Dreamer met his gaze again. "Blue coats. We have not yet seen many men wearing blue coats." She saw the spark of the warrior in her husband's eyes, and she pulled her new daughter even closer. "Have you heard anyone yet speak the name *Ta-sunko-witko* among the Oglala? Do you know who he is with whom you will one day ride against the blue coats?"

He shook his head. "I have not yet heard. I have decided not to send runners to search for him. The Great Spirit will bring him into my life when it is the right time. Even now he would be only five or six summers of age. That means we have many years ahead together, Buffalo Dreamer, before this man called Crazy Horse becomes a warrior. We will not let the coming of more whites spoil our happiness over the birth of another daughter."

Buffalo Dreamer touched his arm. "Stay, Rising Eagle. Do not go south just yet to see the white-topped wagons.

Wait until I am healed, and until our son completes his vision quest. Then we can all go together and see for ourselves, when we leave for the buffalo hunt. Promise me you will wait, my husband. I will worry over you if you go now. It is important that you first concentrate on Brave Horse's vision quest."

Rising Eagle smiled sadly. "You know that I cannot say no to you. Inside the tepee, I am weak. See what you do to me? I will wait."

Buffalo Dreamer smiled in return. "Thank you." She felt drained and tired. "I am thinking the land to the south is not such a good place to go anymore. The white man is changing everything. I do not want to see it yet."

An overwhelming depression fell over her, and she held her husband's hand tightly as she wept . . . for the coming of the white man . . . and for the sure feeling that she would never bear another child.

MAY 1849

The Time When the Horses Grow Fat

CHAPTER THIRTY

BRAVE HORSE WALKED with his father to a high ledge that overlooked a vast expanse of the Black Hills, and a river that rushed and splashed over rocks in the canyon below.

"This is where the spirit of the white buffalo and the black wolf spoke to me and told me I must marry your mother," Rising Eagle told his son. "I traveled many miles to her clan of Brule to speak for her hand. Part of her price was the coat of the great humpbacked bear, and I had to find and kill one of the beasts before her father would consider letting me marry her."

Brave Horse had heard the story many times, but it was custom for the elders to repeat stories. His father was still handsome, strong, and vital at forty-one summers, a man who looked and behaved as though much younger, but to Brave Horse, he was an elder. He was proud of Rising Eagle's status among the Oglala as a holy man and a visionary, and he could think of no greater accomplishment than to be as brave and successful and respected as his father.

"You must have been pleased that my mother was so beautiful," he told his father.

Nearby, his great-uncle and mentor, Bold Fox, prepared a fire with sage blessed by Moon Painter. Soon the search for a special vision would begin.

Brave Horse gathered strength from the look of pride in his father's dark eyes. As the man's firstborn son, he did not want to shame Rising Eagle in any way. His father had fasted with him, wanting to help with his first vision quest by sharing in his suffering. Fasting was important, a way of showing *Wakan-Tanka* a willingness to "empty" oneself so that one might be filled with the Great Spirit.

"I tell you the story about my first vision only because I want you to understand what a special place this is to me," Rising Eagle continued. "It is a good place for your own first vision quest."

Pride burned in Brave Horse's heart. He was beyond hunger now, but his body screamed for water. "I thank you for bringing me here, Father." He followed Rising Eagle to a fire of smoldering sweet grass, prepared by Bold Fox. The scene around Brave Horse began to blur with his dizziness, and he was weak from starvation. Just walking to the snapping, crackling fire was an effort. He sat down cross-legged opposite his father. Rising Eagle laid his prayer pipe across his knees, and resting both his hands on his knees then, he closed his eyes and began a soft chant.

> *See my son here?*
> *He seeks you, oh Great Spirit.*
> *See my son here?*
> *He has a good heart and a brave spirit.*
> *See my son here?*
> *Bless him, Great One, with your presence.*
> *Show him the way.*
> *Bring him truth.*
> *Bring him courage.*
> *See my son here?*
> *He seeks you, O Great Spirit.*

Rising Eagle opened his eyes and met Brave Horse's gaze. "You must sing your own prayer song and beg *Wakan-Tanka* to come to you, to send you a vision to guide you into manhood. Do you wish to shed blood so that the Great Spirit can see how earnest you are in seeking him?"

"Yes, Father." Brave Horse took a deep breath as his father took his hunting knife from its sheath at his side. Brave Horse had made up his mind he would not flinch from the pain, for he was the son of Rising Eagle. He had seen his father bravely suffer the incredible physical sacrifice of the Sun Dance, something he hoped to do one day himself. But before that, he had to start here, seek his first vision, become accustomed to fasting and to lengthy prayers, and most of all, learn to accept pain, for one day he would ride as a warrior. He would risk life and limb for the Oglala, and for the nation of the Lakota. He could think of no greater honor than to do so with the same fierce bravery his father had shown.

Rising Eagle took his hand, then hesitated. Brave Horse knew this was hard for his father: he had never doubted the depth of his father's love for him. It was not easy for the man to bring him pain, but it was necessary. Quickly then, Rising Eagle slit the knife across Brave Horse's palm, then made another slice across his forearm, not deep enough to sever nerves and risk losing use of the arm, but just deep enough to be sure his son would shed plenty of blood in his first sacrifice to *Wakan-Tanka*.

Brave Horse felt proud that he had winced only a little, and now that it was done, the pain was not so bad as long as he held his arm still. Rising Eagle directed him then to hold out his arm and let the blood drip into the sacred fire, then onto Mother Earth. Lighting his prayer pipe and offering it in the four directions, as well as toward the heavens and the earth, Rising Eagle asked the spirits of each direction to bless the pipe and his prayers during this vision quest. At last, he offered the pipe to Brave Horse.

Never had the boy known more love for his father, or felt more proud and honored. This was the first time he had accepted a sacred pipe from an honored *Naca* such as Rising Eagle. This was the most special event so far in his life. Blood still dripping from his wounds, he took the pipe and offered it in the four directions just as his father had done, then drew deeply on it, filling his lungs with the smoke of sweet grass. He could not help choking on it at first, but once the effects of the smoke settled in his lungs, he had less pain and he felt as though he were beginning to float into a realm beyond reality. He began his own prayer song:

> *Great Spirit, I am not yet a man.*
> *Great Spirit, make me so.*
> *Give me courage and power.*
> *Help me find my spirit guide.*
> *Great Spirit, I am not yet a man.*
> *Great Spirit, make me so.*

Brave Horse struggled to remain sitting, reminding himself that he must be strong like his father, and that he must honor his mother, the holy woman who had seen and touched the white buffalo and had eaten of its heart. He was the seed of special people, and he must live up to what was expected of him.

He continued singing his prayer song as both Bold Fox and Rising Eagle joined him in an effort to make the words stronger. For the rest of the day he sang his song, and Rising Eagle never wavered in singing right along with him. Bold Fox's duty was to keep adding sweet grass to the fire and to wave the smoke over him. Very quietly Bold Fox began singing his own song, asking *Wakan-Tanka* to help his "grandson" know the way he should go as he entered manhood.

For the rest of the afternoon and into the night, they prayed and sang. Bold Fox sat down next to Brave Horse and set out a small bowl made from the hoof of a buffalo. From a leather sack he removed a pouch made from a buffalo's intestine. He untied one end of it and squeezed out some of its contents—red paint made from clay, fat, and the juice of crushed bloodroot stems—into the bowl. He began painting Brave Horse's forehead with red stripes, then used two fingers to paint two red stripes down each of the young man's cheeks.

"Red represents all things sacred," Brave Horse heard Bold Fox tell him. "If you wear this color, you will show

Wakan-Tanka that you respect him, Mother Earth, the sun, and all things sacred."

To Brave Horse, the words were a voice out of the darkness, for even though he felt the warmth of a risen sun, he saw no light. He inhaled the smoke from the sweet grass, each breath making him feel more intensely alive, even though his limbs were weak and dizziness overwhelmed him. His stomach groaned with hunger, and he felt light enough to float away.

He tried getting to his feet, but could not feel the ground. He sensed a strong arm helping him, but he could not tell if it belonged to Bold Fox or Rising Eagle. He threw back his head, trying to see the sun, for he could feel its heat against his face and shoulders. He sang louder and began to dance, raising his arms to greet the universe, oblivious to the passing of time, unable to tell a moment from a day.

Finally he saw a light, dim at first. It began to grow brighter, as though traveling toward him very swiftly. He heard a rumbling sound that grew louder as the light came closer. At first he thought it was the sound of approaching buffalo, for the earth shook. But then there came a long wail, similar to the voices of many wolves howling at once, yet it was not a wolf sound at all. He could not quite discern the sound, nor did he recognize the strange black beast that rumbled toward him in the darkness. It was simply a gigantic, dark object, bearing a light before it.

The terrible wailing attacked his ears again, and the black monster charged past him with such speed that it caused him to fall back. He saw fire in its belly as it flew beyond him and vanished into the night: then he saw faces trailing behind the black monster, many white faces. They also faded off into the night, and again Brave Horse heard the odd, almost sad, wailing sound. Behind it came a black horse with wings, flying rather than walking. It settled before him and spoke to him: *"Brave Horse will be your name forever, for the horse is your spirit guide. But there is one horse that will always be your enemy. It is dark, and it is hard like iron and has no legs. This horse you shall not ride, but it will charge back and forth across your land like the beast that it is, belching smoke that clouds the sun. It will carry behind itself many white men—the* wasicus, *who come to destroy. But one day the red horse with the white mane will run faster and farther than the black horse, and it will retake the land to itself, for its blood is good, like the blood of the Lakota. The black horse that brings the white faces has no blood, and no heart. Because of this, it will one day die, but the blood of the Lakota will live forever."*

The iron horse wailed off into the night, and the black horse who had spoken to Brave Horse flew away. Then, through a haze, Brave Horse thought he saw his father's face before weakness overcame him. He fell into Rising Eagle's arms.

CHAPTER THIRTY-ONE

"AN IRON HORSE! How can this be?" Old Many Horses sat talking quietly with Rising Eagle and Bold Fox inside Buffalo Dreamer's tepee. Buffalo Dreamer refilled a wooden bowl with broth made from buffalo fat and turnips, then handed it to her son. For a full day following his vision quest, Brave Horse had lain semiconscious, finally rousing that night to drink some broth, then sleeping soundly all the next day.

Now the evening brought him enough strength to sit up and talk to his father and uncle about what he had seen in his vision. He took his second bowl of broth from his mother and sipped it slowly, obeying his parents' advice to never eat too much or too quickly following a long fast.

Buffalo Dreamer treated the wounds on her son's hand and arm with mixed feelings—proud of his first visionary sacrifice, yet worrying over the physical effects of his fasting and letting of blood. She told herself she must be prepared for many more such things, for Brave Horse was very much his father's son.

She moved to her side of the tepee and sat down beside Yellow Bonnet to listen to the conversation. Four-summers-old Little Turtle slept nearby, and Yellow Bonnet held two-moons-old Little Storm in her lap. Spirit Walker—always a quiet, patient young man—sat on the right side of Rising Eagle.

"An iron horse, large and black and fast," Brave Horse told the two older men. "It was like a great monster, with one light at the front. It spat fire from its belly, and when it passed me by, there were more lights, rows of them, each one showing the face of a *wasicu*."

Rising Eagle scowled. "We must watch for this black beast that breathes fire. It is just another weapon the *wasicus* will send to try to destroy us. I do not fear what has been foretold to my son. I feel only pride that Brave Horse has been successful in finding his spirit guide."

Brave Horse sat up a little straighter and shook his long black hair that fell behind his shoulders.

"When you are fully strong again, we will celebrate the first vision of the son of Rising Eagle," Bold Fox told Brave Horse. "This is a great occasion. You must never fret over a vision, but rejoice in it, for a vision is sent as warning, and to help a man see the way to his future, and to know what animal spirit will always guide him. For me, it is the fox. For your father, the eagle, and for your mother, the white buffalo. Now you are guided by the horse, and I think this means you will be one of our greatest horsemen, and probably you will also *steal* many horses, perhaps some of them from the white travelers."

"I will help him," Spirit Walker finally spoke up.

Bold Fox shook his head. "I think, Spirit Walker, that you are destined to stay in camp when your father and brother make war, so that you can be here for them if they are wounded, for you are a healer, not a fighter, and that is also something of which to be very proud. You hold an important place among the Oglala. Never forget this. There is a place for warriors and a place for healers."

Spirit Walker glanced at Rising Eagle. "Sometimes I still feel I do not belong here, because of my white blood."

Rising Eagle reached out and touched the boy's shoulder. "You have been my son since you were a baby. I held you to the heavens atop Medicine Mountain and you were healed. I promised your mother I would raise you as my own, and we celebrated the adoption ceremony for you, piercing your ears. That means you are Lakota in every way, just as Yellow Bonnet also is considered Lakota now."

* * *

He looked at Yellow Bonnet and smiled. "Being Lakota is not always a matter of blood." He put a fist to his chest. "It is a matter of the heart."

Rising Eagle turned again to Spirit Walker. "It is a matter of being a true human being—" he continued "—one with the earth, the winged ones, and the four-leggeds. A true human being does not leave his filth on the land and in the water. He does not cut down a tree when it is still green and alive. He does not kill an animal just for its meat. He uses every part of it. A true human being loves Mother Earth. He cares for her and respects her. He knows he is no different from the four-leggeds, and his spirit soars with the eagle. He is humbled by the animals."

He glanced at Yellow Bonnet again. "When a human being does these things, he or she believes as a Lakota man or woman, and so he or she becomes Lakota, even if that person's hair is light." He turned again to Spirit Walker. "Or if his eyes are blue." He smiled. "And so you and Yellow Bonnet are also Lakota."

Bold Fox also smiled, nodding to Yellow Bonnet and to Spirit Walker. "It is as my nephew says. You must never doubt that you are both Lakota now." He rose. "And so we have much to celebrate. Not only has Brave Horse been blessed with his first vision, but Running Elk Woman is planning the feast for the wedding ceremony of our son to a Shihenna daughter, Red Clay Woman."

Rising Eagle also rose, nodding to his uncle. "I am glad to see the Lakota and Shihenna becoming so close as to marry between the two nations. This will make us even stronger in the fight against our enemies."

"Thank you for helping me with my vision quest, Bold Fox," Brave Horse told him.

Bold Fox frowned in mock irritation. "I only wanted an excuse to get away from Running Elk Woman. She is so excited about our son's wedding that she rushes about like a busy ant. I think I will take daily hunting trips just to stay away from her."

They all shared in laughter then, and Bold Fox bowed to

Buffalo Dreamer, who had also risen, for Bold Fox was an honored elder. He thanked her for the meal of elk meat she had served him earlier, accompanied by berries picked from wild bushes in the nearby foliage.

"You can thank our new brother-in-law for the berries," Buffalo Dreamer told Bold Fox. "Wind In Grass has done well in choosing camps for us. This is a good place, with many wild turnips and berries." She glanced back at Yellow Bonnet, then to Bold Fox. "Take our daughter with you," she told the old man. "Running Elk Woman needs help, and she has been *uncheedah* to Yellow Bonnet. My daughter should be with her to help plan the wedding feast."

Bold Fox nodded and beckoned to Yellow Bonnet. "Come with me, Granddaughter."

Yellow Bonnet obeyed, laying Little Storm beside her sleeping brother and following Bold Fox out of the tepee. Brave Horse lay down again, still needing rest.

"Walk with me, Rising Eagle," Buffalo Dreamer told her husband.

His eyebrows arched in surprise, and she knew it was because he knew the meaning of the phrase "Walk with me." She wanted to talk about something important. He followed her far enough away from their tepee that the children could not hear. Buffalo Dreamer folded her arms then and faced him. "I believe it is time for our sons to go and sleep in the dwelling of Bold Fox and Running Elk Woman. Bear Dancing is leaving them to marry, and our daughter is a woman now. We call her daughter, but she is not related by blood to our sons, and they are young men. I am sure you remember how hot your blood was at that age. And she whom a young man does not call sister by blood can become very different in his eyes from a relative."

Rising Eagle stared at her for a moment, frowning. Then he arched his eyebrows again. "But Yellow Bonnet *is* their sister."

"Not by blood. And she is beautiful, fascinating because of her yellow hair and blue eyes."

Rising Eagle made no reply at first, then slowly nodded. "I see you are right."

"I thought it best to speak to you first."

Rising Eagle grinned, although Buffalo Dreamer could see the concern in his eyes. "We will send Spirit Walker and Brave Horse to Bold Fox. Since Yellow Bonnet is considered their sister, it would bring shame to us if one of our sons looked at her differently or touched her wrongly." He smiled. "It is hard to realize that our children are of such an age. You and I, we are getting older, Buffalo Dreamer."

She moved her arms around his waist and rested her head against his chest. "Just remember that we cannot rule our children's hearts. I just think that we should be careful to see that they avoid temptation while they are still so young."

He kissed the top of her head. "Temptation is not something only the young enjoy," he reminded her.

Buffalo Dreamer smiled, and Rising Eagle picked her up in his arms, carrying her off into the darkness.

JULY 1849

Time of Ripeness

CHAPTER THIRTY-TWO

THE SCENE WAS too heartbreaking to describe. The large tribe of Oglala migrating south for another hunt moved slowly among the dead buffalo, and even the children remained somber, sensing that this was no time to play and laugh. The dogs did not bark, but a few of them sniffed at the carcasses; yet in spite of their carnivorous instincts, none ate of the buffalo flesh that lay covered with flies and maggots, rotting in the hot sun. Such a thing would normally be a dog's delight, yet even they left it alone, as though the blood of their Lakota owners ran in their own veins, causing them to respect the spirits of these animals and mourn what they saw here.

Buffalo Dreamer rode behind Rising Eagle, five-moons-old Little Storm secured firmly in a cradleboard hanging at Sotaju's side. She could feel her husband's renewed rage at the *wasicus,* for no man from any Indian nation would do this.

Scattered across the open plain ahead were the raw and bloated carcasses of at least a hundred buffalo, their skins gone, the meat and bones left to rot. To the Lakota, that represented hundreds of utensils and weapons; clothing, moccasins, tepee coverings and liners, cradles, drums, ropes, ornaments, saddles, bedding, saddle blankets, all sorts of containers, fire carriers, powder horns, toys, medications; brains for the preparation of hides; soups and paints from the blood; thousands of pounds of meat that could be made into sausages, jerky, and pemmican for long, hungry winters; hundreds of uses for the buffalo hair, the fat, the bones, the bladder; scrotum for rattles, hooves for glue and spoons. The number of things the Lakota could have done with these slain buffalo was almost endless. But someone had wasted all of it except for the hides. Apparently the white men had adopted the idea of hunting buffalo themselves and taking the hides, rather than trading anything to the Lakota for them. And in the process, they had wasted everything else, all that was vital to the survival of Buffalo Dreamer's people.

Rising Eagle halted his horse, and when Buffalo Dreamer drew up beside him, she saw that the look in his eyes was more formidable than anything she had seen there before, even worse than the way he had looked when he and his children had suffered with the spotted disease.

"It is not so much the waste," he said, his voice strained. "But the disrespect . . ." His voice broke and he looked away.

"I understand, my husband," Buffalo Dreamer told him gently. "It is not likely they even thanked the spirit of each one for offering itself."

Rising Eagle swallowed. "When an animal offers its life to you, you honor its death by using every single part of its body for your people. That is why it gives itself to you."

Buffalo Dreamer's eyes stung with tears. "Someday they will suffer for this. The Feathered One told you that. We might never see it, nor even our children. But someday the *wasicus* will destroy themselves, yet the Lakota will live forever."

Olute whinnied and tossed his mane, then moved in a circle, bending his head and behaving restlessly, as though sensing his master's frustration. Rising Eagle gently commanded the animal to settle down, his jaw flexing with repressed anger. He looked at Buffalo Dreamer, his dark eyes slits of fury.

"We *will* live forever, and until *I* die, white men will pay for this injustice. How can *any* man be so wasteful? Now I understand more than ever before what the Feathered One meant when he said these white men would have no respect for the land and the animals! The Shihenna tell us of trees cut while they are still green, filth in the streams, shallow graves, dead horses and those strange animals they call oxen, left behind to attract the wolves and stink up the earth, as well as careless campfires that start grass fires and burn the prairie for as far as a man can see, destroying the very grass upon which the buffalo graze. With that, and slaughters like this, the buffalo will become more difficult to hunt, and if as many white men are coming through this land with their clattering wagons as the Shihenna say, that will frighten away whatever buffalo are yet roaming alive!"

Bold Fox rode closer during his nephew's tirade. "Stay calm, Rising Eagle. We both know that in spite of this, there are so many buffalo that if they ran back-to-back, a man could walk on them for many miles."

Rising Eagle shook his head. "That might be so, but if this is a sign of how white men can waste the gifts of *Wakan-Tanka,* how long will it take them to destroy not just the animals, but the land itself? What will there be for our grandchildren?"

"Rising Eagle," Bold Fox said reassuringly, "our grandchildren will have *Paha-Sapa.* As long as the sacred Black Hills belong to us, we need not worry about what the white man does to the rest of the earth and its creatures, but I realize that does not ease the pain of it. We know these things will happen, for you yourself have seen it in your dreams. Let us fight what we can fight and accept what we must accept, as long as we keep our pride and our honor."

Rising Eagle tossed his hair behind his shoulders, his bare arms and chest gleaming with beads of perspiration from the summer sun. "I most certainly intend to keep my pride and my honor, and I intend to fight this any way I can, to my dying day!"

Wind In Grass came riding toward them then, his black horse running with the wind, his long hair flying back from his face. He had taken the duty of scouting ahead for the clan and had been the one to warn them of the dead buffalo. The tribe had come here, a huge, migrating clan on the hunt, to see for themselves if what Wind In Grass had told them could possibly be true. Some of the women were crying, and many of their group had hurried past the horrible sight, eyes turned away. Now it appeared that Wind In Grass had yet more news for them. He charged up to Rising Eagle, sod flying from under his horse's hooves.

"It is as the Shihenna told us. Come and see! From the edge of the far bluff, following the flat river below it, stand many wagons, more than I have ever seen! And with them are riders in formation. The way they ride, they look like soldiers!" He looked at Buffalo Dreamer. "They wear blue coats."

Buffalo Dreamer felt her blood run cold. She looked at her husband. "We must go and see," she said. "We must only look for now, then learn whatever we can."

"You can do more than that," Wind In Grass told her. "I rode close, and I saw the agent, Broken Hand. He waved a white flag and hailed me even closer. I could tell that the white soldiers were afraid. They kept looking all around, and I saw they were nervous."

"What did Broken Hand have to say?" Rising Eagle asked.

"He asked if I knew the one called Rising Eagle. I answered 'Of course! He is my brother-in-law!' I told him you were nearby, and he seemed glad. He wants to speak with you. He said you should come to the top of the rise there—" Wind In Grass pointed to a hill north of them— "where he will meet you."

"If soldiers are with him, we must talk to him and learn what he wants," Buffalo Dreamer advised. "I wish to see the blue coats for myself and see if they are like the ones in my dreams." She felt needles of terror in her heart at the thought of seeing the white man's soldiers in many numbers.

Rising Eagle smirked with irritation. "Go and tell Broken Hand I will speak with him."

Wind In Grass nodded and charged away, and Rising Eagle turned to Buffalo Dreamer. "We will go and see what Broken Hand wants to tell us *this* time. Already his first promises have been broken."

He rode forward, and Buffalo Dreamer followed, ordering Brave Horse—who kept Little Turtle on his horse with him—and Spirit Walker to stay in back of her. Yellow Bonnet walked farther behind with Little Storm. Several of the women whose horses pulled travois packed with necessities for a migrating camp came last.

Rising Eagle and Buffalo Dreamer reached the far bluff, and there they could not help but stare at the spectacle below. Buffalo Dreamer drew in her breath at the sight: white-topped wagons, too many to count, and far in the distance, a herd of horses and other animals to accompany them. But it was not only the sight of so many white people moving through prime buffalo country that made her gasp. It was the hundred or so men who rode some distance from the wagons, yet alongside them—a strict formation of men, each wearing a blue coat with gold buttons, just like in her vision.

CHAPTER THIRTY-THREE

BUFFALO DREAMER FELT her stomach tighten as Broken Hand rode closer to where Rising Eagle and the other Oglala men of importance waited. A party of about thirty soldiers rode with Broken Hand. Two other white men who were wearing dark suits and tall hats, came by buggy, and they sat straight and stiff, arrogant looks on their faces, as though well-pleased with themselves. In the distance, the rest of the soldiers halted their march.

Broken Hand greeted Rising Eagle and sat down in a circle with the Oglala elders. The two suited men disembarked the buggy, and Buffalo Dreamer noticed they seemed reluctant to join the circle of men, doing so only when Broken Hand barked some kind of order to them. Buffalo Dreamer thought their tight-fitting clothing looked very uncomfortable, especially for such hot weather. Broken Hand himself again wore buckskins, obviously a white man with more common sense than most.

The soldiers who stood behind the three leaders were armed with swords and held long guns propped at their sides, making Buffalo Dreamer very nervous. Rising Eagle's vision had told him he would die by a sword, but surely not yet. First he must ride with a warrior called Crazy Horse.

"Why are the blue coats here?" Rising Eagle opened the conversation. "Have you come to make war?"

"No, Rising Eagle," Broken Hand answered in the Oglala tongue. "I will explain why they are here, but first you must smoke with me. I have brought you a new pipe, a white man's pipe, and a very fine one. I have also brought the white man's tobacco."

By then, several other Oglala had arrived, many more warriors moving to stand behind the circle of elders, creating a formidable appearance that Buffalo Dreamer could tell in turn made the soldiers uneasy.

"Before I accept your gift, we will smoke the pipe of peace," Rising Eagle told Broken Hand. He looked over at Many Horses, who always carried his ceremonial pipe in one hand wherever he went, keeping it constantly stuffed with sweet grass so that the embers in the pipe bowl were always hot. Many Horses nodded to Rising Eagle and puffed the pipe, then raised it to the sky and lowered it to the earth, then pointed it in the four directions before smoking it again. He passed it around then, each man in the circle drawing on it.

When the pipe reached the first of the two fancy-dressed white men, he took it gingerly and just looked at it.

"Smoke it." Broken Hand said the words to him in English, but Buffalo Dreamer had no doubt of what he was saying, for the man seemed averse to sharing the pipe.

"Smoke it!" Fitzpatrick growled.

The pudgy, red-faced man swallowed and raised the pipe, then took a quick little puff, his face crinkling as though in disgust. He immediately coughed and choked, and the Oglala men laughed at him. Pouting, the man handed the pipe to Broken Hand, who in turn smoked it and passed it to the second suited man, who grimaced and wiped off the end of the pipe before smoking it. He, too, coughed, then wiped his lips with the back of his hand. When the pipe finally came back around to the Oglala, Many Horses lay it across his lap, and Rising Eagle addressed Broken Hand.

"Now I will smoke *your* pipe," he told him.

Buffalo Dreamer watched Fitzpatrick stuff white man's tobacco into a pipe that was shaped in a loop design and made of a glossy red wood. It was indeed a beautifully carved pipe, and she gasped slightly when the man struck a long piece of wood against a rock, causing it to instantly flare into a small flame. He used the flame to light the pipe and draw on it, then handed the pipe over to Rising Eagle, along with a pouch of tobacco. Buffalo Dreamer noticed several Oglala men staring in wonder at the burning stick, and Broken Hand held it up.

"This is called a match. If you strike it against something rough, like a rock, it will make a flame for lighting your pipes, or to light your campfires. It is much quicker and easier than rubbing sticks together, or carrying hot coals with you in your buffalo horns. Would you like to have some of these matches?"

The Oglala men looked at each other, and Many Horses nodded to Rising Eagle. "We will let you decide, my nephew," the old man told him. "You are the one who spoke with Broken Hand the first time he came to us. You speak for us again this time."

Several of the others nodded their approval, and Buffalo Dreamer could feel her husband's pride. Rising Eagle took the new pipe and drew on it, breathing in the smoke and sitting quietly before blowing out the smoke and finally answering Broken Hand.

"This is a fine pipe. I thank you for it and for the tobacco. I will take some of your matches, and I will give you something in return before you leave."

Broken Hand nodded and motioned to the man at his right, who had continued to cough off and on ever since drawing on Many Horses's peace pipe. The whole time the round-faced man had sat through the smoking of the peace pipe, Buffalo Dreamer had noticed him glaring at the Oglala with what she saw as a combination of fear and disgust. His face was red from the heat, and perspiration trickled down his temples and sparkled on his upper lip. It was obvious by the look on his face that he hated being here.

The man handed Fitzpatrick a handful of matches almost grudgingly, and afterward he ran a finger between his neck and the stiff collar of his white shirt, clearly very uncomfortable. Broken Hand handed the matches to Rising

Eagle, who in turn gave them to Bold Fox, sitting to his left.

Rising Eagle took another several puffs on his new pipe before speaking again. Broken Hand waited patiently, but Buffalo Dreamer could see that the other two men were getting anxious.

"I ask again why you are here," Rising Eagle finally demanded. "I do not want your soldiers on Lakota land. If they have not come to make war, they should not be here at all."

Broken Hand grinned amiably. "I brought them only to show you that the white man's government does have soldiers, men who ride and shoot well, and who now are being sent into your hunting grounds to let you know that we wish to keep peace and that we will send soldiers to protect our people if necessary."

"I have left your people alone since I captured the white woman and then gave her back to you. Why do you talk of keeping peace when I have not made war against the white man? And you promised that not many of your people would come through our hunting grounds. Now they come through in endless numbers."

Broken Hand puffed his own pipe for a thoughtful moment before answering. "Well, Rising Eagle, something has happened that my government did not plan on. I—" He cleared his throat. "I told you that the number of whites who came through your land would remain few, but something has been found in the land of the setting sun that has caused thousands of my people to migrate from the East to the West. It is called gold, and gold is very valuable to my people. It is found under the earth, and many are going to this place in the West to dig for it. I guess it is a little bit like how you value horses."

Rising Eagle looked at his cohorts, and they all chuckled. Buffalo Dreamer noticed a look of slight relief in the eyes of several of the soldiers at the sound of their laughter, and she thought how easily these Lakota men could kill all of them. Surely they knew that and were nervous.

"You are wrong," Rising Eagle told Broken Hand. "No Lakota man values horses so much that he would leave his homeland forever just to find more. This seems a very foolish thing to me, going so far for this gold. I am beginning to think that white men are never happy with what they have. They are always going places to look for something else."

Broken Hand nodded. "The ways of my people are different from yours, but that does not mean we can't all exist together peacefully. I am here to tell you that because so many thousands of my people are migrating through your hunting grounds, my government has decided to send its soldiers out to protect them along the way, in case your people should be unhappy with this migration and decide to attack my people. Already there has been trouble with the Cheyenne. I must warn you, as I did the first time we met, that the more the Cheyenne and the Lakota kill and harass my people—especially if they steal women and children and livestock—the more soldiers my government will send west. I am trying to protect your people as well as mine, Rising Eagle. I hope that you will believe me when I tell you so."

Rising Eagle puffed his pipe again, studying Broken Hand. "I believe you, but that does not mean I trust all those who sit beside you and stand behind you. You are one of the few whites who speak the truth. That one beside you, the fat one, him I would never trust. I cannot respect a man who shows fear and tells me with his eyes that he hates me and finds smoking our peace pipe disgusting. Such a man is not even worth killing or torturing, for he has a bad spirit. A Lakota man would never gain strength from torturing such a man. I think that before we talk anymore, he should go someplace where I do not have to look at him."

The other Oglala men chuckled, and Buffalo Dreamer covered her mouth, laughing quietly to herself. When Broken Hand explained Rising Eagle's words, the fat man beside him blubbered something in anger, then got up and glared at Rising Eagle before storming away in a huff, going to stand behind the soldiers. Even some of them were snickering at the words.

Broken Hand shook his head, also smiling. "All right, Rising Eagle, is that better?"

"For now." Rising Eagle leaned forward, his elbows resting on his knees. "Now, explain to me, and to the *Nacas* sitting with me here, as well as to my wife, a holy woman who has touched the white buffalo, how it is you can protect my people."

Broken Hand sobered. "Just as I said. The less trouble there is, the fewer soldiers my government will feel obliged to send west; and the fewer soldiers, the less likely it is that my government will decide to make war against the Oglala. We want no trouble, Rising Eagle, and to prove it, my government has decided to hold council with you. Not just with the Oglala, but with all tribes within the Lakota nation—the Sichangu, Itazipchos, Miniconjous, Hunkpapa, all your tribes—and even with the Cheyenne, the Shoshoni, the Crow, the Blackfoot, the Omaha, all of the Indian nations that would like to talk peace. We would like to talk about where it is safe for our people to travel without angering yours, about a vast amount of land we would like to set aside for the Lakota to live on freely, without being bothered by the white man."

Rising Eagle shook his head, grinning. "Is your government made up of fools?" he asked Broken Hand.

The bellies of the Oglala elders again shook with laughter.

"Do they really think they can tell the Lakota where they can and cannot go?" Rising Eagle continued. He waved his hand. "All this land, from west of this great river, south to Medicine Mountain and farther south to the flat river, east to the mighty river that flows past Fort Pierre, and north, as far as that river flows, it *all* belongs to the Lakota. And you are telling me your government wants to talk to us about where we can and cannot go? Surely they all think backwards, for it is *we* who should be telling *them* where they can and cannot go!"

Nods and murmurs moved among the other Lakota present, and Broken Hand looked at the white man to his left and said something. The man answered, and Broken Hand addressed Rising Eagle again. "In many ways, you are right, Rising Eagle, and I ask to be forgiven if I have offended you. This man with me is a commissary from my government. His name is Henry Parker, and he says to tell you that if you come to this Great Smoke we have planned and listen to what we have to say, there will be many gifts sent to the Lakota from my government, very fine things—pipes and tobacco, blankets, cooking utensils, medicine that helps the sick, warm clothing that can be used in times of poor hunting when there are not enough hides for such things, all kinds of food—meat, sugar, flour, salt. I assure you, our intentions are good ones. All we want is peace with the Lakota, and with all the other Indian nations."

Rising Eagle shook his head. "You expect us to come and meet with you at the same place where the Crow and Shoshoni will be? They are our enemy. We cannot speak for them, nor do we want to even stand on the same ground with them. And no one Lakota man can speak for all the Lakota. If I promised you I would never again attack a white man, it would make little difference, because all the rest of these men who sit here with me could still attack white men if they so chose. It is not easy for a Lakota man to tell another what to do, so why do you think any Lakota man would allow a *white* man to tell him what to do?"

Broken Hand sighed as though vexed. He rubbed his forehead, saying something more to the man next to him before answering. "All right, my friend, would you at least promise me this much? Will you promise to think about coming to this Great Smoke? We will have many soldiers there to keep the peace between the Lakota and other tribes. You don't have to mingle with your enemies. You only have to come and listen to what we have to say, and to consider accepting the many gifts we wish to give you to show you our good intentions. In the meantime, we want your promise to leave the migrating whites alone. I assure you, they want nothing more than to get to the land beyond the mountains. They do not wish to settle in Lakota country, so there is no need for you to disturb them."

"They disturb *us!* They leave filth behind, and dead animals to stink up the land. They kill our game, and they kill our buffalo just for the skins and leave behind the meat and bones. This is a desecration of Mother Earth and the beasts that *Wakan-Tanka* provides for man's sustenance. Your people respect nothing, neither man nor beast. And now you say they are going west to dig into Mother Earth to find this gold. It is wrong to hurt and scar the earth that way. They cut down live trees, and I have learned that some of them beat their children. They dress like fools and honor nothing. I see no reason to go to this Great Smoke. I have no desire to make peace with such people, no desire to allow them to pass through our hunting grounds. I would rather kill all of them and burn their wagons, steal their horses, and make their children my own. That sounds much better to me."

The elders straightened proudly and nodded their agreement. Broken Hand rubbed his eyes as though perplexed. "All right, then, how about this? I have given you a very fine pipe, very expensive by my people's standards. I know it is your custom to return gift for gift, so I am asking that as your gift to me, you come to this Great Smoke and listen to what my government wants to tell you. That's all you have to do. No one is saying you have to agree with anything or abide by anything. Just come and listen. Nothing will happen to you or your women and children. I am not trying to trick you and I am not lying to you.

"No matter what happens over the next several years, I want you to remember one thing, Rising Eagle." The man leaned slightly forward. "Thomas Broken Hand Fitzpatrick is your friend. I have traveled and traded and scouted out here for years. I even speak your language."

He leaned back again. "In return for that fine pipe and tobacco I have given you, I want your promise that you will come to Fort Laramie and counsel with my government. You have a lot of time to plan for it. This gathering will not be held until the second summer after this one. It will take my government that much time to send emissaries to all the different tribes and get all of this organized. And it will take some time for my government to prepare and deliver all the gifts we are promising you just for coming and talking with us."

Rising Eagle frowned. "Where is this Fort Laramie?"

Broken Hand puffed on his own pipe for a moment. "It used to be called Fort William, then Fort John. It was just a trading post, but today it is called Fort Laramie and is owned by my government. There are many soldiers there now, and keep in mind that many more can and will be sent if you begin raiding the wagon trains moving through your hunting grounds." The man removed his floppy leather hat and wiped sweat from his brow before continuing. "Do you know where this fort is?"

Rising Eagle nodded. "It is south of the flat river. I have never been there, but I know of it. Our Shihenna friends speak of it."

"Good. And by the way, the white man calls the flat river the North Platte." Fitzpatrick put on an amiable smile. "So, will you favor me with your presence? Try to be there in the late summer, around the month we call August, your Moon of Dry Dust Blowing. That will give you time for your summer hunts and summer celebrations before coming to Laramie."

Rising Eagle again turned to the rest of the *Nacas* who sat there with him. "What do all of you think?"

Bold Fox rubbed his chin. "I think we should go and hear what they have to say."

"It might be wise to listen," said Runs With The Deer. "It is true we have no good feelings for these people, but the one thing we must always consider is the preservation of our women and children, for they are our future. If talk-

ing with these people means not having to go to war and
not risking the lives of our children, then we should counsel with them."

Rising Eagle sighed, then turned to seek out Buffalo
Dreamer. He called her forward. Surprised, she obeyed,
coming to stand behind him. "What do you think, Buffalo
Dreamer?" Rising Eagle asked.

Buffalo Dreamer felt pride and satisfaction that he
would value her opinion, especially in front of the important men of the tribe.

"I agree with your honored uncles, my husband. They
are old and wise, and there is no harm in simply listening
to what the *wasicus* have to say. You must not think of going
there as some kind of defeat. It is instead a matter of pride
and a compliment. Apparently the white man's government is afraid of the power and skills of the Lakota. Already they fear our warriors. But they must also learn that
we do not want war. We want only to keep and protect
what is rightfully ours. This is your chance to tell them so,
and to warn them that if they do try to take any of it or to
harm our people in some way, they will suffer for it. It is
these *white* men who feel defeated right now. That is why
they have come begging to us."

Rising Eagle smiled and nodded. "You are a wise
woman." He turned his attention back to Broken Hand.
"We will come to your counsel and smoke the pipe of peace
with your people. But let it be known that we do not fear
any of them. Most of all, we do not fear your soldiers. Send
as many as you want; if necessary, we will kill all of them."

Broken Hand grinned, putting out his hand. Rising Eagle grasped his wrist, and for the second time, the two men
shook hands on a promise. Buffalo Dreamer hoped that
this was one promise the *wasicus* would keep and that something good would come of this Great Smoke.

"I look forward to seeing you there, Rising Eagle. This
will be a historic gathering, a great moment for your people and for mine. I am sure we can work something out
that will mean a lasting peace for all of us."

Rising Eagle again folded his arms. "I see only one road to peace," he answered. "The white man must stay out of our hunting grounds, and most important, he must stay out of the Black Hills."

Fitzpatrick nodded. "That will be part of our promise. The Black Hills will always belong to the Lakota."

Rising Eagle raised his chin arrogantly. "I will remember your words, Broken Hand. We will see if the white man can keep his promises. So far, he is not very good at such things."

Fitzpatrick smiled with a look of embarrassed shame in his eyes. "I know that. But this time, my government is much more sincere."

Rising Eagle scanned the soldiers behind the man before answering. "I am thinking the white man is sincere only when there is something he wants. And I am thinking more and more that I want these soldiers out of here. They upset my wife."

Fitzpatrick raised his hands defensively. "We are leaving. Just don't underestimate my government's soldiers, Rising Eagle. I don't want your people getting hurt unnecessarily."

Rising Eagle and those with him chuckled among themselves. "Let me tell you something, Broken Hand. We will not bring harm to you or to these men, because I believe your heart is true. But you should know that my wife and I have both had a dream in which many Lakota and Shihenna warriors surrounded many men in blue coats and fought them until they became a pool of blood. So far, our dreams and visions have all become fact, all but this one."

The two men stared at each other with a note of challenge, and then Fitzpatrick slowly nodded. "I can only hope that somehow that is one vision that does *not* become fact."

Rising Eagle did not answer. He stood quietly watching as Broken Hand and the white men in tall hats and their soldiers rejoined the wagon train. Buffalo Dreamer looked to the east.

"Still they come," she said. "Their wagon wheels are making ruts in Mother Earth." She glanced at Rising Eagle and noticed his jaw flex in repressed anger.

"Surely She is in pain," he answered.

NOVEMBER 1850

Deer-Rutting Moon

CHAPTER THIRTY-FOUR

FLORENCE LEANED DOWN and covered William, who had fallen asleep on the floor while playing. Her four-year-old son was dark and handsome, just like his father. She wanted to let his hair grow long, but Abel would not allow it.

She tucked the blanket lightly around him, hoping there was not too much of a draft on her carpeted parlor floor. She was proud of the addition of a parlor and an extra bed-room to her and Abel's small frame house, which sat only a quarter of a mile from what the government now called Fort Laramie.

She leaned back in her rocker then and glanced at Abel, who sat at his desk preparing his sermon for the next day. His responsibilities had grown since the arrival of so many soldiers at the fort. The Indians who hung around the area, the whites who had settled there, and the soldiers, some of whom had wives and families with them—all had their own unique spiritual needs.

"I worry about Rising Eagle coming to the treaty-signing," Florence told Abel. "I have the great hope of see-ing my first son, but Rising Eagle is a wise, visionary man. If he comes here and sees William, one look into our son's eyes and he will know the child is his."

Abel turned from his work with a sigh. "Florence, I can't believe he would be that insightful. All you have to do is tell him you adopted William after his parents died of smallpox or something. He would believe that."

"Maybe. But you don't know him, Abel. You don't know how important it would be to him to know that he has another son, or how determined he would be to take William away with him. Sons mean everything to a Lakota man."

Abel frowned. "Sons mean everything to *any* man."

"Not to all men. Not to men like John Dundee."

Abel took a moment to apply a blotter to the piece of paper that contained his freshly written notes in ink. He turned his chair so that he could face his wife better. "That was a long time ago, Florence. There are the John Dundees of this world, and then there are the Abel Kingsleys. I love William like my own. He means just as much to me as he would to Rising Eagle, and I do not intend to allow anyone to take him from us. Besides, you might not even see Rising Eagle if he does come to the signing. For heaven's sake, woman, do you realize how many Indians will be coming? *Thousands!* I have to admit I find it quite intimidating. And out of those thousands, you expect to find one particular man?"

Florence took a deep breath. "I *have* to find him, Abel. He is the only one who knows what happened to my son. Mary said there was no young man with him who had fingers and toes missing. My heart will not rest until I know exactly what happened to him—if he died soon after they took him, or died later from something else. I have to know how old he was when he died, where he is buried. I will have no peace until I know these things."

Abel leaned back in his chair. "Then by all means, my dear, go and find Rising Eagle, but I will be going with you. I want to meet the man myself . . . I *think*." He grinned at the comment. "Agent Fitzpatrick is the one who brought Mary here, which means he's met and knows Rising Eagle. I'll talk to him about finding him for us."

Florence studied the white man she had learned to love. "You are so patient and understanding, Abel. I am amazed at how much you love William."

"Why shouldn't I? He is bright and handsome and sweet, and *you* love him. What you love, I love. I try to adhere to my Christian teaching, Florence. It isn't always easy, especially to have patience with some of the Indians around here who are drunk most of the time."

Florence dropped her eyes. "As I once was."

"*Was* is the word, my dear. And there are certainly plenty of my own people who are hard to love, and who do their own share of drinking." He looked at William and smiled. "But that boy there, he's easy to love."

A sudden mist filled Florence's dark eyes. "He is. But some of the soldiers here, and the few wives with the officers, they are not so accepting. I have seen how some of them look at me, and at William. I don't mind for myself, but I do not want William to suffer scathing looks and cruel remarks. If things get worse with my people, if there are attacks and killings, the whites here will look down on William just because of his Indian blood. That is so cruel, and so wrong. How will we explain that to him?" She quickly wiped at a tear. "That is the very reason I gave my first son to Rising Eagle. I knew the Lakota would love him and bring him pride and happiness. He could never have had that among the whites. Now these new people come, who know nothing about my people, who think they are all savage heathens with no feelings—"

"Florence," Abel interrupted. "We both have enough love for William to raise him to be an upstanding, responsible, and proud adult. We will send him to a university someday, and he will be a fine example, living proof that being Lakota makes him no different from any other man. He will be just as intelligent, just as proud, just as trustworthy, and just as Christian. He will be fine, Florence."

Florence nodded. "I believe that can happen. But for now, you must include such things in your sermons. You say your Christ taught that we should love all people and accept all people, that we are all equal in God's eyes. The way some of the officers' wives look at me, I know they do not practice these teachings. I would like you to remind them how Christians are to behave. I do not want any of them making remarks to William, or looking down on him."

"Nor do I. You don't have to defend him alone, Florence. Don't forget that."

She wiped at another tear. "Thank you, Abel."

He smiled and turned back to his writing. "As for William and Rising Eagle, you have several months yet to decide how you want to handle things at the treaty-signing. I don't condone lying, but we may have to lie to Rising Eagle about William's true identity. Just trust in God, Florence."

Florence sniffed and sighed, fingering the knitting she had been working on while thinking about the Great Smoke to take place here next summer. That was what many of the Indians were calling the coming treaty-signing. It actually frightened her a little to think of how inventive and powerful the white men were, and how many more of them were in the East. In spite of living like them now, and loving a white man, she could not help the hidden anger she felt at seeing so many *wasicus* coming into Lakota hunting grounds, even if only to pass through. She had learned enough about them to realize that someday they would not just travel through this land—they would come here to stay, and Lakota men like Rising Eagle would never stand for that.

Abel even thought that perhaps someday the railroad would come farther west, and by his description of it, she feared that such a thing would scare away all the buffalo and wild game. She saw only dangerous times ahead for the Lakota—and for her own heart, too, which was bound to be torn between the two, especially if the conflict involved her own son. Maybe *both* her sons, if Little Wolf was still alive. There was only one way to find out. She had to find Rising Eagle; but she would have to make sure Agent Fitzpatrick understood that Rising Eagle must not be told that William was his son by Mary. Rising Eagle *must* believe that William belonged to her and Abel.

EARLY SEPTEMBER 1851

When the Leaves Become Yellow Moon

CHAPTER THIRTY-FIVE

RISING EAGLE HALTED Olute a few hundred yards from Fort Laramie, taking a long look at the scene ahead. "Many have already come," he said to Bold Fox.

Bold Fox quietly nodded. "Many thousands. Many old enemies . . . Crow, Shoshoni."

"I see Shihenna tepees," Looking Horse told them. "And look over there." He pointed to the right. "Some of those tepees have the markings of the Hunkpatila band of the Oglala. We have not seen that band for many years. We should camp near them."

"I agree," Rising Eagle answered, "*if* we stay. I still cannot decide if we should." He wore his finest regalia: a colorfully quilled shirt with beaded fringes and a bone hairpipe choker at his neck. His hair was slicked back into a greased braid into which were wound two strips of brightly beaded rawhide. Coup feathers were wound into the braid, and small, colored stones tied to tiny rawhide strings decorated his pierced ears. At the end of his lance, which was positioned in its sheath at the side of his horse, he'd tied red flannel, depicting that he belonged to the Brave Heart Society.

Bold Fox wore a full headdress of eagle feathers, and Wind In Grass, Looking Horse, Bear Dancing, Many Horses, Standing Rock, Runs With The Deer, and other *Nacas* wore their finest, determined to make their entrance to the Great Smoke the grandest of all the tribes. They were, after all, Lakota: the largest, strongest, most-feared

Indian nation attending this treaty meeting with the white man's government representatives.

Rising Eagle raised his chin as he motioned for all to move forward. He was now *Naca Ominicia,* a member of the highest council among the Lakota, an honor that had been his goal since he was old enough to understand the importance of such a position. He intended to make an intimidating display toward old enemies who were present, and also toward the white man's government representatives. They would see and understand that they were dealing with a formidable foe, one against whom they had better think twice about challenging in any way.

He'd painted white stripes down his cheeks and across his forehead. Yes, he was here to listen to talks of peace, but not at the expense of the Lakota, and not by allowing the white man to claim an inch of Lakota lands or hunting grounds. He would listen to the Great White Father's promises, and he would then decide whether or not he could trust those promises. So far, the white man had not shown him any reason to believe the *wasicu* would abide by any agreements.

The Lakota rode forward four abreast, and Rising Eagle smiled inwardly when he saw several white men and soldiers come out of the central area of the fort to stare. He noticed that a large group of Crow, as well as Shoshoni, also gathered to watch their entrance. He knew they all felt intimidated, as well they should!

He had directed Buffalo Dreamer to ride directly behind the tribal council, the only woman among them with such an esteemed position. He took great pride in the fact that she was his wife. Behind her were the *Tokalas,* the Police Society; then the *Akicitas,* the War Society; then the *Wicasa Itacans,* the Executive Committee that enforced the decisions of the tribal council and appointed the Shirt Wearers; then came the *Wakincuzas,* the Pipe Owners, those who chose campsites; and then the Shirt Wearers, who organized camp moves.

Behind them came the bravest, most accomplished

younger warriors, and those who held the most potential for greatness, including his own son, Brave Horse. Spirit Walker also rode with them, as one who could heal.

At the end of their formidable *Nacas* and warriors came the women, children, and old ones, followed by a large remuda of horses, for Rising Eagle was determined to show enemy tribes just how wealthy were the Lakota in their stock of horses, many of them stolen from those very enemy tribes! Those already here would surely look at this great procession of Lakota with envy and admiration.

The *Nacas* riding in lead formation included not just the Oglala leaders, but also Hunkpapa, Sichangu, Miniconjou, Sihasapa, and Ochenonpa, all seven tribes of the Seven Council Fires. Seldom did all tribes of the Lakota Nation come together this way, but all had been invited, and runners had been sent to organize a gathering at the fork of the North and South Platte rivers so that they could organize this parade, a planned approach to show the representatives of the white man's government and their soldiers just what they were up against if they should consider giving the Lakota Nation any trouble.

Rising Eagle and most of the *Naca Ominicia* had spent many long hours talking about what might happen at this treaty gathering, and it was decided that each man—of his own free will—would be permitted to sign whatever agreement the white man might offer. No one Lakota leader would speak for the entire nation, nor would any man agree to allow white men to even set foot, let alone settle, in *Paha-Sapa*.

A man wearing buckskins rode out from the fort then to welcome them, and Rising Eagle recognized Agent Fitzpatrick. He removed his lance and held it in the air as salutation, telling Bold Fox and the others to wait while he rode forward to meet Broken Hand, who raised his hand in greeting.

"It is good to see you, Rising Eagle. I was afraid you had decided not to come."

Rising Eagle nodded. "We have come to hear what you

have to say, Broken Hand. Our presence does not mean we agree to anything you tell us."

"Understood." Fitzpatrick scanned the vast tribe behind Rising Eagle, then turned his attention back to Rising Eagle himself. "You have brought many thousands with you."

Rising Eagle grinned wryly. "And your soldiers would be wise not to make trouble while we are here."

"The soldiers are here simply to help make sure there are no conflicts among the various tribes that have come to talk. We understand that many of them are your enemies, but this talk is one of peace, Rising Eagle, and an effort to bring peace not just between my people and yours, but between your nation and the other Indian nations. We want the warring among you to stop, as it sometimes ends up affecting our own people. But that is just part of our talks, and it is not our place to discuss these things now. There are many government representatives here, and we will present what we have to say when we can sit down with the leaders of *all* the nations."

He turned and waved his hand, indicating the thousands more already camped around the fort, their tepees and herds of horses stretched out as far as the eye could see.

"I must tell you," Fitzpatrick continued, "that because so many have come, the grass around the fort is grazed out. We have decided to move everyone south to Horse Creek. It is about thirty-five miles from here, and there is plenty of water and plenty of grass for everyone's horses. We were only waiting for the Lakota to arrive. Once we settle in at Horse Creek, my government will come bearing many gifts for all of you. I assure you this council is being held with a sincere interest in reaching an understanding between the Indian nations and our government. We want no more trouble from you, and we do not want to cause more trouble."

Rising Eagle studied the man's eyes. "I believe you, Broken Hand, but I do not think you alone can control what your nation does. However, we will move south with the others and listen to what your leaders have to say."

"We leave in two days. In the meantime, I have been asked to tell you there is someone living here who wishes to talk with you and your wife."

Rising Eagle frowned. "Who would I know at this place who would want to see me?"

"Her name is Florence, and she is Oglala. She said to tell you her name was once Fall Leaf Woman."

Rising Eagle felt surprise and pleasure. "Fall Leaf Woman lives *here?* When last I saw her, she lived at Fort Pierre."

Fitzpatrick nodded. "She has since married a white man, a preacher, what your people would call a priest. They came here to teach a new religion to the Lakota and others who live near the fort. They have a five-year-old son. They would have come out here to greet you, but the boy is very ill and Florence does not want to leave him. They ask that you come there, and Florence said to tell you that if the son she gave you many years ago is still alive, she would hope to see him again."

Rising Eagle nodded. "He is alive. He is called Spirit Walker, and he is a healer. You can tell Fall Leaf Woman that her son now calls our medicine man Grandfather." He could see that Fitzpatrick understood the meaning of the words. The man smiled and nodded.

"Florence will be overjoyed to know her first son still lives and that he is being taught by your medicine man."

"He is alive, and he is himself healed."

Fitzpatrick frowned. "Was he sick? Did he have the smallpox?"

"No. Florence will know what I mean when you tell her."

Fitzpatrick pushed back his hat and turned his horse. "I will tell her. You can settle your people wherever you choose, and tomorrow morning I will come and take you to see Florence and her husband and son."

Rising Eagle nodded his agreement, and Fitzpatrick said good-bye and rode off. Rising Eagle was both surprised and pleased to learn that Fall Leaf Woman was here at Fort

Laramie. He rode back to the rest of the *Nacas* and explained that they could make camp but that in two days, they would move south to Horse Creek. He proceeded on to where Buffalo Dreamer waited, then called Brave Horse and Spirit Walker to join them. Once there, Rising Eagle told his sons the news.

"Fall Leaf Woman is here."

Buffalo Dreamer drew in her breath, putting a hand to her chest.

"My mother?" Spirit Walker asked.

"Yes. She is called Florence now, and she is married to a white man who is a priest. They have a son." He looked at Buffalo Dreamer. "I am glad Fall Leaf Woman gave birth again. Now she has another son, one who can fill the emptiness left when she gave Spirit Walker to us. Perhaps she has changed and no longer drinks the firewater."

Buffalo Dreamer looked at Spirit Walker. "It is your choice, son, if you want to meet your birth mother."

Spirit Walker looked from her to Rising Eagle. "I think of Buffalo Dreamer as my only real mother, but I would like to meet my birth mother, and my new brother. I want Fall Leaf Woman to know that I am not angry with her for having given me away and that I am no longer deformed. And she should also know that I am a healer."

"Seeing you again will make her very happy, I am sure," Buffalo Dreamer told him. "I am glad you have agreed to go to her."

Others moved past them to make a temporary camp until they all moved south to Horse Creek. Rising Eagle thought about how many years had passed since that night he'd killed Fall Leaf Woman's abusive white husband and agreed to take her half-blood son with him to raise. She had been a thin, drunken, sorry-looking woman then, a far cry from the proud, beautiful Fall Leaf Woman he had known before marrying Buffalo Dreamer. What was she like now? He glanced at Buffalo Dreamer and knew she was wondering the same.

"She will be surprised to see that her son is healed," Buffalo Dreamer told him.

Rising Eagle nodded. Indeed, it would surely be quite a shock to her.

CHAPTER THIRTY-SIX

"ARE YOU SURE he believed you?"

Agent Fitzpatrick nodded in reassurance. "I simply told Rising Eagle that you and your husband have a son. I don't see how he will ever know William is his own blood. I didn't say anything about the real mother. And since the boy does not look pure Lakota, and your husband is white, it will be easy to convince Rising Eagle that Willy belongs to you and the preacher. I don't think he will suspect."

"It is important that he never knows, Agent Fitzpatrick. Abel and I would have gone to Rising Eagle ourselves, but I cannot leave my son, sick as he is."

"I understand. I do have some good news for you that might ease your worry about Willy. Rising Eagle told me that the son you gave him to raise is alive and well, and that he is here with them."

Florence gasped and covered her mouth as her eyes teared. She felt Abel's arm come around her for support. "I told you that if we prayed hard enough, you would one day see your son again," he told her.

Florence shook with a sob. "I can't believe it."

Fitzpatrick smiled. "His name is Spirit Walker, and Rising Eagle also said to tell you that he is a healer, that he calls their medicine man Grandfather."

Florence wiped at her eyes and smiled. "It is all such wonderful news! My son a healer! A medicine man!" She looked up at Abel, who smiled and handed her a handkerchief. Florence used it to blow her nose and again wipe at her eyes. "I can hardly wait to see him."

"I will bring them by tomorrow morning. By the way, ma'am, how is Willy?"

Florence shook her head, her emotions torn between joy at learning her Little Wolf, now called Spirit Walker, lived, yet feeling terror and agony over the fact that her William could be dying. He had been sick with a chest congestion and fever for several days now, and the army doctor had done all he could for the child. She loved William just as deeply as if he had come from her own womb, and the thought of losing yet another child, this one to death, was almost too much to bear.

"He's not doing well at all," Abel replied for his wife. "It's really difficult for us."

"Well, maybe seeing Spirit Walker tomorrow will help." The man turned his horse, then suddenly turned back around after riding a few feet away. "Oh! I forgot to tell you. I am not sure what he meant, but Rising Eagle said to tell you that your son is healed."

Florence felt as though the blood was draining from her body. On faltering feet, she stepped away from Abel. "Healed?"

"That's what he said. When I asked him what sickness the boy had once had, Rising Eagle said none. He said you would know what he meant."

Florence grasped the support post of the wooden porch at the front of her home. "That can't be! My son was . . . *deformed!* I mean—" She turned to Abel. "What else could he have meant? To say I would understand can only mean that Spirit Walker's deformities are gone!"

Abel folded his arms and frowned. "That's impossible. He must have meant something else."

Florence turned back to Fitzpatrick, wiping at her eyes again. "You're sure he said it that way? I mean, maybe you interpreted wrongly what he said."

Fitzpatrick shook his head, smiling. "Ma'am, I've been working with the Lakota for quite a while. I know exactly what he said. Besides, he uses a little English now. Must have learned it from William's mother, maybe more from her daughter." He tipped his hat. "I have a lot to do, ma'am. I'll be by tomorrow with Rising Eagle and your son."

The man rode off, and Florence stood staring after him, astonished at what she'd been told. "It can't be," she said, turning back to face Abel. "Abel, those words can only mean one thing."

Abel walked closer and put his hands on her shoulders. "Florence, that's crazy. It's not humanly possible."

Florence pulled away. "Maybe not *humanly* possible, but it is as I once told you long ago. You must understand and respect the spiritual powers of my people." She faced him again. "You preach about the miracles of the Bible, and I tell you again, Abel, that I see no difference between Jehovah and his son, and the Lakota god *Wakan-Tanka* and the Feathered One."

"Florence—"

"No! Listen to me. The one thing I see about your people, even the most religious among them, is that they do not trust enough in the *powers* of Jehovah. I believe that you do; but you, as well as the others I have known, do not understand the spiritual powers of the Lakota, the powerful connection some of them have to *Wakan-Tanka*. Rising Eagle is one of those men. If my son is truly healed, I know in my heart it is because of the prayers of Rising Eagle. He would give his life for another if *Wakan-Tanka* told him to do so. He has shed much blood in sacrifice to *Wakan-Tanka* in his prayers, to show him—"

"Florence, you are a *Christian* now! You are talking like a heathen!"

Florence sucked in her breath and stepped back, shaking her head. "I am trying to tell you how easy it is to reach my people with the Christian religion. I have told you this before. If your God can work miracles, so can ours! For they are the *same*!"

Abel turned away.

"Listen to me, Abel! I am still *Lakota* on the inside. The reason I call myself Christian is because I truly believe that to do so does not mean I must turn away from *Wakan-Tanka*. The only difference I see is that because of Jehovah's son, Christians need not shed blood in offering to their god. The Lakota still believe they must do this. There is no other difference. The Lakota only need to learn that they do not need to suffer the Sun Dance or cut themselves in prayer, but their doing these things does not make them heathens! It is simply their way of worshiping the same god *we* worship! And did Jehovah not require blood offerings in the Old Testament? Do you not see the resemblance? And I have told you that my people believe there was once a great flood. When I learned of such a thing in the Old Testament, I was astonished to realize that some of my people's beliefs are exactly the same as in the Bible!"

Abel faced her again, frowning. "I must say I find all of it hard to believe, Florence."

"I know you do. Just do not be angry with me when I try to explain it to you. I am only trying to help you reach my people. When my son comes tomorrow, if he is truly healed of his deformities, you will believe me. And you will understand the power of Rising Eagle's prayers. You will understand why he had to marry someone more worthy than I. Men like Rising Eagle follow every law of the Lakota, and they obey every command they are given in dreams and visions. It is the way."

Abel sighed, studying her intently for a moment. "For all the white woman's clothing, the way you wear your hair, the way we live now, I will never really understand your Lakota heart, will I?"

"Does that make you love me less?"

He shook his head. "You know it doesn't. I just worry sometimes that someday you will run off to rejoin them. I'm not exactly thrilled about Rising Eagle coming here tomorrow, but I'm happy to know your son is still alive."

Florence walked closer, wrapping her arms around him and resting her head against his chest. "I would never leave you, Abel. In my heart I am Lakota, but I have lived this way with you and your people for too long now. I would not fit in with the others anymore. I only want you to understand and respect my people, their religion, and their ways."

Abel embraced her. "The news about Spirit Walker is certainly welcome, especially with William being so sick. We had better get back inside and check on him again. It's good to have him sleeping decently—"

"Mama!" The word was followed by deep coughing, and Florence immediately left her husband and rushed back into the house. Her son's much-needed rest had again been interrupted by more of the agonizing coughing and wheezing. His face was flushed with fever when Florence sat down on the edge of his bed and pulled him into her arms.

"Willy, my Willy," she soothed, gently rocking him until the coughing finally ceased. By then, Abel was back in the room, kneeling in front of them. "I am so afraid for him," Florence whispered.

Abel reached up and stroked the boy's hair. "All we can do now is pray for him, Florence."

"I can't . . . hardly breathe . . . Mama," the five-year-old whimpered.

"I know, Willy. You must stay sitting up. The doctor said it would help. Mama will hold you . . . you can sleep against my chest." She looked intently at Abel, suddenly taking hope. "Spirit Walker!" she said. "I will have my first-born son pray over Willy."

Abel closed his eyes and hung his head. "Florence, singing and shaking a rattle over Willy is not going to heal him."

"It can! I have seen it happen. And the Lakota have a way with herbs and sweet grass. What harm can it do, Abel? The army doctor has not been able to help him." The joy continued to build in her soul. "Don't you see? Willy is sick, and at the same time, I have discovered that my first son lives. It is meant to be. Spirit Walker was brought here by God to heal his brother."

Abel touched her arm. "If that's what you want to believe. . . . In the meantime, I will continue doing my own praying for our son."

"And you should, for your prayers have much power, Abel. Perhaps if you pray to Jehovah, and Spirit Walker prays to *Wakan-Tanka,* together you can bring the spirit and mercy of God upon our son and make him well."

Abel rose. "I do not doubt your hope, Florence. Now I must go to the church to pray."

Florence clung to her son as Abel left, and she knew her husband was doubtful about everything she had told him. But in her own heart, she had no doubts. Her firstborn son lived, and he was not only healed, but was himself a medicine man. It was a good sign. In spite of the risk of letting Rising Eagle meet William, she had no choice now. William's life was more important than anything, and if indeed Rising Eagle's prayers had healed Spirit Walker, perhaps they could also heal William.

CHAPTER THIRTY-SEVEN

RISING EAGLE HAD decided to wear his best regalia for the meeting with Fall Leaf Woman and her husband. He'd insisted his family do the same. Buffalo Dreamer wore a newly made tunic decorated with a star pattern of many-colored beads, beads also trimming each of the hundreds of fringes on the dress. Two-and-a-half-summers-old Little Storm sat in front of her mother, a dark, chubby little girl with snappy black eyes. Rising Eagle was very proud of his daughter, whose bright smile was the light of his life.

Brave Horse wore a bleached shirt colorfully decked with a spiraling circle of bright red and yellow quills, and Spirit Walker's shirt displayed an array of turquoise, white and red beads and quills in an eagle design. All, including Buffalo Dreamer, wore their hair in two queues that hung over the front of their shoulders and decorated with strips of colorful beads. Rising Eagle, Spirit Walker, and Brave Horse wore white stripes painted down their cheeks and across their foreheads, and both Brave Horse and Rising Eagle sported lances, tomahawks, and long guns tied to their gear.

Brave Horse had painted his roan-colored gelding with white stars and a moon on one shoulder, and with a yellow sun and red eagles on the other. Little Turtle was perched in front of his big brother on Brave Horse's mount.

Rising Eagle took great pride in what a fine family he had. He rode Olute, whose right rump was painted with red hands that represented all the wounds Rising Eagle had suffered, his left rump with black hands for the number of enemies Rising Eagle had killed. He had also painted white stripes for peace on the horse's front left shoulder, and on the right shoulder, red stripes—for war and blood.

Now they all rode closer to the porch of the white frame home that Agent Fitzpatrick had told them was where Florence lived. Rising Eagle could see Florence now, standing on the steps with a white man who wore dark clothing. How different she looked from the last time he had seen her—healthier, happier, her black hair slicked back into a tight knot the way he'd seen white women wear theirs. Gray showed at her temples, reminding him of how many years had passed since this woman first tempted him to lie with her when they were young. He nodded to her and her husband.

"And so we meet again. It has been many summers since the night you gave me your son, Fall Leaf Woman," he told her in the Lakota tongue, deciding to use her more familiar Lakota name. He caught the tears in her eyes . . . and the old admiration.

"Indeed," she answered. She looked him over. "You appear well, Rising Eagle." She stepped closer. "But I see marks on your face that tell me you have suffered the smallpox."

Rising Eagle felt the old anger rising. "The white man's disease stole two of our children, a son and a daughter."

Florence shook her head. "I am so sorry, Rising Eagle." She looked at the rest of the family, then back to him. "My son?"

Rising Eagle glanced at the man in black, pleased to see a mixture of jealousy and intimidation in his gray eyes. He directed his attention at Florence again. "Spirit Walker did not take the sickness."

Relief flooded Florence's eyes. She scanned the entire family again, smiling at Buffalo Dreamer. "You are still so beautiful!"

Buffalo Dreamer smiled in return. "As you are."

Florence shook her head. "Oh, no. I have a thicker waist, and grayer hair." She turned to the man in the black suit, taking his arm and urging him closer. "This is Abel Kingsley," she told Rising Eagle. "He is my husband, and a good man."

Abel reached his hand toward Rising Eagle. Rising Eagle slid off his horse and walked around to face the man, grasping his wrist. He stood a head taller than Abel, and he could tell by their grip that he could easily kill this man. Instinct told him that Kingsley was not a warrior in any sense of the word.

"Tell your husband that I am glad to meet him," he told Florence, "because I can see by how you look that he has made you happy."

Tears slipped down Florence's face. "It is good to know that you care," she answered. She interpreted for Abel as the two men released their grip. After Abel spoke, Florence told Rising Eagle that her husband was also glad to finally meet him. "I have told him all about you," she said. "Everything that happened with Gray Owl and how I happened to end up at Fort Pierre." She looked down then. "All of it." She raised her eyes, and Rising Eagle saw a pleading look there. "My son is with you?"

Rising Eagle turned. "You did not see the blue eyes of the young man on the black horse? Spirit Walker is the one with the eagle design on his shirt. Buffalo Dreamer made it for him."

Florence moved closer to Spirit Walker, putting trembling hands to her face and speaking his name fondly in the Lakota tongue. "At last I see you again! I have dreamed of this day since the night Rising Eagle took you."

"And I am glad to finally meet my birth mother," Spirit Walker answered with a gentle smile.

Rising Eagle could see that Florence struggled to keep from weeping. She stood there shaking her head, looking like she had just seen a ghost. "You are . . . so handsome and—" She reached up and took hold of one of his hands, staring at it for a moment, fingering it over and over. She broke down then, kissing his hand, turning and saying something excitedly to her husband.

Abel Kingsley walked over to Florence, and she showed the man Spirit Walker's hand, weeping and laughing at the same time. Rising Eagle enjoyed the look of pure shock on the face of Abel Kingsley. Abel, too, examined Spirit Walker's hand intently, then said something to Florence, shaking his head and studying Spirit Walker's fingers yet again before looking over at Rising Eagle.

Rising Eagle never felt more proud or accomplished than at this moment, for Abel looked at him not just in surprise, but in near reverence, as well as obvious confusion and disbelief. Surely he knew the story of how Spirit Walker had been born with some of his fingers and toes missing.

Spirit Walker slid down from his horse then, and Florence grasped both his hands, looking him over again. "I do not doubt now that I did the right thing when I gave you to Rising Eagle," she told him. "You are healed! And you in turn have become a healer. Agent Fitzpatrick told me so."

She kissed his hands, then stepped back, eyeing the rest of Rising Eagle's family. "Such a fine family you have," she exclaimed, glancing at the children. She kept hold of Spirit Walker's hand, compelling him to accompany her as she walked closer to Brave Horse. "You look exactly like a young Rising Eagle. You must be the son I saw the night I brought Spirit Walker to your father."

"I am called Brave Horse," the young man told her in the Lakota tongue. He held Little Turtle closer. "This is my brother, Little Turtle, and with my mother is my sister, Little Storm. We also have a white sister, but my father keeps her out of sight. We fear the soldiers will try to take her from us."

Rising Eagle noticed that Florence suddenly took on a look of worry, glancing at her husband. Just then he heard the sound of a child crying. It came from inside the frame house. Florence said something quietly to her husband, who also looked worried. They exchanged words, and Abel Kingsley seemed irritated, then rather reluctantly tolerant. He glanced at Rising Eagle, then hurried into the house.

Florence turned to Rising Eagle, an imploring look in her eyes. "I have something important to ask of you," she said, "and of Spirit Walker." She reached over and took Spirit Walker's hand again. "First I want to thank you, Rising Eagle, for raising such a fine young man. And now I—"

Rising Eagle sensed a deep worry in her soul. "Broken Hand said that you have another son," he told her, "and that he is very sick. Do you want Spirit Walker to pray over him? They are, after all, brothers."

There was that strange, worried look again. Florence stepped back. "Yes. I would like you and Spirit Walker to *both* pray over my son." She looked from Rising Eagle to Buffalo Dreamer, who had dismounted and lifted down Little Storm. Walking closer, Buffalo Dreamer addressed Florence.

"The loss of a child is a terrible thing, Fall Leaf Woman. I will never truly get over losing two of my own. If Rising Eagle's prayers can help, then he and Spirit Walker should pray over your son. You should not have to lose yet another child." She looked up at Rising Eagle. "You must do as she asks, Rising Eagle."

"Thank you, Buffalo Dreamer," Florence told her. "I am so sorry about the children you lost." She turned then to Spirit Walker again. "William is your brother. He is only five summers old, Spirit Walker, and he is very sick with a coughing illness and fever. The white doctor here at the fort has done all he can do. I fear my little William will die if he doesn't get better soon. I talked to my husband last night, and he agreed to let you and Rising Eagle pray over our son. It goes against his deepest religious beliefs, but I have explained to him that *Wakan-Tanka* is no different from the god the white man calls Jehovah."

She looked at Buffalo Dreamer again. "I live like a white woman now, and I dress like one, I cook like a white woman, I live in a house with four walls and a roof that does not let in the sun; but in my heart, I am still Oglala, and I still believe in the healing practices of our medicine men." She turned to Rising Eagle. "Now that I have seen with my own eyes the power of your prayers, Rising Eagle, that brought about the healing of my firstborn, I know that surely if you pray over my William, he will be healed also. There is not much time. The day after tomorrow, all of the Indian nations will move south to Horse Creek for talks. I will not be able to go because of William."

Rising Eagle looked up at Brave Horse, who was still on his horse. "Go and get Moon Painter. Tell him what is wrong and to bring whatever herbs and medicines are necessary."

"Yes, Father." Brave Horse turned his mount and rode away, keeping Little Turtle with him.

"Thank you, Rising Eagle," Florence said, her eyes again misty with tears. She turned to Spirit Walker. "It is so hard to believe that I actually am seeing you again, my son."

Rising Eagle's attention was distracted then by an odd inner calling when the child inside the house began crying harder, then began a wretched coughing. "I would like to see your son now," he told Florence. "Bring him out to us."

Florence held his gaze, an almost pleading look in her eyes. "I . . . I don't know if my husband will let me bring him out here."

Rising Eagle glanced at the house. "It will do no good to pray over him inside a place with hard walls and a roof that does not let in the sunlight. We cannot reach *Wakan-Tanka* with our prayers that way. Perhaps that is why the boy still is not well. He needs to come out where *Wakan-Tanka* can see him."

Florence began wringing her hands, and Rising Eagle could not help wondering at a look of near fear in her eyes.

"I . . . I will ask Abel." She turned to go inside.

"Tell your son not to be afraid," Rising Eagle added. "He is, after all, Oglala."

Florence stood still on the porch steps for a moment. "Yes, he is Oglala." She hurried into the house, and Rising Eagle walked closer to Buffalo Dreamer, frowning. "She is very afraid about something, very troubled. It is more than just her son's illness."

"Perhaps she is just worried about what her husband will say about all of this. He does not believe in our way. Maybe he is afraid you will try to steal the boy."

Rising Eagle glanced at the house again. "Why would I steal him? He belongs to Fall Leaf Woman and her white husband. If she chooses to live here, and if he is a good father, the boy should stay with them."

Just then Florence stepped out of the doorway, followed by her husband, who held a young boy in his arms. Florence seemed suddenly hesitant as she walked closer.

"This is William," she said when they reached where Rising Eagle stood. "We call him Willy."

Rising Eagle noted that the boy's deep-brown hair was cut short, the way white men and boys wore theirs. That saddened him, for there was strength and spirit in a man's hair. The child turned his face from where he had been resting against his father's shoulder, and Rising Eagle could see without touching him that he was fevered. The whites of his coal-black eyes were bloodshot with it, and even though his skin was as dark as any Lakota child's, there was an obvious flush to it, and his breathing was labored.

The boy stared at Rising Eagle, and Rising Eagle held his gaze, noting the child showed no fear at all. Rising Eagle felt an odd piercing pain in his heart at the sight of him, a feeling of oneness, as though this boy should mean much more to him than just the fact that he was part Oglala. He reached out to him, and William willingly left his father's arms and went to him.

Rising Eagle closed his eyes and drew in his breath as William rested his head on his shoulder. *What is this feeling? I could so easily call this one son.*

CHAPTER THIRTY-EIGHT

FLORENCE FELT HER stomach twisting into a knot. She could tell that Rising Eagle suspected there was something different about William, and she scrambled for possible explanations as he stood there holding the boy close, virtually trembling. She looked at Abel. "I told you," she whispered, her eyes tearing.

"You wanted to do this, Florence," he replied softly. "Don't worry. There is no proving anything."

Rising Eagle grasped William under the arms then, holding him up and studying him. The sick child's feet dangled from beneath the flannel gown he wore, and Florence noticed William grasp Rising Eagle's powerful arms. The boy actually giggled, an astonishing surprise, considering he was so sick and had done nothing but sleep and cry for days.

"I feel one with your son," Rising Eagle told Florence in his own tongue. "Buffalo Dreamer, come and look at this boy. He is handsome, and I know he is strong enough to be well again. Florence has a fine son. I am glad for her."

Florence breathed a sigh of relief as Buffalo Dreamer walked closer, carrying Little Storm. "Spirit Walker, come and see your brother," she told the young man. "Touch him, and he will begin to feel better, I am sure."

A smiling Spirit Walker came closer as Rising Eagle lowered William. Spirit Walker touched William's face, and the boy smiled at him.

"William, this young man is your older brother," Florence told her son in English. "He is called Spirit Walker, and he is a healer. He is going to help make you better. Will you go to him?"

William nodded, and Rising Eagle handed the boy over to Spirit Walker. The child put his arms around Spirit Walker's neck and hugged him like a long-lost brother, taking the news as any trusting child would. If his mother said this was his brother, then it was so, and he was excited. Florence suspected that her son simply looked at all of this as an adventure, and she was glad it was enough of a distraction to take the boy's mind off his misery, if only for a short while. She looked at Rising Eagle, and she saw confusion in his eyes.

"Why do I feel such a bond with your son?" he asked. "Is there something you are not saying to me?"

Florence struggled to keep her composure, putting on a forced smile but feeling very anxious because of Rising Eagle's ability to almost see inside another's mind. "No. I think . . ." She glanced at Buffalo Dreamer. "My husband cannot understand everything I say in the Lakota tongue, so I will admit to you why Rising Eagle might feel this way." She looked back at Rising Eagle. "I think it is just because I always hoped . . . wanted . . . *your* son, Rising Eagle. My feelings for you have never died. I care very much about my white husband, and this is the life I have decided to live now. But my heart is Lakota, and when William was born, I saw you in his dark eyes, and sometimes I . . . pretend . . . that he is yours and mine. I think that is probably why you feel the way you do about him."

She wanted to look away from Rising Eagle's intense scrutiny, but she knew that if she did, he would be more suspicious. She held his gaze until he finally nodded.

"I could easily call any child with Lakota blood mine. This you know, because to me, Spirit Walker is my own. And so we share our children, Fall Leaf Woman," he said.

"Your son has become mine, and I feel a bond with your second son. If you asked me, I would take him also, but he belongs to your white husband. No man easily gives up his blood child, and so I would not ask to take this one."

But he is your blood child, she thought. If he knew, he would take him away, and she would not be able to bear it; nor could she allow such heartache for Abel.

"If William's father was as uncaring and abusive as John Dundee was to my first son, I would beg you to take him from me," she told Rising Eagle. "But Abel is a good father. He is loving and caring. William will be raised to be honest and honorable. But he will know a different life from the Lakota, and I think that someday it will be so for all Lakota children. I see it coming, and so some of them must begin learning this new way, Rising Eagle. Even so, I will teach William about the Lakota way and make sure he is proud of his heritage. This I promise."

Rising Eagle nodded. "I in turn am raising a young white woman to be Lakota. What is sad is that there are not many white people who have a good heart, like your husband, and the agent, Broken Hand. From what I have seen so far, most of them have bad hearts, and no vision, no connection with the earth and the animal spirits, no honor or respect for such things. Perhaps you are right about learning each other's ways, but you have lived long among the white man. I see no reason to learn his way, for there is nothing good about how he lives."

"Florence—" Abel interrupted, taking her arm. "What are you talking about? Is everything all right?"

Florence put her hand over his. "Yes." She faced him. "He doesn't suspect," she said softly. "I will explain later." Turning back to Rising Eagle, she continued. "I hope you will go to the talks and listen to what the white man's government has to say. If you don't accept what they want, I am afraid there are bad times ahead for the Lakota."

Rising Eagle put a fist to his chest. "I listen to my heart," he answered, "and to my dreams and visions. No white man can tell me what I should or should not do, or where I can live and hunt. If this is what the talks will be about, it is useless for me to listen."

Florence closed her eyes for a moment, feeling the piercing pain of knowledge, the awareness of just how bad things could get, for she knew enough now about the white man's world—his power, determination, and greed—and about the attitude of warriors like Rising Eagle to know the only outcome could be conflict; and the Lakota had no idea of the kind of weapons, force, and sheer numbers the white man could employ.

"Rising Eagle—" She was interrupted by the arrival of Brave Horse and Moon Painter, who galloped toward them. She breathed deeply at the sight of Brave Horse, who looked so much like his father had at that age. Seeing the young man brought back memories that should be forbidden to a properly married woman.

"I don't like this," Abel said as old Moon Painter dismounted. "The man looks to be a thousand years old. What can he possibly do to help William?"

She faced her doubting husband, grasping his arm. "What good has our *own* doctor done? Please show respect for him, Abel. The older a Lakota man or woman becomes, the more honor they enjoy. They are considered very, very wise, and Moon Painter has healing powers. I have seen it for myself. So does Rising Eagle. You surely cannot doubt that, now that you have seen Spirit Walker. Let them do whatever they deem necessary."

Moon Painter walked up to Spirit Walker and looked closely at William, then chanted something, shaking a rattle over the boy. Florence felt proud that William seemed to understand he was a part of these people, showing no fear. He displayed only curiosity and boyish excitement. The sight of a wrinkled, painted old man like Moon Painter would normally frighten most little white children.

Moon Painter handed his rattle to Spirit Walker then,

telling him to go to a nearby cottonwood tree and build a small fire of sweet grass and begin praying. He took William from Spirit Walker, carrying him to a watering trough in front of Florence's home, then proceeded to remove William's nightgown.

"What is he doing?" Abel exclaimed. Moon Painter lifted William and set him in the trough, pushing him down so that he was completely immersed. Abel started to protest, reaching for his son, but Florence grabbed his arm more tightly, imploring him not to interfere.

"The water will take away his fever," Rising Eagle told Florence, obviously aware that her husband did not like the procedure at all.

"He'll kill him!" Abel said. "A chill will only make him worse!"

"He will be fine, Abel, I assure you," Florence said, watching Moon Painter take the naked, smiling William out of the water and put the gown back on his wet body. "The Lakota have done this for fever ever since I can remember. It's better than letting a fever rage to the point that William loses his mind. It can happen. Look. See? He's smiling. He probably feels better after being cooled down."

"The army doctor is going to be furious when he finds out about this."

"He doesn't need to find out," Florence protested. "Have some faith, Abel. You're the one always telling me that. Maybe God himself brought Rising Eagle and the others here at this particular time. Maybe God is trying to teach you something about my people, and about faith."

Moon Painter handed William to Rising Eagle. "He is special," he told Rising Eagle. "I feel it."

Rising Eagle nodded, taking the boy into his arms again. "I also felt it," he answered. "It is as though the boy carries my blood."

Florence put a hand to her heart to slow its rapid beating.

Rising Eagle carried William over to where Spirit Walker had begun singing over a small, smoky fire. Florence hung back, closing her eyes and asking God to forgive her for having lied to Rising Eagle, and asking at the same time that Moon Painter's healing herbs and Spirit Walker's prayers would make her son well. If he got worse after this, and especially if he died, Abel would probably never forgive her or speak to her again.

CHAPTER THIRTY-NINE

ABEL WATCHED WITH impatience old Moon Painter's singing and chanting, feeling like a fool for allowing this. Still, there was no arguing the fact that Spirit Walker was indeed healed. He wanted to believe that maybe Rising Eagle was lying—that Spirit Walker was just some other half-breed whom Rising Eagle was passing off as Florence's once-deformed son, making himself seem some sort of great healer and a powerful leader. Indian men enjoyed feeling important. That much he'd learned in his years of working with them. But he had also learned that the most honored Indian men would not tolerate lying. Deep inside, he knew Rising Eagle would not lie about something so important, for fear of suffering some kind of horrible consequences from the ire of the Great Spirit.

Maybe Spirit Walker had never been deformed at all. Maybe Florence was so drunk most of the time back then that she'd only thought he was deformed, something she imagined because she feared the life she had led would affect her child; but no matter how much he argued with himself, he knew it was all true. By some miracle, Spirit Walker had been healed. There was no explanation for it but that God himself had chosen to make it so.

That revelation made him angry, mostly with himself for the un-Christian thoughts he was having toward Rising Eagle. He *wanted* Rising Eagle to be a liar. He did not want him to be a man whose prayers were powerful enough to heal, a man who just might possibly have a stronger spiritual connection to a greater power than he did himself.

To make matters worse, he could not help feeling resentful that his wife had once loved the handsome, intimidating, and arrogant Indian leader. No doubt Rising Eagle still held a very special place in her heart. Now the man sat beside a "sacred" fire with William placed between his legs. Rising Eagle held his hands to either side of William's face, pressing them gently against the boy's temples, while Spirit Walker wafted smoke into William's face. Spirit Walker softly repeated some kind of chant, and Moon Painter, whom Abel thought was surely too old and frail to be living at all, sang loudly, shaking his medicine rattle over William.

Rising Eagle's eyes were closed, apparently in prayer, and his wife, one of the most beautiful Indian women Abel had ever seen, sat next to him, her eyes also closed in prayer. Florence sat on the other side of Rising Eagle, also praying; but she held her Bible in her lap, praying to the new god she had learned to worship.

Brave Horse had gone back to the Lakota encampment, taking his little brother and sister with him. Abel could not deny that this encounter with Rising Eagle and his family, seeing the way Rising Eagle lovingly held William, brought a respect on his part toward the Lakota as people with feelings for their families and children no different than his own people's. All this time that he'd worked with them, such things had never been quite so clear to him as now.

And yet, this same man had killed white men, mutilated Florence's brother in a vicious fight, fought a grizzly bear . . . and attacked William's mother, capturing her, raping her, making a slave of her. There was a side to Rising Eagle that no sane man would want to tangle with. Abel could easily picture the man fearlessly charging an enemy. Painted and decked out as he was now, Rising Eagle could readily be imagined dancing around a night fire, or standing atop a mountain crying out to *Wakan-Tanka*.

Was Rising Eagle's god the same as his own? Who was to say? The god of the Bible remained a mystery in many ways, and the Bible did state that there were certain things man did not understand now, but that he would one day understand when he met his Maker in heaven. Maybe then such burning questions would be answered. It was difficult imagining any Sioux making it to heaven, but God in heaven was certainly a more patient Being than any human.

He sat down wearily, deciding that he had no choice now but to wait. To try to stop this would only upset Florence, and she was right about one thing—the army doctor had done no better, so where was the harm? All the attention and ceremony seemed to lift William's spirits and take his mind off of his misery, and there was nothing wrong with that. The boy remained surprisingly calm, and as day moved into night, his fever did come down, and his breathing did begin to improve. Abel decided that for all anyone knew, that would have happened anyway. It was not necessarily the result of Rising Eagle and Moon Painter's prayers.

Still, he could not deny the aura of power and mysticism he felt while sitting here in the night, smoke from the burning sweet grass creating a comforting aroma, old Moon Painter's endless chant-like song bringing a strange peace to his own heart. Yes, there was something here, a feeling of closeness to the earth, the stars, the moon. And although he had to fight sleep through the night, Abel noticed that none of the Lakota seemed to tire at all—not even old Moon Painter, whose energy and persistent praying and singing astounded him.

The old man was tough, that was sure. Rising Eagle was tougher. Abel could just imagine the man in battle, certainly not a man anyone would want to offend. If there were a lot more like him among the Lakota, the U.S. government had indeed chosen a formidable foe. He suspected his government would be surprised to what lengths men like Rising Eagle would go to have their way and keep their hunting grounds.

Deep into the long night, Abel could not help lying down in the grass and dozing off. The next thing he knew,

Florence was stirring him awake. The sun was over the horizon, and birds were singing. He sat up, wincing at an ache in his back from sleeping on the ground. "Good Lord, what time is it?" he asked, yawning and stretching.

"It is about seven o'clock," Florence told him. "And look at our son!"

Able stretched once more and stood up, brushing himself off. Only then did he realize that Rising Eagle and the others were gone . . . except for Spirit Walker, who sat on the porch steps with William. William was dressed, and he was laughing as he tried to talk to his big brother in sign language.

Abel stared, trying to gather his thoughts, feeling as though he had just awakened from a strange dream. He turned to a smiling Florence then. In spite of the dark circles under her eyes from having been awake all night, she seemed energetic and elated.

"What's going on?" Abel asked her.

"William feels much better, and his fever is gone. Did I not tell you there is magic to the prayers of Lakota men such as Rising Eagle and our medicine men? Spirit Walker also prayed very hard, and I sensed the healing in his touch. Rising Eagle and the others have left to prepare for the journey to Horse Creek, but Spirit Walker has chosen to stay here for that time, so that I can spend it with him, and he with me. He also wants to know his little brother better, since it could be months, even years, before he sees him again." She stepped closer, touching his arm. "Isn't it wonderful, Abel? William is much better, and I have a few days, perhaps two or three weeks, to spend with the son I have not seen since he was only a few months old. Prayer is such a wonderful thing, Abel, whether it is to Jehovah or to *Wakan-Tanka!* In my whole life, I have never been this happy!"

An astounded Abel looked from her to the steps where William and Spirit Walker were trying to understand each other. Brothers. Each believed the other to be his true half brother, yet they were not related at all. *How long can we keep that news from William? Should we ever tell him the truth?* "I am at a total loss for words," he told Florence.

"You don't mind that Spirit Walker stays with us for a while, do you?"

At the moment, none of what he was seeing and hearing seemed real to Abel. "No, of course not. He's your son."

"And a very fine, good-hearted young man," Florence added. "He is special, Abel. Moon Painter said that Spirit Walker is meant to be a healer, not a warrior. I am so proud of him."

Abel turned his gaze to what was left of the small fire around which Moon Painter and the others had prayed for William, realizing then that whether he liked it or not, whether he wanted to believe in the mystical powers of the Lakota or not, he was being drawn ever more deeply into their culture and beliefs. He could almost smile at the humor of it, wondering just who was converting whom.

CHAPTER FORTY

BUFFALO DREAMER COULD barely take in all that was happening. Just arriving at Fort Laramie had been an exciting experience, the like of which she would never know again, so many thousands of Indians, many of them ancient enemies, all gathered in one place! She would never have dreamed of seeing such a thing in her lifetime.

They barely settled before meeting Fall Leaf Woman again, after so many years, so many changes. Every day since coming here, it seemed that something new and exciting happened. First the meeting with Fall Leaf Woman and the touching reunion between her and Spirit Walker; and then the healing of the little brother Spirit Walker never knew existed. Now Spirit Walker stayed with his birth mother, which he had every right to do. It was a good thing, but she could not help feeling a strange loss. It was only natural that he would want to know his real mother better, and especially to form a bond with his new brother, and so they had come to Horse Creek without him.

The migration of so many thousands of Indians at the same time was indeed something that would live in her memory forever. Each different clan, on up through the different Indian tribes, dressed and painted themselves in their finest, strutting their best horses, showing off their symbols for wounds, kills, counting coup, as well as displaying special regalia that depicted their status within the tribe. The move became a grand pageant of color and motion, the air filled with shouting and laughter, the barking of dogs, and the squealing of children.

Once everyone arrived at Horse Creek, it took three days to choose campsites and settle in again. Then there came the various processions before the white man's peace commissioners. One thousand Lakota warriors, led by Rising Eagle and his uncles, as well as elders from other clans, paraded proudly before the commissioners and were gifted with a good supply of the white man's tobacco. The Lakota even put on a grand feast for their friends the Shihenna, having decided to make an impression on the white leaders by inviting their old enemies, the Shoshoni and the Arapaho.

Surprisingly, there were no problems. Everyone had a joyous time, and all day and night the air rang with songs and drumming. Night fires lit up the dark figures of dancing warriors and trilling women, and by day, children of different tribes screamed and laughed and played with one another. It seemed as though in half of her waking time, Buffalo Dreamer had completely lost track of the whereabouts of Little Turtle and Little Storm. She constantly had to ask Brave Horse or Yellow Bonnet to go find their little brother and sister.

The days preceding the peace talks were ones of feasting, races, games, and celebration. Yet there was also a strange feeling of foreboding to it all, as though this would be the last of truly good times.

Finally, the peace commissioners, headed by Agent Broken Hand and a man named Mitchell, sat down with the heads of all the nations, and through interpreters they outlined what it was their government wanted, hoping to treaty with all the nations.

During day after day of talks, Buffalo Dreamer sat behind rows of elders, not allowed to sit among them, yet sitting as next in rank of importance, ahead of other warriors, who in turn sat ahead of those women and children who cared to attend the talks. Many of the women stayed behind to tend fires and mind the children who stayed at camp to play.

Buffalo Dreamer did not like what she was hearing, and she knew Rising Eagle would never agree to any of it. The commissioners stated that their government wanted all Indians to stop molesting wagon trains and settlers. They also wanted to be allowed to build more forts on Indian lands, and they wanted peace among the nations. The most ridiculous thing they asked for was that each nation should set boundaries on where their people could live and hunt. They wanted to give the Lakotas and other nations fifty thousand dollars in gifts each year for the next fifty years for their cooperation.

Buffalo Dreamer knew that Rising Eagle must be laughing inside. What did any amount of the white man's money mean to the Lakota? The commissioners would be better off talking in terms of numbers of horses, blankets, beads, or meat. How much in those items did fifty thousand dollars in the paper money represent? Stretching her neck to get a glimpse of Rising Eagle, she saw him hold a fan made of an eagle's wing in front of his face. This meant he totally disagreed with what was being asked. He had already clearly stated to Broken Hand that he would never be told he must stay in one area, or that he could not hunt wherever he chose. These requests were an outrage to the Lakota way of life and were beyond acceptance.

More days were spent arguing with the commissioners over the fact that no one Lakota man could speak for the entire nation. In fact, even among each separate clan, no one man could speak for the rest. Even so, Superintendent Mitchell insisted that someone must represent all the Lakota in signing an agreement to their demands.

Finally, one Brule chief, Conquering Bear, agreed to sign the treaty, mainly because all of them were tired of the talks and wanted to be on their way. It was important to leave soon for the Black Hills, to be sure winter did not trap them on the open plains before they could reach their homeland. And the Brule wanted to get back to their favorite stronghold, farther southwest of the Black Hills.

Buffalo Dreamer almost felt sorry for Conquering Bear, who knew the possible effects of purporting to sign an agreement that represented compliance by all the Lakota Nation. The old man rose, stating to the commissioners that he was not afraid to die but that he had a wife and children and did not wish to leave them in death. He asked to be allowed to stay near the fort, for to say he was signing for all the nation could mean his own life, at the hands of his own people.

He was right. Most men of Rising Eagle's status would be very angry that any one of them would agree to signing the white man's ridiculous paper, daring to say he spoke for all the Lakota in agreeing that they could no longer make war on enemy tribes, could no longer hunt wherever they pleased, could no longer deal out proper punishment to whites who intruded on lands that did not belong to them.

Did the commissioners really intend to declare that all the Lakota had agreed to these things just because one man, or even several men, touched a pen to their piece of paper? She watched as a few other headmen put their mark on the treaty, but she very proudly noted that not one Oglala or Shihenna man signed it. One of the Shihenna leaders, called Black Hawk, stood before the commissioners and told them that he absolutely did not agree to the white men trying to split up Lakota lands. He walked away, as did Bold Fox, Wind In Grass, Runs With The Deer, Moon Painter, Bear Dancing, Many Horses, and others. When Rising Eagle approached the wooden table where the commissioners sat, rather than pick up the pen, he took a knife from his belt. The commissioners' eyes widened, and a couple of soldiers stepped closer, one leveling a rifle at Rising Eagle.

"Don't fire that gun!" Broken Hand ordered.

Broken Hand and Rising Eagle looked at each other, and Rising Eagle just shook his head. "I told you that if the white man only moved through my land and did not kill our game, I would leave him alone. I tell you now that if one white man chooses to set down for good anywhere in Oglala country, or in our hunting grounds, I will not allow it. And if any white man dares to come into *Paha-Sapa*, I will not allow that either. I agree to nothing that is in your papers here. I will live where I choose, and I will hunt where I choose. Your people do not have the right to come here and tell me to do otherwise. I have seen enough to know that most of them have bad hearts. They are not true human beings!"

With that, Rising Eagle slammed his knife into the treaty papers and walked away. The commissioners merely looked at each other and shook their heads, then smiled amiably at the next man who approached to put his mark on the paper. An angry Rising Eagle walked back to where Buffalo Dreamer stood and ordered her to follow him.

"We leave now!" he told her. "This has been a waste of time. We will go and get Spirit Walker and return to *Paha-Sapa*."

Buffalo Dreamer followed, agreeing with his decision but worried over what kind of trouble could ensue from all the misunderstandings that had taken place. Apparently the white man's government really thought that by getting a few marks on a piece of paper, they now had a treaty with the Lakota. Did that mean their soldiers would come after them if a Lakota man attacked a white man? Her vision of many soldiers in blue coats remained vivid in her memory. How long would it be before she saw that vision realized? And if the Lakota and Shihenna did indeed surround the soldiers and kill them all, what was to come after that?

CHAPTER FORTY-ONE

BUFFALO DREAMER AGONIZED for Rising Eagle. Their trip here for the Great Smoke had been a stark awakening to changes in their lives—changes over which they had little control. Not only would they have to deal with white intruders who actually thought they had a right to hunt and settle in Indian lands, but now their adopted son was telling them he had decided to stay with his birth mother and his new brother rather than go home with them to the Black Hills.

Rising Eagle stood outside Florence's home, facing Florence and Abel, William, and Spirit Walker, still silent after several long seconds of contemplating what Spirit Walker had just told him. Buffalo Dreamer had no idea with whom she should sympathize—Spirit Walker, who looked ready to cry; Rising Eagle, who could hardly bear the thought of one of his sons staying in the white world; or Florence, who must herself be torn between the joy of having her firstborn with her again and the knowledge of what his staying would do to Rising Eagle.

"I am a man now, Father," Spirit Walker told Rising Eagle. "Old enough to make these decisions for myself." He swallowed, blinking back tears. "I have told you many times that part of me has never felt as though I belonged with the Lakota. Because of your great spiritual powers, I was healed, and for this I will be eternally grateful. And because of your generosity, I was blessed with being raised by one of the greatest men among the Oglala. You and my uncles taught me well. But there is another side to me, and with the Oglala, I have no blood relatives. Here I have my birth mother, and a brother who shares the same blood."

Buffalo Dreamer noticed that Florence cast an odd look at Abel, as though she felt some kind of guilt. Surely it was only that she felt bad about Spirit Walker deciding to stay with her. Still, it was usually when the subject of William came up that Florence had that look on her face that made it seem she was hiding something.

"You *belong* with us now," Rising Eagle argued. "If you stay here, there will be an empty place in my heart, and in Buffalo Dreamer's heart, as well as in the hearts of your uncles, especially Bold Fox. And what about Moon Painter? He has been teaching you how to become a healer."

A tear slipped down Spirit Walker's face. "Do you think I have not thought about all of that? Do you think I will not miss *Paha-Sapa?* My sisters and brothers? My uncles? Most of all, my adoptive mother and father?" He put a fist to his chest. "You are all here in my heart, forever. I do not know how long I will stay here. I only know that for now, I must do this. Just as you feel the Great Spirit guides you, Father, he also guides me. While you were at the talks at Horse Creek, I had a dream, and the dream foretold that I would one day heal my adopted brother, Brave Horse."

He turned his gaze then to Brave Horse, who sat his mount quietly watching and listening. Behind them, the huge contingent of Lakotas and Dakotas made their way past them, heading north and east—Oglala, Hunkpatila, Brule, Hunkpapa, Miniconjou, Sihasapa, Ochenonpa; the Santee, Yankton and Teton—all striking out for their various homelands. Little Turtle and Little Storm were with Running Elk Woman and Bold Fox. They had all gone ahead, expecting Rising Eagle and the rest of his family to catch up after picking up Spirit Walker along the way. The fact that Spirit Walker might want to stay behind with his birth mother had never crossed their minds. Buffalo Dreamer felt stunned, and she knew it was worse for Rising Eagle.

"In the dream," Spirit Walker continued, "I was dressed like a white man, and I carried the instruments of the white man's doctors, like those I learned about while I remained here. I believe that this dream is a sign that I am to stay here and learn the white man's way of healing. Perhaps between that and our way of healing, I can save even more from dying, whether they are white or Lakota."

Rising Eagle closed his eyes and turned away. "If I had known that bringing you here would lead to this—"

"Father," Spirit Walker interrupted, "you know yourself that I am a healer, not a warrior. You have said it many times, as has Bold Fox. You have sons, *blood* sons, of whom you can be very proud. Already Brave Horse is everything a Lakota man could want in a son, brave and daring, skilled with horses and weapons. I love him like the brother that he is, but always I will be in his shadow, wondering where I truly belong." He stopped to sniffle and swallow, obviously struggling not to break down. "The only way I will ever know my true self is to stay here and learn about that part of me that gave me blue eyes. I have had my whole life to get to know my Lakota brothers and sisters. I have had only these two weeks to become acquainted with the one brother who actually shares my blood. He deserves to have time with me, and just as you taught me the Lakota way, I in turn can teach William the Lakota way, and he can teach me the white man's way. From the things that have happened here, I feel in my heart that someday it will be important that the Lakota know and understand the white man's way. We may have no choice, Father."

Rising Eagle drew in his breath and tipped his head back, looking to the heavens for a moment. Then he turned, facing his son. "Right now we *do* have a choice! And my choice is to never allow any white man to tell me I must believe his way, live his way, live where he tells me to live. The white man has no right being here. *No* right! If he chooses to learn this the hard way, then so be it."

Spirit Walker sniffled again, his shoulders shaking while

he quickly wiped at his nose and eyes with the sleeve of the cotton shirt he wore, a white man's shirt. "Do not leave angry, Father. That is all I ask. You would not argue with anything Brave Horse feels his dreams tell him to do. I ask only the same from you."

Rising Eagle turned to Buffalo Dreamer, appearing lost for words.

"He is right, my husband. If Spirit Walker feels he must do this, then you must let him do it. It is bad for the heart to be angry with your own son who loves you."

Rising Eagle faced Florence and Abel then. "What have you done to make him choose this?"

"Nothing!" Florence answered quickly. "I gave my son to you willingly all those years ago, Rising Eagle, thinking I would never see him again. I would not choose now to try to keep him against his will. This was not an easy decision for him. It is something that he truly feels he must do, and so you must accept it, as any Lakota man allows his sons freedom of choice. I assure you, neither Abel nor I tried to talk him into this. He has grown closer to William, and William also wants him to stay."

Rising Eagle walked closer to William, who stared up at him as though he were a god. "You wish to have Spirit Walker with you?" he asked.

Florence interpreted, and William nodded. "He is my brother," the boy answered.

When Florence told Rising Eagle what William said, Rising Eagle again turned to Spirit Walker. "Indeed, he is your brother." He came close to Spirit Walker and put out his hand. Buffalo Dreamer could tell that her husband dearly wanted to embrace Spirit Walker, but he would not do so in front of the others. "Stay," he told the young man. "But never forget the part of you that is Lakota."

Spirit Walker grasped the proffered wrist. "You know that I can never forget that, Father. Nor would I ever forget you. And when you come through here to hunt, I hope that you will come and see me."

Rising Eagle shook his head. "I think that I will never return to this place. But you know where to find us if your heart should ever lead you back to the Black Hills and the home of your childhood."

Spirit Walker nodded, more tears spilling down his face as his lips remained tightly pressed. Rising Eagle turned away, and Buffalo Dreamer went to Spirit Walker, embracing him tightly.

"May the Great Spirit go with you, son," she said, unable to quell her own tears. She pulled away and glanced at Florence and Abel. "And with you."

Florence nodded, her own eyes wet with tears. Buffalo Dreamer turned. If the parting must be done, then let it be done quickly.

Brave Horse rode close to Spirit Walker. *"Wakan-Tanka nici un,"* he told his brother. "I will miss you forever, Spirit Walker. The memories of our days growing up together will be good ones."

"May the Great Spirit be with you, too, my brother. My vision tells me that someday you will need me, and I will be there for you."

Brave Horse nodded, and Buffalo Dreamer could tell he was deeply touched. He turned his horse and kicked it into a run to catch up with the others. Rising Eagle lifted Buffalo Dreamer onto Sotaju's back, then leaped onto Olute. He charged away, letting out a long cry, as though one of mourning.

Buffalo Dreamer remained a moment longer, wanting one last look at the young man she had called son since he was a deformed, sickly infant. "Good-bye, my son." Tears spilled down her cheeks as she turned her horse and rode almost blindly toward the thousands of migrating Lakota. For a while, she rode along beside them, not sure of where her own family was, not caring at the moment.

Finally, she drew a deep breath and told herself there was no choice but to go on. Her children were growing and changing, and soon she would have no little ones left. Each would have to make his and her own choices.

She urged Sotaju into a gentle lope, searching through

the seemingly endless migration, maneuvering around *travois,* greeting other women, watching for dogs and for little children who might stray into Sotaju's path, until at last she spotted Rising Eagle, who stood at the edge of the huge contingent of Lakota, talking to a man about the same age as he, both men watching two young men racing some distance away.

Curious, Buffalo Dreamer rode closer, and when Rising Eagle turned to her, she was almost startled by the proud, determined look in his eyes. She had expected to see continued sorrow, but apparently something had happened to change that.

"Again my dreams prove to carry great power," he told her. "So much so that even I am surprised."

Buffalo Dreamer frowned. "What do you mean, my husband?"

He said nothing at first but instead turned to watch the race. Buffalo Dreamer realized then that one of the riders was their own Brave Horse. The other looked like a boy half his age. He rode like the wind, giving Brave Horse a run for it, losing the race by hardly more than his horse's nose. Both young men let out war whoops and charged back toward Rising Eagle.

"That young one is called Curly," Rising Eagle told Buffalo Dreamer, "of the Hunkpatila band, the ones we have seldom associated with until now. His father calls him Curly because of his light wavy hair that is nothing like the straight black hair of the Lakota—yet he carries no white blood."

Buffalo Dreamer watched the young men come closer, and she could see what Rising Eagle meant about the younger boy's appearance. Indeed, he hardly looked Lakota, but he certainly rode like one, and he carried the arrogant, proud stance of an older warrior. "I do not understand what you are telling me, Rising Eagle."

Rising Eagle faced her. "I am telling you that Curly is the son of this man beside me, who is convinced that the boy will one day be a man of great notice. His father hopes that his son will prove worthy enough that one day he can rename him, after himself, which to the Hunkpatila is a token of great respect."

Buffalo Dreamer glanced at the other man, a handsome Oglala warrior, who only grinned at her oddly, as though carrying some great secret. She looked back at Rising Eagle. "You are confusing me. What does any of this have to do with your dreams?"

Rising Eagle folded his arms and smiled as Brave Horse and Curly bantered back and forth about who had truly won the race. "As Brave Horse and I were riding together, Curly came charging past," he told Buffalo Dreamer. "He nudged Brave Horse and challenged him to a race. His father tells me that before he did this, Curly turned to his father and said, "See that young man ahead of us? We will be good friends.' He did not even know Brave Horse, yet he said this. And then he challenged Brave Horse to the race. Somehow he knew . . . he just knew."

"Knew what?"

Rising Eagle turned to the man next to him. "Buffalo Dreamer, this is Curly's father. From here on, I believe he and I will also be good friends, for I have invited him to sit with us at our fire tonight so that I can tell him why this must be so, why I believe his son and ours—and even I myself are destined to be known in Lakota history. Stories will be told about us. Even you are a part of this, because I believe we will all become part of your vision of the Lakota riding down on soldiers until they become a pool of blood."

The two young men dismounted, shoving each other back and forth and laughing. Brave Horse was older and bigger, but Curly charged into him, knocking him over. Brave Horse rose and flipped Curly over his head. The younger boy landed on his back, laughing.

Buffalo Dreamer put her hands on her hips and faced her husband. "Explain yourself, husband, unless you prefer not to eat tonight."

Rising Eagle looked at the man next to him, who

shrugged. "He has not even let *me* in on what he means," the man told her. "But I do not mind sharing a meal over your fire." He laughed and told Curly to mount up again. "We must catch up with the rest of our clan, son."

Rising Eagle took hold of the ropes to Curly's horse, holding the mount there for a moment so the boy could not leave yet. "You will understand when I tell you the name of Curly's father," he told Buffalo Dreamer. "It is *Tasunko-witko*."

Buffalo Dreamer sucked in her breath, looking up at Curly and feeling suddenly removed from reality. "Crazy Horse!" she whispered.

There was no denying the special fire that glowed in the boy's eyes.

My son has been against the people
Of unknown tongue,
He has done a brave thing;
For this I give him a new name,
The name of his father,
And of many fathers before him.
I give him a great name,
I call him Crazy Horse.

—THE WORDS OF YOUNG CRAZY HORSE'S FATHER AFTER THE YOUNG MAN SHOWED EXTREME BRAVERY IN A BATTLE WITH ARAPAHO INDIANS, IN WHICH YOUNG CRAZY HORSE CHARGED AMONG HIS ENEMY COUNTING COUP WHILE THE ARAPAHO SHOT AT HIM WITH ARROWS . . . ARROWS THAT, STRANGELY, NEVER TOUCHED HIM.

1858

AUTHOR'S NOTE

I hope you have enjoyed *Mystic Visions* and will look forward to its sequel, *Mystic Warriors*, due approximately in the spring of 2001. If you would like to read about events leading up to *Mystic Visions*, look for a copy of *Mystic Dreamers*, published in hardcover in April 1999, and in paperback in April 2000.

For information about other books I have written, send a SASE to me at P.O. Box 1044, Coloma, Michigan 49038; or contact my Web site at www.parrett.net/~bittner. Thank you!

Read on for a sneak preview of

MYSTIC WARRIORS,

the exciting conclusion
to the Lakota saga.

CHAPTER ONE

"Take a look!" Cooper Baird said, as he handed his spy-glass to Clement Dees. "First one I've ever seen. I've heard of white buffalo, but in all the years I've trapped and hunted out here, I've never seen one."

Clement steadied the spyglass while Cooper remained crouched beside him. "That robe's made of white buffalo skin all right," Clement answered. He kept his voice to a low whisper. "From what I can tell, there's nobody down there but one brave and his squaw." He handed back the spyglass. "Shouldn't be too hard a job for four men."

Cooper swatted at a fly on his cheek. "You never can tell with the Sioux. There's likely plenty more nearby. Don't forget what happened to them soldiers under that Lieu-tenant Grattan. The Sioux are feelin' their oats, right boast-ful and ready for more killin', most likely; kind of like a wolf. Once it gets the scent of blood, it's ready for more."

"In this case it's one man and his squaw, not a whole war party," Clement argued.

Both men slithered down the rise that hid them from the Indian camp below. Cooper shoved his spyglass into a loop on his belt. "As long as we keep things quiet and don't end up with a war party on us. I seen the remains of Grattan and his men. It weren't a pretty sight, let me tell you. Most of the bodies could hardly be recognized, all chopped up and riddled with arrows." He brushed off his already-soiled buckskins. "Still in all, we can get good money for some-thin' like that white robe, it bein' so rare and all. I say we try for it."

Clement shrugged. "You're the one who was just gripin' about the mood the Sioux are in. It's a big risk."

Cooper headed toward the gully where he and his hunting party were camped. He whistled softly to signal two more men waiting in the brush. Clement was right. This was not a good time to be out here hunting buffalo, but the animal's hide was garnering a damned good price back in St. Louis. Hunting the great beasts was becoming the new sport, a damned exciting one for men who liked the challenge. Cooper liked nothing better than trying something he'd never done before, including the idea of stealing a sacred white buffalo robe from the Sioux.

He ducked into the thick brush surrounding the camp, followed by Clement. Bob Powers and Jim Liskey waited there for them, both men holding pieces of jerky, their most practical nourishment in times when making a fire meant danger. No white man in these parts wanted to be spotted by the enemy. Sidearms, knives, and rifles were kept handy.

Liskey nodded to both arriving men before biting off a piece of the hard, dry meat. "See any buffalo?" He wiped at his nose with the sleeve of his stained buckskin shirt.

Cooper winced at the sight of Liskey's left eye, which was really nothing but a sewn-up hole. A large white scar ran from above the eye down across the man's cheek and lips. A drunken Sioux brave had done that to him. No one hated Indians more than Jim Liskey. "Saw somethin' even better than buffalo. There's a white buffalo robe spread out on tepee skins the other side of the hill."

Liskey's eyebrows shot up in surprise. "White?"

"White. Never seen anything like it, and it's already cleaned and stretched. All we need to do is go down there and take it from an Indian camp."

"That easy, huh?" Powers replied, snorting in laughter. "No, thanks."

"There's only one tepee, a man and woman camped alone."

"And probably a couple thousand more nearby," Liskey

grumbled. "You know how wily the Sioux are. Least ways, *I* know. If you want your hide roasted over an open fire, go get the damned robe by yourself."

"I've got an idea for gettin' it with no trouble," Cooper answered.

"The robe is laid out over tepee skins, maybe to air out," Clement added. "Looks like some squaw is down there lookin' for turnips or somethin'. There's a brave with her, sittin' off smokin' his pipe. Looks to us like they're alone, probably feelin' right cocky after the Grattan thing; but that don't matter much, long as it's just the one Indian."

Liskey shrugged. "If it's true they're alone, why don't you just pick off the man with your buffalo gun and go get the robe? You could bring along the squaw for all of us to share."

"Sounds tempting," Cooper answered. "But you were right that there could be a couple thousand more someplace nearby. Them bastards can pop up out of the tall grass like prairie dogs. Don't forget that any Sioux in these parts are likely ripe for another fight. I don't aim to go shootin' off my gun and let them know we're here."

Powers chuckled. "That damn fool Grattan deserved what he got, goin' up against half the Sioux nation with a lousy thirty inexperienced soldiers. And what for? Just because one Sioux warrior shot an old, lame cow that belonged to a damned Mormon. The cow wasn't worth a shit to begin with."

"I don't give a damn about how many soldiers died or what the reason was," Cooper grumbled. "All I know is I want that white robe. You three willing to help me get it?"

The other three glanced at each other warily.

"I don't know," Powers answered skeptically.

"What's your plan?" Clement asked.

"I figure on sneakin' down there and doin' it quietly, after dark," Cooper said. "If one or two of you can create some kind of distraction, I can make off with the robe. We could have our horses someplace nearby and ride off, hard and fast, right toward Fort Kearny. We're only a day's ride from there. Fact is, the soldiers would probably be righ glad to know there's some Sioux so close by. Last I heard they was gettin' ready for a new campaign against the mur derin' bastards under a Colonel Harney, I think. We car furnish them with some information when we get there."

Liskey rubbed at his shriveled eye socket. "I hope the kill every last one of the bastards."

Cooper snorted, gathering phlegm at the back of hi throat, then coughing it up and spitting it out. "We ain' gonna' kill these. Not if we can help it. That's my orders."

"Why not?" Clement asked. "Seems to me the easies way to get the robe."

Cooper scratched at the several-day-old stubble on hi face. "And that's the best way to bring the whole lot o them after us. All I want is the robe, and with nobody hur and no horses stole, they won't be so likely to come afte us. They might not even know why we were there till later That will give us time to get away." He grinned. "And a far as I know, we'll be the first to arrive in St. Louis an al bino robe."

"They're sacred, you know." Powers said.

"Sacred?" Clement removed a floppy, leather hat.

"The white buffalo. The Sioux consider them sacred You can bet that robe means a hell of a lot to whoeve owns it. And if you steal it, you might regret it."

Cooper chuckled. "How's that?"

Powers shrugged. "Who knows? You might have al kinds of bad luck once you steal it. The Sioux religion i pretty powerful stuff. You mess with somethin' sacred t them, and you could have a heap of trouble on you hands."

Cooper shared in the snickers of Liskey and Clement shaking his head. "It's *their* religion, not mine," Cooper said derisively. "I don't have *any* religion, and I ain't supersti tious. I ain't worried about some damn object a bunch o wild Indians think has magical powers. The only magica powers that robe has is the magic to put money in ou pockets."

"Whoever is in charge at Fort Kearny won't take kindly to us stirrin' up the Sioux again," Clement reminded him.

"They don't need to know nothin' about it. We'll hide the white robe and just ride in like a huntin' party done with its job. Besides, the Sioux are riled up over other things. They'll stir up enough trouble all on their own." He took a piece of jerked meat from his pants pocket and bit down on one end of it, yanking off a piece. "You three gonna help me?"

They all grinned and nodded. Cooper thought how nice it was going to be getting back to St. Louis. He wouldn't mind being the center of attention because of that fine white robe. He bit off another piece of meat, feeling very satisfied.

CHAPTER TWO

Buffalo Dreamer lay next to Rising Eagle, listening to the distant cries of coyotes. A west wind rustled the leaves of the nearby cottonwood trees. Her husband sighed and rolled to his side, resting his head on his hand as he faced her.

"There is much change in the air," he said softly.

Buffalo Dreamer stared up at the twinkle of a few stars she could see through the smoke hole of the tepee. The view was clear tonight, for she'd made no fire. "A new season will come soon," she answered.

"It is not just the seasons of which I speak," Rising Eagle answered. "Our children are mostly grown. Brave Horse is a man now, a warrior of twenty-one summers; and one day soon we will give our adopted daughter away in marriage. Little Turtle is growing fast and already doing well in the warrior games, anxious to become a man. Songbird is learning much from Running Elk Woman. She is still young, but eager to be grown."

"Running Elk Woman has been a good replacement for my mother. Your aunt has become like a grandmother to our daughter." Buffalo Dreamer swallowed a sudden urge to cry. "I still miss my mother so."

Rising Eagle sighed deeply. "I often think about all the loved ones we lost to the white man's spotted disease, all the friends who have left us over the years, many due to the white men and their soldiers. When we were young life was good, free, and happy. Now all these changes because of the *wasicus*. No matter what we do, they keep coming

All the soldiers we killed not long ago will be replaced by twice as many . . . and they will come again."

"And we will continue defeating them until they give up," Buffalo Dreamer assured him. She reached up in the darkness and touched his face. "Don't forget that in my dream of long ago, our people surrounded and killed many more soldiers than were killed last summer. That means we have more victories ahead of us, and as long as we possess the robe of the white buffalo, we have much power."

Rising Eagle moved on top of her, resting on his elbows. "It will all have to happen soon. My hair is showing gray at the edges. Soon I will be considered an elder, and I will not have enough power and strength to ride against the enemy."

Buffalo Dreamer laughed lightly in spite of her misty eyes. She could not see him well in the darkness with only a sliver of a moon; but she knew her husband was also smiling. "You will always have power," she answered, running her hands over his still-muscled arms. "You are a holy man, a man of vision, one who has seen and heard the words of the Feathered One. As far as your physical strength . . ." She moved her hands up and over his shoulders. "You have not changed, my husband, and you still do not have the big belly of an elder."

Rising Eagle leaned down and licked at her lips. "You are the one who has not changed. We have been together for twenty-three summers, and still your hair shows no gray. You have borne many children." He ran a hand over a naked breast, down over her waist and around under her hips. "But your body is still that of a young woman . . . and I still burn for you."

The warm night required no clothing. Buffalo Dreamer could feel her husband's hardness pressing against her groin. "Then I should put out the fire," she said seductively, moving her own hands down along his back, to his bare hips, around to touch that part of him that still made her ache to feel him inside her. She opened herself to him, groaning when he entered her, taking delight in these two days they had chosen to spend alone while others watched over their two youngest children. There were times when a man and woman had to do these things, knowing hard times may lie ahead, knowing their own bodies were aging, and that moments like these would become more rare.

For the next several minutes they reveled in lovemaking, taking and giving, sharing each other's ecstasy, loving in the most intimate, most intense way a man and woman could love.

Buffalo Dreamer's pride in Rising Eagle had not waned over the years. She was herself a holy woman, the only one among their people who'd seen and touched the white buffalo. Her dreams often evoked visions of the future.

Rising Eagle was a man of even greater vision, a man with healing powers, and the only warrior in generations who'd seen and heard the Feathered One, the great Being who spoke for *Wakan-Tanka*. He was a man held in high esteem by the entire Lakota Nation, and he'd chosen her because of a vision. A stranger when first he came for her, she'd learned to love him deeply.

She felt his life spill into her. She would never stop wishing that life could take hold again, but she knew it was not to be. Instinctively, she'd known that after the birth of her youngest child, Songbird, she would never have another. Now it was grandchildren she would look forward to, but she still enjoyed the pleasures of lovemaking.

Rising Eagle could have his pick of any young maidens he chose, yet he had kept his long-ago promise that he would never take another wife. He honored his word, unlike the white man. The whites seemed to honor nothing they had promised. It was a white man's disease that had stolen away two of their children, Buffalo Dreamer's mother, and many friends and loved ones . . . a white man's disease that had left small, white, pitted scars on Rising Eagle's handsome face.

He rolled away. "Tomorrow we will return to the main camp. We need to hunt more buffalo before the weather changes. Those who go to Laramie for promised supplies bring back only rotten meat and blankets eaten by moths. It is just as I told the others when I refused to sign any treaties. We cannot depend on the white man to keep any of his promises. We can only rely on the hunt for survival. We will move into Crow and Shoshoni country if that is the only way to find more buffalo. We will drive them out, as we have done in the past, in spite of the white man's orders to make no more war against other tribes."

"Apparently the soldiers learned a good lesson last summer when we killed all those who attacked Conquering Bear and the Brule. They have not disturbed us since."

"Perhaps not. But we must remember we cannot ever trust them. We must always be on guard."

Just then one of the four horses tethered outside whinnied. Then another.

Both Rising Eagle and Buffalo Dreamer quickly sat up. Rising Eagle grabbed his hatchet and a knife, and Buffalo Dreamer reached for her tunic, slipping it over her head as her husband, still naked, ducked outside to determine what had disturbed the horses. Buffalo Dreamer thought she heard something behind the tepee. She quickly grabbed her own knife and darted outside. "Who is there?" she shouted in her own tongue.

She heard a man cry out then, over near the horses. She ran in that direction, yelling Rising Eagle's name.

"I am here!" he called to her.

She hurried toward the sound of his voice, several yards past where the horses were tethered. When her eyes adjusted to the darkness, she could see Rising Eagle standing over a man writhing on the ground. The culprit wore buckskins, and his hair was dark and tangled. She did not need to see him well to tell that he was a white man. She could tell by his smell, a sweet, sweaty, dirty smell she'd already learned most white men had. It made her nose curl.

"He was trying to steal a horse," Rising Eagle told her. He looked around. "I think there were more. I heard them running away."

"What were white men doing out here with so many of

our people close by? Don't they know we'll kill any white man we see?"

"They're probably buffalo hunters," Rising Eagle sneered. "The kind who kill the sacred beast just for its hide, leaving the rest to rot!" He looked down at the man he'd just caught and stabbed. He kicked him onto his back, and the man groaned. "Good. He is still alive. We will take him to the bigger camp and let the women and elders decide what to do with him!"

Buffalo Dreamer could feel the eagerness in his voice. They would make this man suffer for the way he and his kind were destroying the buffalo. The Lakota would make an example of this white man for others who dared to come into their hunting grounds. He would not die quickly or easily.

"We should bring the horses closer," she said.

"Hush!"

Buffalo Dreamer quieted as her husband listened with keen ears. Then she, too, heard the sound of horses riding off.

"They are going," Rising Eagle said quietly. "They have left their wounded friend behind. I'm not surprised." He looked down once more at the man at his feet. "We can leave the horses where they are. I do not think they will be back."

"Are you hurt, Rising Eagle?"

"No." He kicked at the wounded man once more. "We will leave this one here until morning. Let him suffer." He put a hand around her waist and walked with her back to their tepee.

"I thought I heard one of them near the tepee," Buffalo Dreamer said as they walked. "But then I heard someone cry out. I was afraid it was you, so I—" She drew in her breath, grasping Rising Eagle's arm. "The robe!" She left him then, her heart pounding as she ran. She reached the tepee, feeling around the area where she'd left the robe spread over tepee skins to air in the sun all that day. It was not there.

"No! No!" she whimpered. She got down on her hands and knees and felt around on the ground, hoping it had simply slipped down. Tears welled in her eyes as she searched in the grass, her stomach tightening into a painful knot. "It's gone! Rising Eagle, the robe is gone!" she cried out.

She felt his presence then, felt his own horror.

"I have lost it!" Buffalo Dreamer wept. "I was careless, and I lost it! I did not think anything could happen with us out here alone." She sucked in her breath with a great sob as she felt Rising Eagle grasp her arms and pull her up.

"But we were *not* alone," he said, obvious rage in the words. "Again the white man has come to try to destroy us! Again they show no honor for what is pure and *sacred!*"

"This is a bad, bad omen, Rising Eagle," Buffalo Dreamer wept. "It will be a curse on our people, and it is my fault!"

He gripped her arms tighter and gave her a light shake. "It is *not* your fault! It's just another sign of how evil the white man is. *They* are the ones who will suffer! As soon as it is light, I will follow the tracks of whoever stole the robe. I will find him and I will *kill* him!"